ANTHONY POWELL

A Buyer's Market

A Novel

FONTANA BOOKS
BY AGREEMENT WITH
HEINEMANN

First published in 1952 by William Heinemann Ltd
First issued in Fontana Books 1967
Seventh Impression July 1978

© Anthony Powell, 1952

Made and printed in Great Britain by
William Collins Sons & Co Ltd Glasgow

FOR OSBERT AND KAREN

A DANCE TO THE MUSIC OF TIME

**

A BUYER'S MARKET

ANTHONY POWELL was born in London in 1905. His father was a soldier, of a family mostly soldiers or sailors, which moved from Wales about a hundred and fifty years ago. He was educated at Eton and Balliol College, Oxford, of which he is now an Honorary Fellow.

From 1926 he worked for about nine years at Duckworths, the publishers, then as scriptwriter for Warner Brothers in England. During the war he served in the Welch Regiment and Intelligence Corps; acting as Liaison Officer with the Polish, Belgian, Czechoslovak, Free French and Luxembourg forces, being promoted major.

Before and after World War II he wrote reviews and literary columns for various papers, including the *Daily Telegraph* and the *Spectator*. From 1948-52 he worked on the *Times Literary Supplement*, and was Literary Editor of *Punch*, 1952-58.

Between 1931 and 1949, Anthony Powell published five novels, a biography, *John Aubrey and His Friends*, and a selection from Aubrey's works. The first volume of his twelve-volume novel, *A Dance to the Music of Time*, was published in 1951, and the concluding volume, *Hearing Secret Harmonies*, appeared in 1975. In 1976 he published the first volume of his memoirs, *To Keep the Ball Rolling*, under the title *Infants of the Spring*.

In 1934 he married Lady Violet Pakenham, daughter of the fifth Earl of Longford. They have two sons. They live in Somerset, to which they moved in 1952.

Books by Anthony Powell

ONE

The last time I saw any examples of Mr. Deacon's work was at a sale, held obscurely in the neighbourhood of Euston Road, many years after his death. The canvases were none of them familiar, but they recalled especially, with all kind of other things, dinner at the Walpole-Wilsons', reviving with a jerk that phase of early life. They made me think of long-forgotten conflicts and compromises between the imagination and the will, reason and feeling, power and sensuality; together with many more specifically personal sensations, experienced in the past, of pleasure and of pain. Outside, the spring weather was cool and sunny: Mr. Deacon's favourite season of the year. Within doors, propped against three sides of a washstand, the oil-paintings seemed, for some reason, appropriate to those surroundings, dusty, though not displeasing; even suggesting, in their way, the kind of home Mr. Deacon favoured for himself and his belongings: the sitting-room over the shop, for example, informal, not too permanent, more than a trifle decayed. His haunts, I remembered, had bordered on these northern confines of London.

Accumulations of unrelated objects brought together for auction, acquire, in their haphazard manner, a certain dignity of their own: items not to be tolerated in any inhabited dwelling finding each its own level in these expansive, anonymous caverns, where, making no claim to individual merit, odds and ends harmonise quietly with each other, and with the general sobriety of background. Such precincts have something of museums about them, the roving crowd on the whole examining the assembled relics with an expert, unselfconscious intensity, not entirely commercial or acquisitive.

On these particular premises almost every man-made thing seemed represented. Comparatively new mowing machines: scabbardless and rusty cavalry sabres: ebony fragments of African fetish: a nineteenth-century typewriter, poised uncertainly on metal stilts in the midst of a tea-set in Liverpool ware, the black-and-white landscapes of its design irreparably chipped. Several pillows and bolsters covered with the Union Jack gave a disturbing hint, that somewhere beneath, a corpse awaited burial with military honours. Farther off, high rolls of linoleum, coloured blue, green and pink, were ranged against the wall like pillars, a Minoan colonnade from which wicker armchairs and much-used pieces of luggage formed a semicircle. Within this open space, placed rather like an emblem arranged for worship, stood the washstand round which the pictures were grouped. On its marble top rested an empty bird-cage, two men-at-arms in lead, probably German, and a dog-eared pile of waltz music. In front of a strip of Axminster carpet, displayed like faded tapestry from the side of a nearby wardrobe in pitch pine, a fourth painting stood upside down.

All four canvases belonged to the same school of large, untidy, exclusively male figure compositions, light in tone and mythological in subject: Pre-Raphaelite in influence without being precisely Pre-Raphaelite in spirit: a compromise between, say, Burne-Jones and Alma-Tadema, with perhaps a touch of Watts in method of applying the paint. One of them—ripping away from its stretcher at the top—

was dated 1903. A decided weakness of drawing was emphasised by that certitude—which overtakes, after all, some of the greatest artists—that none of Mr. Deacon's pictures could possibly have been painted at any epoch other than its own : this hallmark of Time being specially attributable to the painter's inclination towards large, blank expanses of colour, often recklessly laid on. Yet, in spite of obvious imperfections, the pictures, as I have said, were not utterly unsympathetic in that situation. Even the forest of inverted legs, moving furiously towards their goal in what appeared to be one of the running events of the Olympic Games, were manifested to what might easily have been greater advantage in that reversed position, conveying, as they did, an immense sense of nervous urgency, the flesh tints of the athletes' straining limbs contrasting strangely with pink and yellow contours of three cupids in debased Dresden who tripped alongside on top of a pedestal cupboard.

In due course two bucolic figures in cloth caps, shirt-sleeves, and green baize aprons held up Mr. Deacon's pictures, one by one, for examination by a small knot of dealers : a depressed gang of men, looking as if they had strayed into that place between more congenial interludes on the race-course. I was not sure how this display might strike other people, and was glad, when exposure took place, that no unfriendly comment was aroused. The prodigious size of the scenes depicted might in itself reasonably have provoked laughter; and, although by that time I knew enough of Mr. Deacon to regard his painting as nothing more serious than one of a number of other warring elements within him, open ridicule of his work would have been distressing. However, all four elevations were received, one after another, in apathetic silence; although

the " lot " was finally knocked down for a few pounds
only, bidding was reasonably brisk : possibly on account
of the frames, which were made of some black substance,
ornamented with gold in a floral pattern, conceivably of
the painter's own design.

Mr. Deacon must have visited the house at least half a
dozen times when I was a child, occasions when, by some
unlikely chance, I had seen and spoken with him more than
once; though I do not know why our paths should have
crossed in this manner, because he was always reported
" not to like children ", so that our meetings, such as they
were, would not have been deliberately arranged on the part
of my parents. My father, amused by his conversation,
was in the habit of referring to Mr. Deacon's painting
without enthusiasm; and when, as he sometimes did, Mr.
Deacon used to assert that he preferred to keep—rather
than sell—his own works, the remark usually aroused
mildly ironical comment at home after he was gone. It
would not be fair, however, to suggest that, professionally,
Mr. Deacon was unable to find a market for his classical
subjects. On the contrary, he could always name several
faithful patrons, mostly business people from the Midlands. One of these, especially, spoken of as a " big iron
man "—whom I used to envisage as physically constructed
of the metal from which he derived his income—would, for
example, come down from Lancashire once a year : always
returning northward in possession of an oil sketch of
Antinous, or sheaf of charcoal studies of Spartan youth at
exercise. According to Mr. Deacon, one of these minor
works had even found its way into the ironmaster's local
art gallery, a fulfilment which evidently gave great satisfaction to the painter; although Mr. Deacon would mention
the matter in a deprecatory sort of way, because he dis-

approved of what he called " official art," and used to speak
with great bitterness of the Royal Academy. When I met
him in later life I discovered that he disliked the Impres-
sionists and Post-Impressionists almost equally; and was,
naturally, even more opposed to later trends like Cubism,
or the works of the Surrealists. In fact Puvis de Chavannes
and Simeon Solomon, the last of whom I think he regarded
as his master, were the only painters I ever heard him speak
of with unqualified approval. Nature had no doubt intended him to be in some manner an adjunct to the art
movement of the Eighteen-Nineties; but somehow Mr.
Deacon had missed that spirit in his youth, a moral separate-
ness that perhaps accounted for a later lack of integration.

He was not rich, although his income, in those days,
allowed the preservation of a fairly independent attitude
towards the more material side of being an artist. He had
once, for example, turned down the opportunity to decorate
the interior of a fish restaurant in Brighton—where he
lived—on grounds that the sum offered was incommen-
surate with the demeaning nature of the work demanded.
His means had also enabled him to assemble what was said
to be an excellent little collection of hour-glasses, silhouettes,
and bric-à-brac of various kinds. At the same time he liked
to describe how, from time to time, in order to avoid the
expense and responsibility of domestic staff, he deliberately
underwent long periods of undertaking his own cooking.
" I could always earn my living as a chef," he used to say;
adding, in joke, that he would look " enormously ornamental " in a white cap. When travelling on the Continent
he commonly went on foot with a haversack on his back,
rather than by trains, which he found " stuffy and infinitely
filled with tedious persons." He was careful, even rather
fussy, about his health, especially in relation to personal

cleanliness and good sanitation; so that some of the more sordid aspects of these allegedly *terre-à-terre* excursions abroad must at times have been a trial to him. Perhaps his Continental visits were, in fact, more painful for managers of hotels and restaurants frequented by him; for he was a great believer in insisting absolutely upon the minute observance by others of his own wishes. Such habits of travelling, in so much as they were indeed voluntary and not to some degree enforced by financial consideration, were no doubt also connected in his mind with his own special approach to social behaviour, in which he was guided by an aversion, often expressed, for conduct that might be looked upon either as conventional or conservative.

In this last respect Mr. Deacon went further than my Uncle Giles, whose creed of being " a bit of a radical " was also well publicised within his own family circle; or, indeed, wherever he might find himself. My uncle, however, dealt in substance he knew and, although he would never have admitted as much, even to some extent revered, merely desiring most aspects of that familiar world to be more nicely adjusted to his own taste. Mr. Deacon, on the other hand, was in favour of abolishing, or ignoring, the existing world entirely, with a view to experimenting with one of an entirely different order. He was a student of Esperanto (or, possibly, one of the lesser-known artificial languages), intermittently vegetarian, and an advocate of decimal coinage. At the same time he was strongly opposed to the introduction of " spelling reform " for the English language (on grounds that for him such changes would mar *Paradise Lost*), and I can remember it said that he hated " suffragettes."

These preferences, with the possible exception of decimal

coinage, would have been regarded as mere quirks in my
uncle; but, as they were presented in what was almost
always a moderately entertaining manner, they were tolerated by my parents to a far greater degree than were
similar prejudices disseminated by Uncle Giles, whose
heartily deplored opinions were naturally associated in the
minds of most of his relations with threat of imminent
financial worry for themselves, not to mention potential
scandal within the family. In any case, aggressive personal
opinions, whatever their kind, might justly be regarded as
uncalled for, or at best allowed only slight weight, when
voiced by a man whose career had been so uniformly unsuccessful as had that of my uncle. Mr. Deacon's per-
suasions, on the other hand, could be regarded with tolerance as part of the stock-in-trade of a professional artist, by
no means a failure in life, and to be accepted, however unwillingly, as the inevitable adjunct of a Bohemian profession : even valuable in their way as illustrating another side
of human experience.

At the same time, although no doubt they rather enjoyed
his occasional visits, my parents legitimately considered Mr.
Deacon an eccentric, who, unless watched carefully, might
develop into a bore, and it would not be precisely true to
say that they liked him; although I believe that, in his way,
Mr. Deacon liked both of them. The circumstances of their
first meeting were unrecorded. An introduction may have
taken place at one of the concerts held at the Pavilion,
which they sometimes attended when my father was
stationed near Brighton in the years before the war.
During that period a call was certainly paid on Mr. Deacon
in his studio : several small rooms converted to that use at
the top of a house in one of the quiet squares remote from
" the front." He had chosen this retired position because

the sight of the sea disturbed him at his work : a prejudice
for which psychological explanation would now certainly
be available.

I never saw the studio myself, but often heard it spoken
of as well stocked with curiosities of one kind or another.
We moved from that neighbourhood before the war came
in 1914, and, I suppose, lost touch with Mr. Deacon; but
for a long time I remember the impression of height he
gave when, one day after tea, he presented me with a
wooden paint-box—the pigments contained in tubes—the
heavy scent of the tobacco he smoked hanging round the
pleats and belt of his Norfolk jacket, a garment already
beginning to look a little old-fashioned, and the sound of his
voice, deep and earnest, while he explained the range of
colours to be found within the box, and spoke of the
principles of light and shade : principles—I could not help
reflecting as I examined the canvases in the sale-room—
which his brush must have so often and so violently abused.

By the stage of life when I happened on these four
pictures, I had, of course, during our brief latter-day
acquaintance, had opportunity to observe Mr. Deacon in
surroundings rather different from my parents' domestic
interior, where I had first heard his peculiarities discussed;
and I had also, by the time I found myself in the auction-
room, talked over his character with persons like Barnby,
who knew him at closer range than I myself ever experienced. All the same, I could not help pondering once again
the discrepancy that existed between a style of painting that
must have been unfashionable, and at best aridly academic,
even in his early days; and its contrast with the revolutionary principles that he preached and—in spheres other
than æsthetic—to some considerable extent practised. I
wondered once again whether this apparent inconsistency

of approach, that had once disconcerted me, symbolised
antipathetic sides of his nature; or whether his life and
work and judgment at some point coalesced with each other,
resulting in a standpoint that was really all of a piece—as
he himself would have said—that " made a work of art."

Certainly I could not decide that question there and then
in the auction-room among the furniture and linoleum, to
the sound of bidding and taps of the hammer, even in the
light of later circumstances in which I had known him,
and I have never really succeeded in coming to a positive
conclusion on the subject. Undoubtedly his painting, in
its own direction, represented the farthest extremity of Mr.
Deacon's romanticism, and I suppose it could be argued
that upon such debris of classical imagery the foundations
of at least certain specific elements of twentieth century art
came to be built. At the same time lack of almost all
imaginative quality in Mr. Deacon's painting resulted,
finally, in a product that suggested not " romance "—far
less " classicism "—as some immensely humdrum pattern
of everyday life : the Greek and Roman episodes in which
he dealt belonging involuntarily to a world of cosy bar-
parlours and " nice cups of tea "—" At least when thought
of," as Barnby used to say, " in terms of pictorial repro-
duction in, say, photogravure "—even though Barnby himself, in some moods, would attempt a defence at least of
certain aspects of Mr. Deacon's art. In short, the pictures
recalled something given away with a Christmas Number,
rather than the glories of Sunium's marbled steep, or that
blue Sicilian sea that had provided a back-cloth for the Victorian Hellenism propagated at school by my housemaster,
Le Bas. Mr. Deacon's painting might, indeed, have been
compared, though at a greatly inferior level of the imagination's faculties, with Le Bas's day-dreams of Hellas; and

perhaps, in the last resort, Mr. Deacon, too, would have been wiser to have chosen teaching as a career. Undeniably there was something didactic about his manner, although, as a child, I had naturally never speculated on his idiosyncrasies, of which I knew only by hearing them particularised by my parents or the servants.

This touch of pedantry had been apparent at a later date, when we ran across Mr. Deacon in the Louvre, during summer holidays taken soon after the termination of the war, when my father was still on duty in Paris. That afternoon, although I did not immediately recognise him, I had already wondered who might be the tall, lean, rather bent figure, moving restlessly about at the far end of the gallery; and his name, spoken again after so many years, at once identified him in my mind. When we had come up with him he was inspecting with close attention Perugino's St. Sebastian, for the better examination of which, stooping slightly, he had just produced a small magnifying-glass with a gold rim. He wore a thickish pepper-and-salt suit—no longer cut with belt and side-pleats—and he carried in his hand a hat, broad-brimmed and furry, the general effect of the whole outfit being, perhaps intentionally, a trifle down-at-heel: together with the additionally disturbing suggestion that his slightly curved torso might be enclosed within some form of imperfectly fitting corset. His grey hair, which needed cutting, was brushed straight back, showing off a profile distinguished rather than otherwise: a little like that of an actor made up to play the part of Prospero, the face heavily lined and grave, without conveying any sense of dejection.

He recognised my parents at once, greeting them with an odd, stilted formality, again like an old-fashioned actor's. My father—who was not in uniform—began to explain that he was attached to the staff of the Conference. Mr. Deacon, listened with an absorbed expression, failed or, perhaps it would be truer to say, pretended for reasons of his own to misunderstand the nature of this employment. In his resonant, faintly ironical voice, he asked: "And what might you be conferring about?"

At that period Paris was full of missions and delegates, emissaries and plenipotentiaries of one kind and another, brought there by the traffic of the Peace Treaty; and probably my father could not imagine why Mr. Deacon should appear to want further details about his job (which had, I believe something to do with disarmament), a matter which could, after all, at least in its details, be only of professional interest. He certainly did not guess that Mr. Deacon must have decided for the moment to close his eyes to the Conference, together with much—if not all—that had led to its existence; or, at least, preferred, anyway at that juncture, to ignore all its current circumstances. My father's reply, no doubt intentionally discreet, was therefore worded in general terms; and the explanation, so far as could be seen, took Mr. Deacon no farther in discovering why we were at that hour in the Louvre.

"In connection with those *expositions* the French love so much?" he suggested. "So you are no longer *militaire*?"

"As a matter of fact, they have not given nearly so much trouble as you might expect," said my father, who must have taken this query to be a whimsical manner of referring to some supposed form of intransigence over negotiation on the part of the French staff-officer constituting his "opposite number."

"I don't know much about these things," Mr. Deacon admitted.

The matter rested there, foundations of conversation

changing to the delineation of St. Sebastian: Mr. Deacon suddenly showing an unexpected grasp of military hierarchy—at least of a somewhat obsolete order—by pointing out that the Saint, holding as he did the rank of centurion—and being, therefore, a comparatively senior non-commissioned or warrant officer—probably possessed a less youthful and altogether more rugged appearance than that attributed to him by Perugino: and, indeed, commonly, by most other painters of hagiographical subjects. Going on to speak more generally of the Peruginos to be found throughout the rest of the gallery, Mr. Deacon alleged that more than one was labelled " Raphael." We did not dispute this assertion. Questioned as to how long he had himself been living in Paris, Mr. Deacon was vague; nor was it clear how he had occupied himself during the war, the course of which he seemed scarcely to have noticed. He implied that he had " settled abroad " more or less permanently; anyway, for a long time.

" There really are moments when one feels one has more in common with the French than with one's own countrymen," he said. " Their practical way of looking at things appeals to a certain side of me—though perhaps not the best side. If you want something here, the question is : Have you got the money to pay for it ? If the answer is ' yes,' all is well; if ' no,' you have to go without. Besides, there is a freer atmosphere. That is something that revolutions do. There is really nowhere else in the world like Paris."

He was living, he told us, " in a little place off the Boul' Mich'."

" I'm afraid I can't possibly ask you there in its present state," he added. " Moving in always takes an age. And I have so many treasures."

He shook his head after an inquiry regarding his painting.

"Much more interested in my collections now," he said. "One of the reasons I am over here is that I have been doing a little buying for friends as well as for myself."

"But I expect you keep your own work up now and then."

"After all, why should one go on adding to the detritus in this transitory world?" asked Mr. Deacon, raising his shoulders and smiling. "Still I sometimes take a sketchbook to a café—preferably some little estaminet in one of the working-class quarters. One gets a good head here, and a vigorous pose there. I collect heads—and necks—as you may remember."

He excused himself politely, though quite definitely, from an invitation to luncheon at the Interallié, a club of which he had, apparently, never heard; though he complained that Paris was more expensive than formerly, expressing at the same time regret at the "Americanisation" of the Latin Quarter.

"I sometimes think of moving up to Montmartre, like an artist of Whistler's time," he said.

Conversation waned after this. He asked how long we were staying in France, seeming, if anything, relieved to hear that we should all of us be back in England soon. On parting, there was perhaps a suggestion that the encounter had been, for no obvious reason, a shade uncomfortable; in this respect not necessarily worse than such meetings are apt to turn out between persons possessing little in common who run across each other after a long separation, and have to rely on common interests, by then half-forgotten. This faint sense of tension may also have owed something to Mr. Deacon's apparent unwillingness to go even so far in comparing autobiographical notes as might have been thought allowably free from the smallest suggestion of an undue display of egotism; especially when conversation was limited chiefly because one side lacked any idea of what the other had been doing for a number of years.

" I was glad to see Deacon again," my father said afterwards, when, that afternoon, we were on our way to tea at the Walpole-Wilsons' flat in Passy. " He looked a lot older."

That must have been almost the last time that I heard either of my parents refer to Mr. Deacon or his affairs.

However, the meeting at the Louvre, among other experiences of going abroad for the first time, remained in my mind as something rather important. Mr. Deacon's reappearance at that season seemed not only to indicate divorce of maturity from childhood, but also to emphasise the dependence of those two states one upon the other. " Grown-up " in the " old days," Mr. Deacon was grown-up still : I myself, on the other hand, had changed. There was still distance to travel, but I was on the way to drawing level with Mr. Deacon, as a fellow grown-up, himself no longer a figment of memory from childhood, but visible proof that life had existed in much the same way before I had begun to any serious extent to take part; and would, without doubt, continue to prevail long after he and I had ceased to participate. In addition to this appreciation of his status as a kind of milestone on the winding and dusty road of existence, I found something interesting—though not entirely comfortable—about Mr. Deacon's personality. He had given me a long, appraising glance when we shook hands, an action in itself, for some reason, rather unexpected, and later he had asked which were my favourite pictures in the gallery, and elsewhere, in the same deep, grave voice with which he had formerly explained his views on tone values: listening to the reply as if the information there contained might possess considerable importance for himself.

This apparent deference to what was necessarily unformed opinion seemed so flattering that I remembered him clearly long after our return to England; and, six or seven years later, when I saw the signature " E. Bosworth Deacon " in the corner of an oil-painting that hung high on the wall of the innermost part of the hall in the Walpole-Wilsons' house in Eaton Square, the atmosphere of that occasion in the Louvre, the talk about the Conference and St. Sebastian, the feeling of constraint—of embarrassment, almost—the visit, later in the day, to the Walpole-Wilsons themselves, came back all at once very clearly: even the illusion of universal relief that belonged to that historical period: of war being, surprisingly, at an end: of the imminence of " a good time ": of all that odd sense of intellectual emancipation that belonged, or, at least, seemed, perhaps rather spuriously, to belong, to the art of that epoch: its excitement and its melancholy mingling with kaleidoscopic impressions of a first sight of Paris. All these thoughts briefly and speedily suggested themselves, when, taking off my overcoat on my first visit to the house in Eaton Square—after I had come to live in London—I observed Mr. Deacon's picture. The canvas, comparatively small for a " Deacon," evidently not much considered by its owners, had been placed beyond the staircase above a Victorian barometer in a polished mahogany case. The subject was in a similar vein to those other scenes lying in the sale-room: the gold tablet at the foot of the frame baldly stating, without mentioning the artist's name, " *Boy-hood of Cyrus*." This was in fact, the first " Deacon " I had ever set eyes upon.

The importance that *Boyhood of Cyrus* eventually assumed had, however, nothing to do with the painter, or the merits, such as they were, of the picture itself : its significance being attained simply and solely as symbol of the probable physical proximity of Barbara Goring, Lady Walpole-Wilson's niece. his association of ideas was, indeed, so powerful that even years after I had ceased to be a guest at the Walpole-Wilson table I could not hear the name " Cyrus " mentioned—fortunately, in the circumstances, a fairly rare occurrence in everyday life—without being reminded of the pains of early love; while at the time of which I write almost any oil-painting illustrative of a remotely classical scene (such as one sees occasionally in the windows of dealers round St. James's normally specialising in *genre* pictures) would be liable to recall the fact, if by some unlikely chance forgotten, that I had not seen Barbara for a longer or shorter period.

I must have been about twenty-one or twenty-two at the time, and held then many rather wild ideas on the subject of women : conceptions largely the result of having read a good deal without simultaneous opportunity to modify by personal experience the recorded judgment of others upon that matter : estimates often excellent in their conclusions if correctly interpreted, though requiring practical knowledge to be appreciated at their full value.

At school I had known Tom Goring, who had later gone into the Sixtieth, and, although we had never had much to do with each other, I remembered some story of Stringham's of how both of them had put up money to buy a crib for Horace—or another Latin author whose works

they were required to render into English—and of trouble
that ensued from the translation supplied having contained
passages omitted in the official educational textbook. This
fact of her elder brother having been my contemporary—
the younger son, David, was still at school—may perhaps
have had something to do with finding myself, immediately
after our first meeting, on good terms with Barbara;
though the matter of getting on well with young men in
no circumstances presented serious difficulty to her.

"Do be quick, if you are going to ask me for a dance,"
she had said, when her cousin, Eleanor Walpole-Wilson,
had first introduced us. "I can't wait all night while you
make up your mind."

I was, I must admit, enchanted on the spot by this com-
portment, which I found far from discouraging. On some
earlier occasion a dowager had referred to Barbara in my
presence as "that rather noisy little Goring girl," and the
description was a just one. She was small and dark, with
hair cut in a square "bob," which—other girls used to com-
plain—was always hopelessly untidy. Her restlessness was
of that deceptive kind that usually indicates a fundamental
deficiency, rather than surplus of energy, though I cannot
claim, either in principle, or with particular reference to
Barbara herself, to have speculated on this diagnosis until
many years later. I remember, however, that when we met
fortuitously in Hyde Park one Sunday afternoon quite a
long time later (as it seemed to me), I still retained some
sense of proportion about her, although we had by then
seen a good deal of each other. She was walking in the
Park that afternoon with Eleanor Walpole-Wilson, fated
apparently to be witness of the various stages of our relationship. I had not managed to get away from London that
week-end, and to fall in by chance with these two seemed

a wonderful piece of luck. That was the last day for many months that I woke up in the morning without immediately thinking of Barbara.

" Oh, what fun to meet like this," she had said.

I felt immediately a sense of extraordinary exhilaration at this harmless remark. It was June, and there had been rain the day before, so that the grass smelt fresh and luxuriant. The weather, though warm, was not disagreeably hot. The precise location of our meeting was a spot not far from the Achilles statue. We strolled, all three, towards Kensington Gardens. The Row was empty. Sparkles of light radiated this way and that from the clusters of white statuary and nodular gilt pinnacles of the Albert Memorial, towards which we were steadily moving. Eleanor Walpole-Wilson, a square, broad-shouldered girl, rather above the average in height, wore her hair plaited in a bun at the back, which always looked as if it were about to come down at any moment: and did sometimes, in fact, descend piecemeal. She had brought with her Sultan, a labrador, and was trying to train this dog by blasts on a whistle, which she accompanied with harsh, mono-syllabic shouting. That enterprise, the training of Sultan, was in keeping with Eleanor's habit of behaviour, as she was always accustomed to act, in principle, as if London were the country, an exercise of will she rarely relaxed.

We ascended the steps of the Albert Memorial and inspected the figures of the Arts and Sciences loitering in high relief round the central mass of that monument. Eleanor, still blowing her whistle fitfully, made some comment regarding the muscles of the bearded male figure belonging to the group called " Manufactures " which caused Barbara to burst out laughing. This happened on the way down the steps at the south-east corner, approaching the statues symbolising Asia, where, beside the kneeling elephant, the Bedouin for ever rests on his haunches in hopeless contemplation of Kensington Gardens' trees and thickets, the blackened sockets of his eyes ranging endlessly over the rich foliage of these oases of the mirage.

For some reason Eleanor's words seemed immensely funny at that moment. Barbara stumbled, and, for a brief second, took my arm. It was then, perhaps, that a force was released, no less powerful for its action proving somewhat delayed; for emotions of that kind are not always immediately grasped. We sat on chairs for a time, and then walked to the north side of the park, in the direction of the Budds' house in Sussex Square, where the girls were invited to tea. When I said good-bye at the gates I experienced a sense of unaccountable loss, similar in its suddenness to that earlier exhilaration of our meeting. The rest of the day dragged, that feeling of anxiety—which haunts youth so much more than maturity—descending, coupled with almost unbearable nervous fatigue. I dined alone, and retired early to bed.

My parents' acquaintance—not a very close one—with the Walpole-Wilsons dated from that same period of the Peace Conference during which we had run across Mr. Deacon in the Louvre, a time when Sir Gavin Walpole-Wilson had also been working in Paris. He had by then already left the Diplomatic Service, and was associated with some voluntary organisation—of dubious practical importance, so my father used to hint—devoted to the assistance of certain specialised categories of refugee; for Sir Gavin's career had been brought to a close soon after receiving his K. C. M. G., as Minister to a South American republic. There had been trouble connected with the dispatch of a telegram; His Majesty's Government, so it subsequently appeared, having already recognised the Leader of the Opposition as Head of the State in place of the Junta that had enjoyed power for some years previously. It was generally agreed that Sir Gavin, whatever the misdemeanour, had been guilty of nothing worse than a perfectly correct effort to " keep in " with both sides: coupled, possibly, with a certain denseness of comprehension regarding potential fallibility of Foreign Secretaries, and changes recently observable in the political stature of General Gomez; but he had taken the matter to heart, and resigned. Pressure from above may have made this course involuntary, a point upon which opinion varied.

Although not at all inclined to under-estimate the personal part he had played in the Councils of Europe, or, indeed, of the World, Sir Gavin was apt to give the impression that he was always anxious, even in the smallest matters, to justify himself; so that an air of supposing life to have treated him less generously than his talents deserved made him, although a far more forceful personality, sometimes seem to resemble Uncle Giles. He was, for example, also fond of proclaiming that he set little store by rank—rank, at least, when contrasted with ability—a taste which he shared with my uncle. It was possible that in days before his marriage Sir Gavin may have suffered similar financial anxieties, for I believe his own family had been far from rich, with difficulty scraping together the money then required for entering the Diplomatic Service. After retirement—I had, of course, not known him before—he wore his hair rather long, and favoured loose, shaggy suits. A firm belief that things were more likely than not to go wrong was another characteristic of Sir Gavin's approach to life, induced no doubt by his own regrets. Indeed, he could not be entirely absolved from suspicion of rather enjoying the worst when it happened : at times almost of engineering disaster of a purely social kind.

" For lust of knowing what we should not know," he was fond of intoning, " we take the Golden Road to Samarkand."

This quotation may have offered to his mind some explanation of human adversity, though scarcely applicable in his own case, as he was a man singularly lacking in intellectual curiosity, and it was generally supposed that the inopportune step in his career had been the result of too much caution rather than any disposition to experiment in that exploration, moral or actual, to which the lines seem to refer. That trait, as it happened, was more noticeable in his wife. She was one of the two daughters of Lord Aberavon, a shipping magnate, now deceased, to whom, as I had discovered in due course, *Boyhood of Cyrus* had once belonged; Mr. Deacon's picture, for some inexplicable reason, being almost the sole residue from wholesale disposal on the collector's death of an accumulation of paintings unsympathetic to the taste of a later generation. Lady Walpole-Wilson suffered from " nerves," though less oppressively than her sister, Barbara's mother, who even regarded herself as a semi-invalid on that account. Indeed, I had scarcely ever seen Lady Goring, or her husband : for, like his niece, Eleanor, Lord Goring shunned London whenever possible. He was said to be an expert on scientific methods of cultivation, and possessed an experimental fruit farm that was, I believe, rather famous for daring methods.

Uncle Giles was fond of calling people richer or in a general way more advantageously placed than himself, against whom he could at the same time level no specifically disparaging charge, " well connected enough, I don't doubt," a descriptive phrase which he would sometimes indiscriminately apply; but I suppose that the Gorings might truthfully have been so labelled. They used to take a house in Upper Berkeley Street for the first part of the summer, though dinner-parties were rare there, and not as a rule convivial. Most of the responsibility for Barbara's " season " fell on her aunt, who probably regarded her niece's lively character as an alleviation of difficulties posed by her own daughter, rather than any additional burden on the household.

Lady Walpole-Wilson, for whom I felt a decided affection, was a tall, dark, distinguished-looking woman, with doe-like eyes, to whose appearance some vice-regal or ambassadorial marriage seemed appropriate. Her comparative incapacity to control her own dinner-parties, at which she was almost always especially discomposed, seemed to me a kind of mute personal protest against circumstances—in the shape of her husband's retirement—having deprived her of the splendours, such as they were, of that position in life owed to her statuesque presence; for in those days I took a highly romantic view, not only of love, but also of such things as politics and government: supposing, for example, that eccentricity and ineptitude were unknown in circles where they might, in fact, be regarded—at least so far as the official entertaining of all countries is concerned—almost as the rule rather than the exception. I can now see that Lady Walpole-Wilson's past experience may have made her aware of this tendency on the part of wives of distinguished public figures to be unable, or unwilling, to make suitable hostesses: a knowledge, coupled with her natural diffidence, that caused her to give an impression sometimes that at all costs she would like to escape from her own house: not because dispensation of hospitality was in itself in the least disagreeable to her as much as on account of accumulated memories from the past of wounded feelings when matters had "gone wrong."

To these sentiments was no doubt added the self-inflicted embarrassment implicit in the paraphernalia of launching a daughter—and, if it could be remarked without unkindness, "what a daughter"—on to an obdurate world; not to mention grappling with purely hypothetical questions, such as the enigma, universally insoluble, of what other mothers would think of the manner in which she herself, as a mother, was sustaining this load of care. In this last affliction Sir Gavin's attitude was often of no great help, and it is hard to say whether either of them really believed that Eleanor, who had always been more or less of a "problem"—there were endless stories of nose-bleeds and headaches—would ever find a husband. Eleanor had always disliked feminine pursuits. When we had met in Paris before either of us had grown up, she had told me that she would at that moment much prefer to be staying with her cousins in Oxfordshire: an attitude of mind that had culminated in detestation of dances. This resentment, since I had known her in those early days, did not seem as strange to me as to many of the young men who encountered her for the first time at the dinner-table, where she could be both abrupt and sulky. Barbara used to say: " Eleanor should never have been removed from the country. It is cruelty to animals." She was also fond of remarking: " Eleanor is not a bad old girl when you get to know her," a statement unquestionably true; but, since human life is lived largely at surface level, that encouraging possibility, true or false, did not appreciably lighten the burden of Eleanor's partners.

The Walpole-Wilsons, accordingly, provided not only the foundation, but frequently the immediate locality, also, for

my association with Barbara, whom I used to meet fairly
often at dances, after our walk together in the park. Sometimes we even saw a film together, or went to a matinée.
That was in the summer. When she came to London for
a few weeks before Christmas, we met again. By the opening of the following May I was beginning to wonder how
the situation was to be resolved. Such scuffles as had, once
in a way, taken place between us, on the comparatively
rare occasions when we found ourselves alone together,
were not exactly encouraged by her; in fact she seemed only
to like an intermittent attack for the pleasure of repulsing
it. Certainly such aggression carried neither of us any
farther. She liked ragging; but ragging—and nothing
more—these rough-and-tumbles remained. "Don't get
sentimental," she used to say; and so far as it went, avoidance of sentiment— as much as avoidance of sentimentality
—appeared, on her side, a genuine inclination.

This affair with Barbara, although taking up less than
a year, seemed already to have occupied a substantial proportion of my life; because nothing establishes the timeless-
ness of Time like those episodes of early experience seen,
on re-examination at a later period, to have been crowded
together with such unbelievable closeness in the course of
a few years; yet equally giving the illusion of being so infinitely extended during the months when actually taking
place. My frame of mind—perhaps I should say the state of
my heart—remained unchanged, and dances seemed point-
less unless Barbara was present. During that summer *Boyhood of Cyrus* developed its mystic significance, representing on my arrival in front of it a two-to-one chance of seeing
Barbara at dinner. If we both ate at the Walpole-Wilsons',
she was at least under my eye. She herself was always
quite unaware of the sentimental meaning thus attached to

Mr. Deacon's picture. When first asked about it, she could not for a long time make out what picture I spoke of; and once, when we were both in the hall at the same time and I drew her attention to where it hung, she assured me that she had never before noticed its existence. Eleanor was equally vague on the subject.

" Are they going bathing?" she had asked. " I don't care for it."

This matter of being able to establish Barbara's whereabouts for a specific number of hours brought at least limited relief from agonies of ignorance as to what her movements might be, with consequent inability to exercise control over her in however slight a degree; for love of that sort—the sort where the sensual element has been reduced to a minimum—must after all, largely if not entirely, resolve itself to the exercise of power: a fact of which Barbara was, of course, more aware than I.

These torments, as I have said, continued for a number of months, sometimes with great severity; and then one afternoon, when I was correcting proofs in the office, Barbara rang up and asked if I would dine at Eaton Square that evening for the Huntercombes' dance. I decided immediately that I would put off Short (my former undergraduate acquaintance, now become a civil servant), with whom, earlier in the week, I had arranged to have a meal, and at once agreed to come. I had experienced the usual feeling of excitement while talking with her on the telephone; but suddenly as I hung up the receiver—thinking that perhaps I was leaving Short rather ruthlessly in the lurch so far as his evening was concerned—I found myself wondering whether I was still in love. Barbara's voice had sounded so peremptory, and it was clear that someone else had failed her at the last moment. In that there was, of course, nothing to be taken reasonably amiss. Obviously I could not expect to sit next to her at dinner every night of our lives—unless I married her; perhaps not even then. And yet my heart seemed a shade lighter. Was the fever passing? I was myself still barely conscious of its declension. I had not at that time met Barnby, nor had opportunity to digest one of his favourite maxims: " A woman always overplays her hand."

I had, naturally, given a good deal of thought at one time or another to the question of love. Barbara did not represent the first attack. There had been, for example, Peter Templer's sister, Jean, and Madame Leroy's niece, Suzette; but Jean and Suzette now seemed dim, if desirable, memories; and I felt, for no particular reason, more sure now of the maturity of my approach. At the same time there was certainly little to boast about in my handling of the problem of Barbara. I could not even make up my mind —should anything of the sort have been practicable— whether or not I really wanted to marry her. Marriage appeared something remote and forbidding, with which desire for Barbara had little or no connection. She seemed to exist merely to disturb my rest: to be possessed neither by lawful nor unlawful means: made of dreams, yet to be captured only by reality. Such, at least, were the terms in which I thought of her as I approached the Walpole-Wilsons' that evening.

Taxis were drawing up in the late sunshine before several of the houses in the square, and young men in tails and girls in evening dress, looking rather selfconscious in the bright daylight, were paying fares or ringing front-door bells. It was that stagnant London weather without a breath of air. One might almost have been in the Tropics. Even Archie Gilbert, who had immediately preceded me in the

hall—he had never been known to be late for dinner—
looked that night as if he might be feeling the heat a little.
His almost invisibly fair moustache suggested the same
piqué material as the surface of his stiff shirt; and, as usual,
he shed about him an effect of such unnatural cleanliness
that some secret chemical process seemed to have been
applied, in preparation for the party, both to himself and
his clothes: making body and its dazzling integument,
sable and argent rather than merely black and white, proof
against smuts and dust. Shirt, collar, tie, waistcoat, handkerchief, and gloves were like snow: all these trappings,
as always apparently assumed for the first time: even
though he himself looked a shade pinker than usual in the
face owing to the oppressive climatic conditions.

His whole life seemed so irrevocably concentrated on
" débutante dances " that it was impossible to imagine
Archie Gilbert finding any tolerable existence outside a tail-
coat. I could never remember attending any London dance
that could possibly be considered to fall within the category
named, at which he had not also been present for at least
a few minutes; and, if two or three balls were held on the
same evening, it always turned out that he had managed
to look in at each one of them. During the day he was said
to " do something in the City "—the phrase " non-ferrous
metals " had once been hesitantly mentioned in my presence
as applicable, in some probably remote manner to his daily
employment. He himself never referred to any such subordination, and I used sometimes to wonder whether this
putative job was not, in reality, a polite fiction, invented on
his own part out of genuine modesty, of which I am sure
he possessed a great deal, in order to make himself appear
a less remarkable person than in truth he was: even a kind
of superhuman ordinariness being undesirable, perhaps, for

true perfection in this rôle of absolute normality which he
had chosen to play with such *éclat*. He was unthinkable
in everyday clothes; and he must, in any case, have required
that rest and sleep during the hours of light which his
nocturnal duties could rarely, if ever, have allowed him.
He seemed to prefer no one woman—débutante or chaper-
one—to another; and, although not indulging in much conversation, as such, he always gave the impression of being
at ease with, or without, words; and of having danced
at least once with every one of the three or four hundred
girls who constituted, in the last resort, the final cause, and
only possible justification, of that social organism. He
appeared also to be known by name, and approved, by the
mother of each of these girls : in a general way, as I have
said, getting on equally well with mothers and daughters.

Even Eleanor's consistently severe manner with young
men was modified appreciably for Archie Gilbert, and we
had hardly arrived in the drawing-room before she was
asking him to help her in the forcible return of Sultan to
the huge wicker hutch, occupying one complete corner of
the room, in which the labrador had his being. Together
Archie Gilbert and Eleanor dragged back the dog, while
Sultan thumped his tail noisily on the carpet, and Lady
Walpole-Wilson protested a little that the struggle would
mar the beauty of Archie Gilbert's clothes.

Her own eagerness of manner always suggested that Lady
Walpole-Wilson would have enjoyed asking congenial
people to her parties if only she could have found people
who were, indeed, congenial to her; and she was, of course,
not the only hostess who must, from time to time, have
suffered a twinge of misgiving on account of more than
one of the young men who formed the shifting male popula-

tion of the London ballrooms. Supposing most other people to live a more amusing life than herself, her humility in this respect was combined with a trust, never entirely relinquished, that with a different collection of guests in the house things might take a turn for the better. This inward condition, in which hope and despair constantly gave place to one another, undeniably contributed to a lack of ease in her drawing-room.

Sir Gavin was moving about dramatically, even rather tragically, in the background. He was, as I have suggested, inclined to affect a few mild eccentricities of dress. That evening, for example, he was wearing an old-fashioned straight-ended white tie like a butler's : his large, almost square horn-rimmed spectacles, tanned complexion, and moustache, bristling, but at the same time silky, giving him a rather fierce expression, like that of an angry rajah. Although deeper-chested and more weather-beaten, he certainly recalled Uncle Giles. Walking, as he did at times, with a slight limp, the cause of which was unknown to me —possibly it was assumed to indicate a certain state of mind—he took my arm almost fiercely, rather as if acting in an amateur production of Shakespeare; and, no doubt because he prided himself on putting young men at their ease, drew my attention to another guest, already arrived in the room before Archie Gilbert and myself. This person was standing under Lavery's portrait of Lady Walpole-Wilson, painted at the time of her marriage, in a white dress and blue sash, a picture he was examining with the air of one trying to fill in the seconds before introductions begin to take place, rather than on account of a deep interest in art.

" Have you met Mr. Widmerpool?" asked Sir Gavin, disconsolately, suddenly dropping his energetic demeanour, as if suffering all at once from unaccountable foreboding about the whole party.

Widmerpool's advent in Eaton Square that night did not strike me at the time as anything more than a matter of chance. He had cropped up in my life before, and, if I considered him at all as a recurrent factor, I should have been prepared to admit that he might crop up again. I did not, however, as yet see him as one of those symbolic figures, of whom most people possess at least one example, if not more, round whom the past and the future have a way of assembling. We had not met for years; since the summer after I had left school, when both of us had been trying to learn French staying with the Leroys in Touraine —the place, in fact, where I had supposed myself in love with Suzette. I had hardly thought of him since the moment when he had climbed ponderously into the *grognard's* taxi, and coasted in a cloud of white dust down the hill from La Grenadière. Now he had exchanged his metal-edged glasses for spectacles with a tortoise-shell frame, similar, though of lesser proportions, to those worn by his host, and in general smartened up his personal appearance. True to the old form, there was still something indefinably odd about the cut of his white waistcoat; while he retained that curiously piscine cast of countenance, projecting the impression that he swam, rather than walked, through the rooms he haunted.

Just as the first sight of *Boyhood of Cyrus,* by its association with Mr. Deacon and life before the war, had brought back memories of childhood, the sight of Widmerpool called up in a similar manner—almost· like some parallel scene from Mr. Deacon's brush entitled *Boyhood of Widmerpool*—all kind of recollections of days at school. I re-

membered the interest once aroused in me by Widmerpool's
determination to become a success in life, and the brilliance
with which Stringham used to mimic his movements and
manner of speech. Indeed, Widmerpool's presence in the
flesh seemed even now less real than Stringham's former
imitations of him : a thought that had often struck me
before, now renewed unexpectedly in the Walpole-Wilson's
drawing-room. Widmerpool still represented to my mind
a kind of embodiment of thankless labour and unsatisfied
ambition. When we had met at La Grenadière, he had
talked of his activities in London, but somehow I had never
been able to picture his life as an adult; idly fancying him,
if thought of at all, for ever floundering towards the tape
in races never won. Certainly it had not once ocurred to me
that I should meet him at a dinner-party given for a dance,
although I recalled now that he had talked of dances; and,
when I came to consider the matter, there was not the smallest reason why he should not turn up upon an occasion such
as this—at the Walpole-Wilson's house or anywhere else.
That had to be admitted without question. He seemed in
the best of spirits. We were immediately left together by
Sir Gavin, who wandered off muttering to himself in a dissatisfied undertone about some impenetrable concerns of his
own.

"Good gracious, Jenkins," said Widmerpool, in that
thick voice of his which remained quite unchanged, " I had
no idea that you were a dancing man."

" I had formed the same wrong impression about yourself."

" But I have never seen you anywhere before." He
sounded rather aggrieved.

" We must be asked to different parties."

This reply, made on the spur of the moment without

any suggestion of seriousness—certainly not intended to dis-
credit the dances frequented by Widmerpool—must, for
some reason, have sounded caustic to his ears. Perhaps I
had inadequately concealed surprise felt on learning from
his manner that he evidently regarded himself as a kind of
standard "spare man ": in short something closely akin to
Archie Gilbert. Whatever the cause, the words had
obviously given offence. He went red in the face, and
made one of those awkward jerks of the body which
Stringham used to imitate so deftly.

" As a matter of fact, I have been about very little this
summer," he said, frowning. " I found I had been working
a shade too hard, and had to—well—give myself a bit of a
rest."

I remembered the interest he had always taken, even
while still a schoolboy, in his own health and its diurnal
changes. In France it had been the same. A whole afternoon had been spent in Tours trying to find the right
medicine to adjust the effect on him of the local wine, of
which the Leroys' vintage, drunk the night before, had been
of disastrously recent growth.

" Then, the year before, I got jaundice in the middle of
the season."

" Are you fit again now?"

" I am better."

He spoke with gravity.

" But I intend to take care of myself," he added. " My
mother often tells me I go at things too hard. Besides, I
don't really get enough air and exercise—without which
one can never be truly robust."

" Do you still go down to Barnes and drive golf-balls into
a net?"

" Whenever feasible."

He made not the smallest acknowledgment of the feat of memory on my part—with which, personally, I felt rather satisfied—that had called to mind this detail (given years before at the Leroys') of his athletic exercises in outer London. The illusion that egoists will be pleased, or flattered, by interest taken in their habits persists throughout life; whereas, in fact, persons like Widmerpool, in complete subjection to the ego, are, by the nature of that infirmity, prevented from supposing that the minds of others could possibly be occupied by any subject far distant from the egoist's own affairs.

"Actually, one can spend too much time on sport if one is really going to get on," said Widmerpool. "And then I have my Territorials."

"You were going to be a solicitor when we last met."

"That would hardly preclude me from holding a Territorial officer's commission," said Widmerpool, smiling as broadly as his small mouth would allow, as if this were a repartee of quite unusual neatness.

"Of course it wouldn't."

His remark seemed to me immensely silly.

"I am with a firm of solicitors—Turnbull, Welford and Puckering, to be exact," he said. "But you may be sure that I have other interests too. Some of them not unimportant, I might add."

He smiled with some self-satisfaction, but clearly did not wish to be questioned further, at least there and then, regarding his professional activities. That was reasonable enough in the circumstances. However, his next words surprised me. Giving a short intake of breath, he said in a lower voice, with one of those unexpected outbursts of candour that I remembered from La Grenadière: "Do you know our host and hostess well? I have been on excellent terms with the family for a number of years, but this is the first time I have been asked to dinner. Of course I really know the Gorings better."

This admission regarding his invitation to dine at Eaton Square was apparently intended to convey some hint, or confession, of past failure; although at the same time Widmerpool seemed half inclined by his tone to impart the news of his better acquaintance with the Gorings equally as a matter for congratulation. Indeed, he was evidently unable to decide in his own mind whether this allegedly long familiarity with the Walpole-Wilsons was—in the light of this being his first appearance in the house—something to boast of, or conceal.

Our conversation, taking place intermittently, while people continually arrived in the room, was several times broken off when one or other of us was introduced to, or spoke with, another guest. Two of the girls present I had not met before. The taller, Lady Anne Stepney, wore an evening dress that had seen better days : which looked, indeed, rather like an old nightdress furbished up for the occasion. She seemed quite unconcerned about her decidedly untidy appearance, her bearing in some respects resembling Eleanor's, though she was much prettier than Eleanor, with large dark eyes and reddish hair. Her name was familiar to me, for what reason I could not at first recall. The lively, gleaming little Jewess in a scarlet frock, who came into the room on the heels of Lady Anne, was announced as " Miss Manasch," and addressed by the Walpole-Wilsons as " Rosie." Both girls were immediately, and simultaneously, engaged by Archie Gilbert, who happened to be free at their moment of entering the room.

Over by the window, Margaret Budd, a beauty, was talking to Pardoe, a Grenadier; and laughing while he demon-

strated with a small shovel taken from the fireplace a scoop-
ing shot, successful or the reverse, that he, or someone
known to him had recently performed on the links. When
she laughed, Margaret looked like an immensely—almost
ludicrously—pretty child. She was, as it were, the female
equivalent of Archie Gilbert: present at every dance, always lovely, always fresh, and yet somehow quite unreal.
She scarcely spoke at all, and might have been one of those
huge dolls which, when inclined backwards, say " Ma-ma "
or " Pa-pa ": though impossible to imagine in any position
so undignified as that required for the mechanism to produce these syllables: equally hard to conceive her dis-
hevelled, or bad-tempered, or, indeed, capable of physical
passion—though appearances may be deceptive in no sphere
so much as the last. Never without a partner, usually
booked up six or seven dances ahead, this was her third
or fourth season—so Barbara had once pointed out—and
there had, as yet, been no sign of her getting engaged.
" Margaret is rather a Guardee's girl," Barbara had added,
evidently intending the label to imply no great compliment
in her own eyes.

Widmerpool's presence reminded me that Margaret was
cousin of the Budd who had been Captain of the Eleven
one year at school; and I remembered the story Stringham
had told me, years before, of Widmerpool's pleased acceptance—delight almost—on being struck in the face with a
banana thrown by that comparatively notable cricketer. I
could not help toying with the fantasy that some atavistic
strain, deep-seated in the Budd family, might cause Margaret to assail Widmerpool in similar manner; perhaps
later in the evening when dessert, tempting as a missile,
appeared at the Walpole-Wilson's table. Such a vision was
improbable to an almost infinite degree, because Margaret

was the kindest, quietest creature imaginable; really, I think, almost wholly unaware, in gentle concentration on herself, of the presence of most of the people moving about her. Even her laughter was rare, and its audible provocation before dinner that evening by his strokes in the air with the shovel did Pardoe credit.

From a girl's point of view, there was no doubt something to be said for considering Pardoe the most interesting person present that evening. He had recently inherited a house on the Welsh Border (Jacobean in architecture, though with more ancient historical associations going back to the Wars of the Roses), together with enough money, so it was said, to " keep up " the estate. He was an agreeable, pink-faced ensign, very short, square, and broad-shouldered, with a huge black moustache, brushed out so forcibly that it seemed to be false and assumed for a joke. Such affluent young men were known to have a tendency to abandon dances and frequent night-clubs. Pardoe, however, was still available, so it appeared; no one could tell for how long. Unlike Archie Gilbert, he had a great deal to say for himself—though his newly acquired possessions made small-talk scarcely necessary—and, as he modestly treated his own appearance as a matter for laughter, the moustache was a considerable asset in his anecdotes. He had at last abandoned the shovel, and, mildly interested in music had become engaged in some operatic argument with Miss Manasch. To this discussion Sir Gavin, from the background where he had been hovering, his moustache bristling more than ever, now cut in with the emphatic words :

" No one could sing it like Slezak."

" Did you ever hear him in *Lohengrin*?" demanded Pardoe, taking the ends of his own moustache with both hands, as if about to tear it off and reveal himself in a new identity.

"Many a time and oft," said Sir Gavin, defiantly. "But what was that you were saying about *Idomeneo*?"

All three of them embarked clamorously on a new musical dispute. The rest of us chatted in a desultory way. Barbara arrived late. She was wearing her gold dress that I knew of old did not suit her; and that spirit of contradiction that especially governs matters of the heart caused the fact that she was not looking her best to provoke in me a stab of affection. Even so, I was still able to wonder whether the situation between us—between myself and her, would perhaps be more accurate—remained quite unchanged; and, as I let go of her small cluster of fingers—each one of which I was conscious of as a single entity while I held her hand—I thought that perhaps that night I should not, as in past months, experience the same recurrent torments as she danced with other men. As soon as she had come into the room, Widmerpool skirted the sofa and made towards her, leaving me with the impression that I might in some manner have appeared unfriendly to him after our comparative intimacy in France. I decided to try to correct this apprehension, should it exist, later in the evening when suitable opportunity might arise.

The minutes passed: conversation flagged. The Louis Seize clock standing on a wall-bracket gave out a threatening tick-tock. One of the male guests had still not yet turned up. In those days, at that sort of party, there were no drinks before dinner; and, while Eleanor told me about her Girl Guides, the evening sun deflected huge golden squares of phosphorescent colour (spread rather in the manner advocated by Mr. Deacon, giving formal juxtaposition to light and shade) against the peacock-green shot-silk shadows of the sofa cushions. Outside, the detonation of loudly-slammed taxi doors, suggesting the opening of a cannonade, had died down. In place of those sounds some cats were quarrelling, or making love, in the gardens running the length of the square. I began to long for the meal to begin. After total silence had fallen on the room for the second time, Lady Walpole-Wilson, apparently with an effort, for her lips faltered slightly when she spoke, came to a decision to await the late-comer no further.

"Let's go down in a troop," she said, "and—as Mr. Tompsitt is so unpunctual—not bother about 'taking in'. I really do not think we can delay dinner any longer."

In speaking to each other the Walpole-Wilsons were inclined to give an impression that they were comparative strangers, who had met for the first time only a week or two before, but at this remark her husband, no doubt wanting food as much as—perhaps even more than—the rest of those present, replied rather gruffly: "Of course, Daisy, of course."

He added, without any suggestion of complaint—on the contrary, if anything, with approbation: "Young Tompsitt is always late."

The news that Tompsitt had been invited would once have filled me with dismay. Even at that moment, sudden mention of his name caused an instinctive hope that his absence was due to illness or accident, something that might prevent him from putting in any appearance at all, preferably grave enough to exclude him from dances for many months: perhaps for ever. He was one of various young men moving within Barbara's orbit whose relationship with her, though impossible to estimate at all precisely, was yet in a general way disturbing for someone who might have claims of his own to put forward in that quarter. In that respect Tompsitt's connection was of a particularly distasteful kind in that Barbara evidently found him not unattractive; while his approach to her, or so it seemed to me, was conditioned entirely by the ebb and flow of his own vanity : no inconsiderable element when gauged at any given moment, though laying a course hard for an unsympathetic observer to chart. That is to say he was obviously flattered by the fact that Barbara found him, apparently, prepossessing enough; and, at the same time, not sufficiently stirred within himself to spend more than comparatively brief spells in her company, especially when there were other girls about, who might be supposed, for one reason or another, to represent in his eyes potentially superior assets.

That was what I used, perhaps unjustly, to reflect; at the same time having to admit to myself that Tompsitt's attitude towards Barbara posed, from my own point of view, a dilemma as to what, short of his own bodily removal, would constitute a change for the better. His relative lack of enthusiasm, though acceptable only with all kinds of unpalatable reservations, had, in its way, to be approved; while apprehension that his feelings towards Barbara might suddenly undergo some violent emotional stimulation was—or had certainly been until that evening—an ever present anxiety. At last, however, I felt, anyway on second thoughts, fairly indifferent as to whether or not Tompsitt turned up. Inwardly I was becoming increasingly convinced of this, and I might even have looked forward to Tompsitt's entry if there had been serious threat of dinner being further delayed on his account.

In the dining-room I found myself sitting at the oval-ended table between Barbara and Anne Stepney, the second

of whom was on Sir Gavin's right. The Walpole-Wilsons
defied prevailing mode by still employing a table-cloth, a
preference of Sir Gavin's, who prided himself on combining
in his own home tastes of " the old school " with a progres-
sive point of view in worldy matters. The scented geranium
leaf usually to be found floating in the finger-bowls could
be attributed to his wife's leaning towards a more exotic
way of life. Beyond Barbara was Archie Gilbert, probably
placed on Lady Walpole-Wilson's left to make up for
having Tompsitt—or rather an empty chair, where in due
course he would sit, if he had not forgotten the invitation—
on her right. Tompsitt, a protégé of Sir Gavin's, was not
greatly liked either by Eleanor or her mother.

This chasm left by Tompsitt divided Margaret Budd,
who had Widmerpool on her other side, from her hostess.
Widmerpool's precise channel of invitation to the house
was still obscure, and the fact that he himself seemed on
the whole surprised to find himself dining there made his
presence even more a matter for speculation. He had been
placed next to Eleanor, who had presumably been consulted on the subject of seating accommodation at the
dinner table, though he seemed by his manner towards her
to know her only slightly, while she herself showed signs,
familiar to me from observing her behaviour on past occasions, of indifference, if not dislike, for his company.
Barbara had been the only member of the party greeted by
him as an old acquaintance, though she had done no more
than wring him rather warmly by the hand when she arrived, quickly passing on to someone else, at which he had
looked discouraged. Pardoe sat between Eleanor and Miss
Manasch—who brought the party round once more to Sir
Gavin. The table had perhaps not been easy to arrange.
Its complications of seating must have posed problems that

accounted for Lady Walpole-Wilson's more than usually agitated state.

" There does not seem any substantial agreement yet on the subject of the Haig statue," said Widmerpool, as he unfolded his napkin. " Did you read St. John Clarke's letter?"

He spoke to Eleanor, though he had glanced round the table as if hoping for a larger audience to hear his views on the matter. The subject, as it happened, was one upon which I knew Eleanor to hold decided opinions, and was therefore a question to be avoided, unless driven to conversational extremities, as she much preferred statement to discussion. The fact of broaching it was yet another indication that Widmerpool could not have seen a great deal of her at all recently.

" Surely they can find someone to carve a horse that looks like a horse."

She spoke with truculence even at the outset.

" The question, to my mind," said Widmerpool, " is whether a statue is, in reality, an appropriate form of recognition for public services in modern times."

"Don't you think great men ought to be honoured?" Eleanor asked, rather tensely. "I do."

She clenched her lips tightly together as if prepared to contest the point to the death—with Widmerpool or anyone else.

" Nobody—least of all myself—denies the desirability of honouring great men," he said in return, rather sharply, " but some people think the traffic problem—already severe enough in all conscience—might be adversely affected if any more space is taken up by monuments in busy thoroughfares."

" I can't see why they can't make a model of a real

horse," said Barbara. "Couldn't they do it in plaster of Paris or something. Don't you think?"

This last question, propitiatory in tone, and addressed in a fairly low voice to myself, could still make me feel, for reasons quite subjective in origin, that there might be something to be said for this unconventional method of solving what had become almost the chief enigma of contemporary æsthetic.

"Need there be a horse?" asked Lady Walpole-Wilson, putting a brave face on the discussion, though evidently well aware, even apart from Eleanor's potential pronouncements on the subject, of its manifold dangers.

"You can't very well have him sitting at his desk," said Sir Gavin, bluffly, "though I expect that was where he spent a good deal of his time. When I saw him in Paris at the time of the Conference——"

"Why shouldn't he be on a horse?" demanded Eleanor, angrily. "He used to ride one, didn't he?"

"We all agree that he used to ride one," said Widmerpool, indulgently this time. "And that, if commemoration is to take the form proposed, the Field-Marshal should certainly be represented mounted on his charger. I should have supposed there was no doubt upon that point."

"Oh, I don't know," said Pardoe, shooting out his moustache once more. "Why not put him in a staff-car? You could have the real thing, with his flag flying at the bonnet."

"Of course if you want to make a joke of it . . ." said Eleanor, casting a look of great contempt in Pardoe's direction.

Archie Gilbert and Margaret Budd appeared to hold no strong convictions regarding the statue. Miss Manasch made the practical suggestion that they should pay off the sculptor of the work under discussion, if—as it certainly appeared—this had not met with general approval, and make a fresh start with another candidate who might provide something of a more popular nature.

"I think they ought to have got Mestroviç in the first place," said Lady Anne, coldly, during the silence that followed Miss Manasch's proposal.

This unexpected opinion was plainly issued as a challenge; but controversy regarding the memorial was now cut short by the sudden arrival in the dining-room of Tompsitt.

After somewhat perfunctory apology for his lateness, he sat down between Lady Walpole-Wilson and Margaret Budd, though without taking a great deal of notice of either of them. Lady Walpole-Wilson shot him a look to suggest her collusion in his apparent inclination to assume that the time for regrets and excuses was now long past; though her glance was also no doubt intended to urge—even to plead with—him to make amends best by showing himself agreeable to his neighbour, since Eleanor had relapsed into further argument that demanded Widmerpool's close attention, leaving Margaret Budd, for all her beauty, high and dry so far as personal attention was concerned.

However, now that he had arrived, formal conversation seemed the last thing to which Tompsitt was at all disposed. He smiled across the table to Barbara, who had crooked her finger at him as he entered the room. Then, picking up the menu, he studied it carefully. The card was inscribed for some reason—probably because she had looked in at tea-time and Eleanor hated the job—in Barbara's own scratchy, laborious hand that I knew so well; not because I had ever received many letters from her in the course of our relationship, but on account of the fact that such scrawled notes as I possessed used to live for months in my pocket, seeming to retain in their paper and ink some atom of Barbara herself to be preserved and secreted until our next meeting. I wondered whether that schoolgirl script breathed any such message to Tompsitt, as it broke the news that he was about to eat the identical meal he must have consumed at every dinner-party—if given specifically for a London dance—that he had ever attended.

He was a large, fair young man, with unbrushed hair and a grey smudge on the left-hand side of his shirt-front: cramming for—perhaps by then even admitted to—the Foreign Office. Sir Gavin held strong views on "broadening the basis" of the selection of candidates for governmental service, and he took an interest in Tompsitt as prototype of a newer and less constricted vehicle for handling foreign affairs. Certainly Tompsitt's appearance was calculated to dispose effectually of the myth, dear to the public mind, of the "faultlessly dressed diplomat," and he had been educated—the details were elusive—in some manner not absolutely conventional: though his air of incivility that so delighted Sir Gavin could no doubt have been inculcated with at least equal success at any public school. It was perhaps fair to regard him a young man rather different from those normally recruited for the purpose, and, in return for this patronage, Tompsitt, supercilious in his manner to most people, accorded a deep respect to Sir Gavin's utterances; although, a posture not uncommon in such dual relationships, this deference sometimes took the more flattering form of apparent disagreement. They had met a year or two before at a gathering of some local branch of the League of Nations Union, where Sir Gavin had given a talk on "Collective Security."

All the time he was reading the menu, Tompsitt smiled

to himself, as if exceedingly content to exist in a world from which most, if not all, surrounding distractions had been effectively eliminated. It had to be agreed that there was some forcefulness in his complete disregard for the rest of the party. Lady Walpole-Wilson began to look rather despairing. Widmerpool, on the other hand, seemed to share, as if by instinct, Sir Gavin's approbation for Tompsitt, or at least felt distinct interest in his personality, because after a time he ceased to give his views on the Horse in Sculpture, and cast several searching glances down the table. Sir Gavin, whose conversation was habitually diversified by a murmur of "m'm . . . m'm . . . m'm . . ." repeated under his breath while his interlocutor was speaking—a technique designed to discourage over-long disquisitions on the other side—did no more than nod approvingly at Tompsitt. For the first few minutes of dinner Sir Gavin had contrived to monopolise the conversation of the girls he sat between. Now, however, he concentrated more particularly on Miss Manasch, from whom, with much laughter and by-play on his part, he appeared to be attempting to extract certain concrete opinions supposedly held by her father regarding the expansion of the Donners-Brebner Company in the Balkans. His attitude suggested that he also found Miss Manasch rather unusually attractive physically.

Now that the small, though appreciable, disturbance caused by Tompsitt's entry had finally settled down, the moment had come for some sort of conversational skirmish to begin between Lady Anne Stepney and myself. Ever since we had been introduced, I had been wondering why her name suggested some episode in the past: an incident vaguely unsatisfactory or disturbing. The mention of Donners-Brebner now reminded me that, the uneasy recol-

lections were in connection with this girl's sister, Peggy,
whom Stringham on that night years before at the Donners-
Brebner building had spoken, perhaps not very seriously,
of marrying. In fact, I remembered now that he had been
on his way to dinner with their parents, the Bridgnorths.
That was the last time I had seen Stringham; it must have
been—I tried to remember—four or five years before. The
link seemed to provide a suitable topic to broach.

"Have you ever come across someone called Charles
Stringham? I think he knows your sister."

"Oh, yes," she said, "one of Peggy's pompous friends,
isn't he?"

I found this a staggering judgment. There were all kinds
of things to be said against Stringham's conduct—he could
be offhand, even thoroughly bad-mannered—but "pompous" was the last adjective in the world I ever expected to
hear applied to him. It occurred to me, a second later, that
she used the word with specialised meaning; or perhaps—
this was most probable—merely intended to imply that her
sister and Stringham were asked to grander parties than
herself. Possibly she became aware that her remark had surprised me, because she added: "I hope he isn't a great
friend of yours."

I was about to reply that Stringham was, indeed, a "great
friend" of mine, when I remembered that by now this
description could scarcely be held to be true, since I had
not seen nor heard of him for so long that I had little or
no idea what he was doing with himself; and, for all I
knew, he might almost have forgotten my existence. I had
to admit to myself that, for my own part, I had not thought
much about him either, since we had last met; though
this sudden realisation that we now barely knew one
another was, for a moment, oddly painful. In any event,

nothing seemed to have come out of his talk of wanting to marry Peggy Stepney, and mention of his name had been, in the circumstances, perhaps tactless.

" I haven't seen him for three or four years."

" Oh, I thought you might know him well."

" I used to."

" As a matter of fact, Peggy hasn't spoken of Charles Stringham for ages," she said.

She did not actually toss her head—as girls are sometimes said to do in books—but that would have been the gesture appropriate to the tone in which she made this comment. It was evident that the subject of Stringham could supply no basis for discussion between us. I searched my mind for other themes. Lady Anne herself showed no sign of making any immediate contribution. She left the remains of her clear soup, and fixed her eyes on Miss Manasch; whether to satisfy herself about technical detail regarding the red dress, or to observe how well she was standing up to Sir Gavin's interrogation, which hovered between flirtation and apprisement how best to handle his investments, I was unable to decide. Whatever the question, it was settled fairly quickly in her mind during the brief period in which soup plates were removed and fried sole presented.

" What do you do?" she asked. " I think men always enjoy talking about their work."

I had the disturbing impression that she was preparing for some sort of a war between the sexes—as represented by herself and me—to break out at any moment. What vehement rôle she saw herself as playing in the life that surrounded us was problematical; some deep-felt resentment, comparable to Eleanor's and yet widely differing from hers, clearly existed within her : her clothes, no doubt outward and visible sign of this rebellion against circum-

stance. I told her my firm specialised in art books, and
attempted to steer a line from Mestrović with unsuccessful
results. We talked for a time of Botticelli, the only painter
in whom she appeared to feel any keen interest, a subject
which led to the books of St. John Clarke, one of which
was a story of Renaissance Italy. This was the author
mentioned by Widmerpool as writing to *The Times* regarding the Haig statue.

" And then there was one about the French Revolution."

" I was on the side of the People," she said, resolutely.

This assertion opened the road to discussion deeper, and
altogether more searching, than I felt prepared to pursue
at that stage of dinner. As it happened, there were by then
signs all round the table of conversation becoming mori-
bund. Lady Walpole-Wilson must have noticed this falling
off, because she remarked at large that there were two
dances being given that evening.

" And both in Belgrave Square," said Archie Gilbert.

He sounded relieved that for once at least his self-imposed
duties would not keep him travelling all over London; his
worst nights being no doubt those experienced—as must
happen once in a way—on occasions when a party was
given in some big house at Richmond or Roehampton,
while there was also, on the same night, perhaps more than
one ball to be attended in the heart of London.

" The Spaniards are having some sort of a reception
there, too," said Tompsitt, who, having satisfied his immediate hunger, seemed disposed to show himself more
genial than earlier. " At their new Embassy."

" I'm rather glad we don't have to attend those big
official crushes any more as a duty," said Lady Walpole-
Wilson, with a sigh. " We had to turn out in honour of
Prince Theodoric the other night, and, really, it was too

exhausting. Now that one is rather out of touch with that world one does so much prefer just to see one's own friends."

"Is Prince Theodoric over for long?" asked Widmerpool, assuming an air of importance. "I understand he is here largely for economic reasons—I believe Donners-Brebner are considering big expansions in his country."

"Base metals, for one thing," said Tompsitt, with at least equal *empressement*. "There has also been talk of installing a railway to the coast. Am I right, Sir Gavin?"

At the phrase "base metals" there had passed over Archie Gilbert's face perhaps the most imperceptible flicker of professional interest, that died down almost immediately as he turned once more to speak with Barbara of dance bands.

"No doubt about it," said Sir Gavin. "I used to see a lot of Theodoric's father when I was chargé d'affaires there. We often went fishing together."

"Gavin was a great favourite with the old King," said Lady Walpole-Wilson, as if it were a matter of mild surprise to her that her husband could be a favourite with anyone. "I am afraid Prince Theodoric's brother is quite a different sort of person from their father. Do you remember that awkward incident when Janet was staying with us and how nice the King was?"

Sir Gavin glanced across the table at his wife, possibly apprehensive for a moment that she seemed inclined to particularise more precisely than might be desirable at the dinner table this contrast between father and son. Perhaps he did not wish to bring up the episode, whatever it had been, in which "Janet"—his sister—had been involved.

"Theodoric, on the other hand, is a serious young man," he said. "A pity, really, that he is not King. The party

given for him at their Legation was certainly dull enough—
though personally I enjoy such jollifications as, for example,
the court ball when our own King and Queen visited Berlin
in 1913."

"For the wedding of the Kaiser's daughter?" Tompsitt
asked, briskly.

"Princess Victoria Louise," said Sir Gavin, nodding
with approval at this scoring of a point by his satellite. "I
went quite by chance, in place of Saltonstall, who——"

"Though, of course, it makes one feel quite ill to think
of dancing with a German now," said Lady Walpole-Wilson, anxiously.

She had taken the war hard.

"Do you really think so, Lady Walpole-Wilson?" said
Widmerpool. "Now, you know, I can feel no prejudice
against the Germans. None whatever. French policy, on
the other hand, I regard at the moment as very mistaken.
Positively disastrous, in fact."

"They did the Torch Dance," said Sir Gavin, not to be
put off nostalgic reminiscences so easily. "The King and
the Tsar danced, with the bride between them. A splendid
sight. Ah, well, little we thought . . ."

"I loved the Swiss Guard when we were in Rome last
winter," said Miss Manasch. "And the Noble Guard were
divine, too. We saw them at our audience."

"But what a demoralising life for a young man," said
Lady Walpole-Wilson. "I am sure many of them must
make unsuitable marriages."

"I can just imagine myself checking a Papal Guards-
man's arms and equipment," said Pardoe. "Sergeant-
Major, this halbert is filthy."

"I'd love to see you in those red and yellow and blue

stripes, Johnny," said Miss Manasch, with perhaps a touch
of unfriendliness. "They'd suit you."

Discussion as to whether or not ceremony was desirable
lasted throughout the cutlets and ice. Lady Anne and
Tompsitt were against pomp and circumstance; Eleanor
and Widmerpool now found themselves on the same side
in defending a reasonable degree of outward show. Tompsitt was rather pleased at the general agreement that he
would go to pieces in the Tropics as a result of not changing
for dinner, and certainly, so far as his evening clothes were
concerned, he put his principles into practice.

"You should cart our Regimental Colour round," said
Pardoe. "Then you'd all know what heavy ceremonial
means. It's like a Salvation Army banner."

"I'm always trying to get a decent Colour for the
Guides," said Eleanor, " and not have to carry about a thing
like a child's Union Jack. Not that anyone cares."

"You won't be too long, Gavin, will you?" said Lady
Walpole-Wilson at this, hastily rising from the table.

By then I had only exchanged a word or two with
Barbara, though this, in a way, was a mark of intimacy
rather than because she had been unwilling to talk, or because any change had already consciously taken place in
our relationship. Most of dinner she had spent telling
Archie Gilbert rather a long story about some dance. Now
she turned towards me, just before she went through the
door, and gave one of those half-smiles that I associated
with moments—infrequent moments—when she was not
quite sure of herself: smiles which I found particularly
hard to resist, because they seemed to show a less familiar,
more mysterious side of her that noisiness and ragging were
partly designed to conceal. On that occasion her look

seemed to be intended perhaps to reconcile the fact that throughout the meal she had allowed me so little of her attention. Sir Gavin assured his wife that we would "not be long" in further occupation of the dining-room; and, when the door was closed, he moved the port in the direction of Pardoe.

"I hear you're letting your shooting," he remarked.

"Got to cut down somewhere," said Pardoe. "That seemed as good a place as anywhere to begin."

"Outgoings very heavy?"

"A lot of things to be brought up to date."

The two of them settled down to discuss Shropshire coverts, with which Sir Gavin had some familiarity since his father-in-law, Lord Aberavon, had settled on the borders of that county during the latter part of his life; though the house had been sold at his death. Archie Gilbert, having successfully undertaken the operation of releasing the ladies from the room, returned to the chair next to mine. I asked who was giving the other dance that night.

"Mrs. Samson."

"What will it be like?"

"Probably better than the Huntercombes'. Mrs. Samson has got Ambrose—though of course the band is not everything."

"Are you going to Mrs. Samson's."

He gave the ghost of a smile at what he must have regarded as a question needlessly asked.

"I expect I shall look in."

"Is it for Daphne?"

"For Cynthia, the youngest girl," he said, with gentle reproof at the thoughtlessness once more shown in putting this inquiry, which betrayed an altogether insufficiently serious approach to the world of dances. "Daphne has been out for ages."

On the other side of the table Widmerpool seemed, for some reason, determined to make a good impression on Tompsitt. Together they had begun to talk over the question of the Far East; Tompsitt treating Widmerpool's views on that subject with more respect than I should have expected him to show.

"I see the Chinese marshals have announced their victory to the spirit of the late Dr. Sun Yat-sen," Widmerpool was saying.

He spoke rather as if he had himself expected an invitation to the ceremony, but was prepared to overlook its omission on this occasion. Tompsitt, pursing his lips, rather in Widmerpool's own manner, concurred that such solemn rites had indeed taken place.

"And the Nationalists have got to Pekin," Widmerpool pursued.

"But who are the Nationalists?" asked Tompsitt, in a measured voice, gazing round the table with an air of quiet aggression. "Can anyone tell me that?"

Neither Archie Gilbert nor I ventured any attempt to clarify the confused situation in China; and not even Widmerpool seemed disposed to hazard any immediate interpretation of conflicting political aims there. There was a pause, at the end of which he said: "I dare say we shall have to consider tariff autonomy—with reservations, of course."

Tompsitt nodded, biting his lip a trifle. Widmerpool's face assumed a dramatic expression that made him look rather like a large fish moving swiftly through opaque water to devour a smaller one. Sir Gavin had begun to grow restive as scraps of this stimulating dialogue were wafted across to him, and he now abandoned the subject of Salopian pheasants in favour of trenchant examination of Celestial affairs.

"To speak of treaty-revision before China has put her house in order," he announced rather slowly, between puffs of his cigarette, "is thought by some—having regard to the *status quo*—substantially to put the cart before the horse. The War-Lords——"

"A cousin of mine in the Coldstream went out last year," Pardoe interrupted. "He said it wasn't too bad."

"Was that at Kowloon?" asked Widmerpool, speaking somewhat deferentially. "I hear, by the way, they are sending the Welsh Guards to Egypt instead of a Line regiment."

"You spoke of treaty revision, Sir Gavin," said Tompsitt, ignoring Widmerpool's adumbrations on the incidence of the trooping season. "Now it seems to me that we should strike when the iron is hot. The iron has never been hotter than at this moment. There are certain facts we have got to face. For example——"

"Some of them were under canvas on the race-course," said Pardoe. "Not that there were any starters, I should imagine." And, presumably with a view to disposing finally of the Chinese question and turning to subjects of more local interest, he added: "You know, legalising the tote is going to make a big difference to racing."

Sir Gavin looked dissatisfied with the turn taken by—or rather forced on—the conversation; possibly, in fact certainly, possessing further views on the international situation in the East which he was not unwilling to express. However, he must have decided that time did not allow any return to these matters, for he made, as it were, a mystic circle before himself in the air with the decanter, as if to show that the fate of China—and of racing, too for that matter—was in the lap of the gods.

"Nobody having any port," he stated, rather than asked. "Then I suppose we shall be getting into trouble if we don't make a move. Anyone for along the passage?"

"Yes," said Tompsitt, setting off impatiently.

While we waited for him, Sir Gavin expatiated to Pardoe whom he seemed, for some reason, particularly to enjoy lecturing, on the advantages to be gained for the country by mustering young men of Tompsitt's kind.

"Had the smooth type too long," he remarked, shaking his head a number of times.

"Need something crisper these days, do we?" inquired Pardoe, who, standing on tiptoe, was straightening his white tie reflected in the glass of the barometer hanging under *Boyhood of Cyrus*.

"All very well a century ago to have a fellow who could do the polite to the local potentate," explained Sir Gavin. "Something a bit more realistic required these days."

"A chap who knowns the man-in-the-street?"

Sir Gavin screwed his face into an expression calculated to convey that such was the answer.

"Where does he come from?" asked Pardoe, who did not seem absolutely convinced by these arguments, and still fiddled with his tie.

Sir Gavin seemed rather pleased by this question, which gave him further opportunity for stating uncompromisingly his confidence in Tompsitt's almost congenital *bona fides*.

"Goodness knows where he comes from," he affirmed vigorously. "Why should you or I be concerned with that —or any of us, for that matter? What we need is a man who can do the job."

"I quite agree with you, sir," said Widmerpool, breaking unexpectedly into this investigation. "Professionalism in diplomacy is bad enough, in all conscience, without restricting the range of the country's diplomatic representation to a clique of prize pupils from a small group of older public schools."

Sir Gavin looked rather taken aback, as I was myself, at such a sudden assertion of considered opinion regarding the matter in hand—and also at being called "sir"—even though Widmerpool's views seemed so closely identified with his own. However, Widmerpool did not attempt to amplify his proposition, and circumstances, represented by the return of Tompsitt, prevented a more exhaustive examination of the problem.

In his distrust of "smoothness" and hankering for "realism," Sir Gavin once more reminded me of Uncle Giles, but such reflections were interrupted by the necessity of making a decision regarding means of transport to the Huntercombes' house. The Walpole-Wilsons' cars were both, for some reason, out of commission—Eleanor had driven one of them against the mounting-block in the stable yard at Hinton Hoo—and Pardoe's sports-model two-seater was not specially convenient for a girl in a ball dress; although I could imagine Barbara wishing to travel in it if she had a chance. As it happened, Pardoe's general offer of "a lift" was immediately accepted by Tompsitt, which settled the matter so far as the rest of the party were concerned: this residue being divided between two taxis. I found myself in Lady Walpole-Wilson's vehicle, with Barbara, Miss Manasch, and Archie Gilbert; Eleanor, Anne Stepney, Margaret Budd, and Widmerpool accompanying Sir Gavin. We all packed ourselves in, Archie Gilbert and

I occupying the tip-up seats. The butler slammed the taxi door as if glad to be rid of us.

" I hope the others will be all right," said Lady Walpole-Wilson, as our conveyance moved off uncertainly, though I could not guess what her fears might be for potential ill that could befall the group under the command of her husband.

" Aren't we going to be too early, Aunt Daisy?" Barbara said. " It is so awful when you are the first to arrive. We did it at the Cecils."

I thought I could feel her foot against mine, but a moment later, found the shoe in question to belong to Miss Manasch, who immediately removed her own foot; whether because aware of a pressure that had certainly been quite involuntary, if, indeed, it had taken place at all, or merely by chance, I was unable to tell.

" I do hope Eleanor will not insist on going home as soon as we arrive," said Lady Walpole-Wilson, more to herself than to the rest of the company in the taxi.

As we covered the short distance to Belgrave Square, she dropped her bag on the floor, recovering it before anyone else could help, opened the clasp, and began to rummage in its depths. There she found whatever she had been seeking. Archie Gilbert was sitting next to the door by which we should descend, and now she made as if to offer him some object concealed in her hand, the thing, no doubt a coin, for which she had been searching in the bag. However, he strenuously denied acceptance of this.

" Please," said Lady Walpole-Wilson. " You must."

" On the contrary."

" I insist."

" No, no, absurd."

" Mr. Gilbert!"

" Really."

" I shall be very cross."

" Not possibly."

During the several seconds that elapsed before we finally drew up, delayed for a time by private cars and other taxis waiting in a queue in front of our own, the contest continued between them; so that by the moment when the taxi had at last stopped dead in front of the Huntercombes' house, and Archie Gilbert, flinging open the door, had reached the pavement, I was still doubtful whether or not he had capitulated. Certainly he had ejected himself with great rapidity, and unhesitatingly paid the taxi-driver, brushing aside a proffered contribution.

There seemed no reason to suppose, as Barbara had suggested, that we might have come too early. On the contrary, we went up the carpeted steps into a hall full of people, where Sir Gavin, whose taxi had arrived before our own, was already waiting impatiently for the rest of his party. His reason for personal attendance at a dance which he would not have normally frequented was presumably because the Huntercombes lived near the Walpole-Wilsons in the country. In fact there could be no doubt that a good many country neighbours had been asked, for, even on the way up the stairs, densely packed with girls and young men, some of them already rather hot and flushed, there was that faint though perceptible flavour of the hunt ball to be observed about some of the guests. While putting away our hats, curiosity had overcome me, and I asked Archie Gilbert whether he had, in fact, refused or accepted Lady Walpole-Wilson's money. At the coarseness of the question his smile had been once again somewhat reproving.

"Oh, I took it," he said. "Why not? It wasn't enough. It never is."

These words made me wonder if, after all, some faint trace of dissatisfaction was concealed deep down under that armour of black-and-white steel that encased him; and, for a moment, the terrible suspicion even suggested itself that, night after night, he danced his life away through the ballrooms of London in the unshakable conviction that the whole thing was a sham. Was he merely stoical like the Spartan boy—clad this time in a white tie—with the fox of bitterness gnawing, through stiff shirt, at his vitals. It was a thought in its horror to be dismissed without further examination. Such cynicism could hardly be possible. His remark, however, had for some reason recalled the occasion when I had been leaving the Templers' house and Mr. Farebrother had added his shilling to the chauffeur's tip.

"Have you ever come across someone called Sunny Farebrother?" I asked.

"Of course I've met him. Quite interested in the metal market, isn't he? He is rather well known in the City for his charm."

I saw that I had been right in supposing that the pair of them had something in common. Archie Gilbert had, indeed, sounded surprised that I should ever have been in doubt about his knowing Farebrother. Meanwhile, we had proceeded almost to the top of the stairs and were about to reach the first-floor landing, where a big man-servant with a huge bottle nose was bawling out the names of the guests in a contemptuous, raucous voice that well suggested his own keen enjoyment of the duty.

". . . Sir Gavin and Lady Walpole-Wilson . . . Miss Walpole-Wilson . . . Captain Hackforth . . . Mr. Cavendish . . . Lady Anne Stepney . . . Miss Budd . . . Miss Manners

... Mr. Pardon ... Mr. Tompsey ... Lady Augusta Cutts
... Miss Cutts ... Lord Erridge ... Miss Mercy Cutts ...
Lord and Lady Edward Wentworth . . . Mr. Winter-
pool . . ."

It was a fearful struggle to get through the door into the
ballroom. Even the bottle-nosed man, familiar with such
tumult as he must have been, had to pause and smile
broadly to himself once or twice; but whether amused at
the confusion of the crowd, or at the hash he was himself
making of their individual names, it was impossible to
guess. The whining of the band seemed only to encourage
the appalling tussle taking place on stairs and landing.

> "I took one look at you—
> That's all I meant to do—
> And then my heart—stood still . . ."

Hanging at the far end of the ballroom was a Van Dyck
—the only picture of any interest the Huntercombes kept
in London—representing Prince Rupert conversing with a
herald, the latter being, I believe, the personage from whom
the surviving branch of the family was directly descended.
The translucent crystals of the chandeliers oscillated faintly
as the dancers below thumped by. A knot of girls were
standing not far from the door, among them Eleanor, who,
in a purposeful manner, was pulling on a pair of long white
gloves. These gloves, always affected by her, were evidently
a kind of symbol assumed in connection with her own attitude towards dances; at once intended to keep her partners
physically farther from her, at the same time creaking
ominously, as if voicing the audible disapproval of their
wearer, whenever she moved her arms. We took the floor
together. Eleanor danced well, though implacably. I asked

how long she had known Widmerpool, mentioning that we had been at school together.

"Uncle George used to get his liquid manure from Mr. Widmerpool's father when he was alive," said Eleanor curtly. "We tried some at home, but it was a failure. Different soil, I suppose."

Widmerpool's old acquaintance with Barbara's family, and his own presence that night at the Walpole-Wilsons', were now both satisfactorily explained. There could be no doubt that the fertiliser mentioned by Eleanor was the basic cause of the secrecy with which he had always been inclined to veil his father's business activities; for, although there was, of course, nothing in the faintest degree derogatory about agricultural science—Lord Goring himself was, after all, evidence of that fact—I had been associated with Widmerpool long enough to know that he could not bear to be connected personally with anyone, or anything, that might be made, however remotely, the subject of ridicule which could recoil even in a small degree upon himself. He was, for example, as I discovered much later, almost physically incapable of making himself agreeable to a woman whom he regarded as neither good-looking nor, for some other reason, worth cultivating: a trait vested, perhaps, in a kind of natural timidity, and a nature that required a sense of support from the desirable qualities of company in which he found himself. This characteristic of his, I can now see, was an effort to obtain a kind of vicarious acquisition of power from others. Accordingly, any sense of failure or inadequacy in his surroundings made him uncomfortable. The mere phrase "artificial manure" told the whole story.

However, when it became clear that Eleanor did not much like him, I found myself, I hardly knew why, assuring her that Widmerpool, at school and in France, had always been quite an amiable eccentric; though I could not explain, then or now, why I felt his defence a duty; still less why I should have arbitrarily attributed to him what was, after all, an almost wholly imaginary personality, in fact one in many respects far from accurate. At that time I still had very little idea of Widmerpool's true character: neither its qualities nor defects.

"They had a small house on the Pembringham estate while experimenting with the manure," said Eleanor. "Aunt Constance is frightfully kind, when she isn't feeling too ill, you know, and used to ask them over quite often. That was where I first met him. Now his mother has taken a cottage near *us* at Hinton. Barbara doesn't mind Mr. Widmerpool. Of course, she has often met him. I don't really care for him very much. We were absolutely at our wits' end for a man to-night, so he had to come. Have you ever seen his mother?"

I did not hear Eleanor's views on Mrs. Widmerpool, because at that moment the music ceased; and, after clapping had died down and couples round us dispersed, the subject of Widmerpool and his family was quickly forgotten.

The ball took its course: dance-tune following dance-tune: partner following partner. From time to time, throughout the course of the evening, I saw Widmerpool ploughing his way round the room, as if rowing a dinghy in rough water, while he talked energetically to girls more often than not unknown to me; though chosen, no doubt, with the care devoted by him to any principle in which he was interested. He did not, as it happened, appear to be dancing much with any member of the Walpole-Wilson dinner-party, perhaps regarding them, when considered as individuals, as unlikely to lead to much that he could personally turn to profit. Later on in the evening, while sitting out with Miss Manasch, I was suddenly made aware of him again when he stumbled over her foot on his way upstairs.

"I know who he is!" she said, when he had apologised and disappeared from sight with his partner. "He is the Frog Footman. He ought to be in livery. Has he danced with Anne yet?"

"Anne Stepney?"

"They would be so funny together."

"Is she a friend of yours?"

"We were at the same finishing school in Paris."

"They didn't do much finishing on her, surely?"

"She is so determined to take a different line from that very glamorous sister of hers."

"Is Peggy Stepney glamorous?"

"You must have seen pictures of her."

"A friend of mine called Charles Stringham used to talk about her."

"Oh, yes—Charles Stringham," said Miss Manasch. "*That* has been over a long time. I think he is rather a fast young man, isn't he? I seem to have heard."

She laughed, and rolled her beady little eyes, straightening her frock over plump, well-shaped little legs. She looked quite out of place in this setting; intended by nature to dance veiled, or, perhaps, unveiled, before the throne of some Oriental potentate—possibly one of those exacting rulers to whom Sir Gavin's well-mannered diplomatists of the past might have appealed—or occupying herself behind the scenes in all the appetising labyrinth of harem intrigue. There existed the faintest suspicion of blue hairs upon her upper lip, giving her the look of a beauty of the Byronic era.

"Anne Stepney said he was pompous. As a matter of fact, I haven't seen him for ages."

"Anne thinks Charles Stringham pompous, does she?," said Miss Manasch, laughing again quietly to herself.

"What do you think?"

"I don't know him. At least only by reputation. I have met his mother, who is, of course, too wonderful. They say she is getting rather tired of Commander Foxe and thinking of having another divorce. Charles was more or less engaged to Anne's sister, Peggy, at one stage, as I suppose you know. That's off now, as I said. I hear about Peggy occasionally from a cousin of mine, Jimmy Klein, who has a great passion for her."

"Is Charles about to marry anyone at the moment?"

"I don't think so."

I had the impression that she knew more about Stringham than she was prepared to divulge, because her face assumed an expression that made her features appear more Oriental than ever. It was evident that she possessed affiliations with circles additional to—perhaps widely different from—those to be associated with Walpole-Wilsons, Gorings, or Huntercombes. Only superficially invested with the characteristics of girls moving within that world, she was at once coarser in texture and at the same time more subtle. Up to that moment she had been full of animation, but now all at once she became melancholy and silent.

"I think I shall leave."

"Have you had enough?"

"Going home seems the only alternative to sitting among the coats," she said.

"Whatever for?"

"I comb my hair there."

"But does it need combing?"

"And while I tug at it, I cry."

"Surely not necessary to-night?"

"Perhaps not," she said.

She began to laugh softly to herself once more; and, a minute or two later, went off with some partner who appeared satisfied that the moment had come to claim her. I set about looking for Barbara, with whom at the beginning of the evening I had danced only once. She was in one of the rooms downstairs, talking excitedly to a couple of young men, but she seemed not unwilling to leave their company.

"Let's sit this one out," she said.

We made our way outside and to the garden of the square. Guests like Archie Gilbert, who had been asked to both dances, and no doubt also a few who had not enjoyed that privilege—were passing backwards and forwards from one party to another. The reception at the Spanish Embassy, mentioned by Tompsitt, was still in full swing, so far as could be seen. Now and then a breath of air lightened the heavy night, once even causing the shrubs to sway in what was almost a breeze. The windows of both ballrooms stood open, music from the rival bands playing sometimes in conflict, sometimes appearing to belong to a system of massed orchestras designed to perform in unison.

> "We'll have a—Blue Room a——
> New room for—two room——
> Where we will raise a family . . .
> Not like a—ballroom a——
> Small room a—hall room . . ."

An equally insistent murmur came from the other side of the square:

"In the mountain greenery——
Where God makes the scenery . . .
Ta-rum . . . Ta-roo . . ."

"Why are you so glum?" said Barbara, picking up some
pebbles and throwing them into the bushes. "I must tell
you what happened at Ranelagh last week."

In the face of recent good resolutions, I tried to take her
hand. She snatched it away, laughing, and as usual in such
circumstances said: "Oh, don't get sentimental."

This tremendous escape, quite undeserved, sobered me.
We walked round the lawns. Barbara talked of Scotland,
where she was going to stay later in the summer.

"Why not come up there?" she said. "Surely you can
find someone to put you up?"

"Got to work."

"Of course they don't need you all the time at the office."

"They do."

"Have you ever danced reels? Johnny Pardoe is going to
be there. He says he'll teach me."

She began to execute capers on the lawn. Stopping at
last she examined her arm, holding it out, and saying:
"How blue my hand looks in the moonlight."

I found myself wondering whether, so far from loving
her, I did not actually hate her. Another tune began and
we strolled back through the garden. At the gate Tompsitt
came up from somewhere among the shadows.

"This is ours, I think."

In his manner of speaking, so it seemed to me, he contrived to be at once uncivil and pedantic. Barbara began
to jump about on the path as if leaping over imaginary
puddles, while almost at the top of her small, though shrill,
voice she said: "I can't, really I can't. I must have made

a muddle. I am dancing with Mr. Widmerpool. I have put him off till now, and I really must."

"Cut him," said Tompsitt.

He sounded as if taking Barbara away from her rightful partner would give him even more pleasure than that to be derived from dancing with her himself. I wondered if she had called Widmerpool "Mister" because her acquaintance with him had never been brought to a closer degree of intimacy, or if she spoke facetiously. From what Eleanor had said, the latter seemed more probable. It suddenly struck me that after all these years of knowing him I still had no idea of Widmerpool's Christian name.

"Shall I?" said Barbara. "He would be terribly angry."

Suddenly she took each of us by the hand, and began to charge along the pavement. In this unusual manner we reached the door of the Huntercombes' house. By the time we had ceased running even Tompsitt seemed, in the last resort, rather taken aback; the combined movement of the three of us—rather like that of horses in a troika—being probably as unexpected for him as for myself. Barbara, for her part, was delighted with her own violent display of high spirits. She broke free and rushed up the steps in front of us.

In the hall, although the hour was not yet late, a few people were already making preparations to leave. As it happened, Widmerpool was standing by the staircase, looking, I thought, a little uneasy, and fingering a tattered pair of white gloves. I had seen him with just that expression on his face, waiting for the start of one of the races for which he used so unaccountably to enter: finishing, almost without exception, last or last but one. When he saw Barbara, he brightened a little, and moved towards us.

"The Merry Widow Waltz," he said. "I always like

that, don't you? I wish I had known Vienna in the old days before the war."

Barbara once more seized Tompsitt and myself by whichever arm was nearest to her. She said to Widmerpool: "My dear, I have made a muddle again. I have told all sorts of people that I will dance this one with them, but—as I can't possibly dance with all three of you—let's all go and have some supper instead."

"But I've already had supper——" began Widmerpool.

"So have I," said Barbara. "Of course we have all had supper. We will have some more."

"*I* haven't had supper," said Tompsitt.

Widmerpool did not look at all pleased at Barbara's proposal; nor, for that matter, did Tompsitt, who must have realised now that instead of carrying Barbara gloriously away from a dashing rival—he had probably failed to catch Widmerpool's name at the dinner-party—he was himself to be involved in some little game played by Barbara for her own amusement. Perhaps for that reason he had felt it more dignified to deny a previous supper; for I was fairly sure that I had seen him leaving the supper-room earlier that night. I could not help feeling pleased that Barbara had insisted on my joining them, although I was at the same time aware that even this pleasure was a sign that I was by now myself less seriously concerned with her; for a few weeks before I should have endured all kind of vexation at this situation. Widmerpool, on the other hand, was by no means prepared to give in at once, though his struggles to keep Barbara to himself were feeble enough, and quite ineffectual.

"But look here," he said. "You promised——"

"Not another word."

"But——"

" Come along—all of you."

Almost dragging Widmerpool with her, she turned, and set off towards the door of the supper-room; bumped heavily into two dowagers on their way out, and said : " Oh, sorry," but did not pause. As I passed these ladies, I caught the words " Constance Goring's girl," spoken by the dowager who had suffered least from the impact. She was evidently attempting to explain, if not excuse, this impetuosity on some hereditary ground connected with Barbara's grandfather. Her more elderly and bedraggled companion, who seemed to have been badly shaken, did not appear to find much solace in this historical, or quasi-scientific, approach to Barbara's indifferent manners. They went off together up the stairs, the elder one still muttering angrily, while Tompsitt and I followed Barbara and Widmerpool to one of many tables decorated with blue hydrangeas in gilt baskets.

The room was still fairly full of people, but we found a place in the corner underneath a picture of Murillo's school in which peasant boys played with a calf. A large supper-party, making a good deal of noise, were seated at the next table, among them Pardoe, who was telling a complicated story about something that had happened to him—or possibly a brother officer—when " on guard " at the Bank of England.

" The first thing is to get some lemonade," said Barbara, who never touched any strong drink, in spite of behaviour that often suggested the contrary.

Clearly Widmerpool had been outraged by the loss of his dance. This annoyance, on the face of it, seemed scarcely reasonable, because by that stage of the evening several " extras " had been played, causing the numbers of dances to become confused, so that there had been plenty of excuse for an unimpeachable mistake to have been made; and obviously Barbara was the kind of girl, at best, to be expected to be in a chronic state of tangle about her partners. However, such considerations seemed to carry no weight whatever with Widmerpool, who sat in silence, refusing food and drink, while he gloomily crumbled a roll of bread. Barbara, who possessed a healthy appetite at all times of day or night, ordered lobster salad. Tompsitt drank —in which I joined him—a glass of what he called "The Widow." The wine had the effect of making him discourse on racing, a subject regarding which I was myself unfortunately too ignorant to dispose as summarily as I should have wished of the almost certainly erroneous opinions he put forward. Barbara embarked upon an account of her own experiences at Ascot, of no great interest in themselves, though at the same time hardly justifying the splenetic stare which Widmerpool fixed on her, while she unfolded a narrative based on the matter of starting prices for runners in the Gold Cup, associated at the same time with the question whether or not she had been finally swindled by her bookmaker.

She was, as usual, talking at the top of her voice, so that people at surrounding tables could hear most of what she said. Owing to this very general audibility of her remarks, she became in some way drawn into an argument with Pardoe, who had apparently been a member of the same Ascot party as herself. Although Barbara's voice was not without a penetrating quality, and Pardoe, who spoke, as it were, in a series of powerful squeaks, could no doubt make the welkin ring across the parade-grounds of Wellington Barracks or Caterham, they did not, for some reason, contrive to reach any mutual understanding in their attempts to make their respective points of view plain to each other; so that at last Barbara jumped up from her seat, saying: "I'm going across to tell him just what did happen."

There was a vacant chair next to the place where Pardoe sat. If Barbara ever reached that place, there could be little doubt that she would spend the rest of her time in the supper-room—perhaps the remainder of her time at the dance—discussing with Pardoe bets, past, present, and future; because he had abandoned any effort to talk to the girl next to him, who was, in fact, amusing herself happily enough with two or three other young men in the neighbourhood. The consequence of these various circumstances was for a decidedly odd incident to take place, with Widmerpool for its central figure: an incident that brought back to me once more expressive memories of Widmerpool as he had been at school. This crisis, as it might reasonably be called, came about because Widmerpool himself must have grasped immediately that, if Barbara abandoned our table at that moment, she would be lost to him for the rest of the time both of them were under the Huntercombes' roof. That, at least, seemed the only possible explanation of the action he now took, when—just as Barbara stood up, in preparation to leave us—he snatched her wrist.

"Look here, Barbara," he said—and he sounded in actual pain. "You can't leave me like this."

Certain actions take place outside the normal course of things so unexpectedly that they seem to paralyse ordinary capacity for feeling surprise; and I watched Widmerpool seize hold of Barbara in this way—by force—without at the precisely operative moment experiencing that amazement with which his conduct on this occasion afterwards, on reconsideration, finally struck me. To begin with, his act was a vigorous and instantaneous assertion of the will, quite out of keeping with the picture then existing in my mind of his character; for although, as I have said before, I no longer thought of him exactly as that uneasy, irrelevant figure he had seemed when we were both schoolboys, his behaviour in France, even when latent power of one kind or another had been unquestionably perceptible in him, had equally suggested a far more plodding manner of getting what he wanted.

In any case, he had been always inclined to shrink from physical contact. I remembered well how, one day at La Grenadière, Madame Leroy's niece, Berthe, standing in the garden and pointing to the river, which shone distantly in a golden glow of evening light, had remarked : " Quel paysage féerique," and touched his arm. Widmerpool, at that instant, had started violently, almost as if Berthe's plump fingers were red-hot, or her pointed nails had sharply entered his flesh. That had been several years before, and there was no reason why he should not have changed in this, as in certain outward respects. All the same, it was wholly unexpected—and perhaps a little irritating, even in the light of comparative emancipation from regarding Barbara as my own especial concern—to watch him snatch at her with those blunt, gnarled fingers. Tompsitt, at that critical moment attempting to get hold of more champagne, did not notice this gesture of Widmerpool's. The grabbing movement had, indeed, taken only a fraction of a second, Widmerpool having released Barbara's wrist almost as soon as his fingers had closed upon it.

If she had been in a calmer mood, Barbara would probably, in the light of subsequent information supplied on the subject, have paid more attention to the strength, and apparent seriousness, of Widmerpool's feelings at that moment. As it was, she merely said: "Why are you so sour to-night? You need some sweetening."

She turned to the sideboard that stood by our table, upon which plates, dishes, decanters, and bottles had been placed out of the way before removal. Among this residue stood an enormous sugar castor topped with a heavy silver nozzle. Barbara must suddenly have conceived the idea of sprinkling a few grains of this sugar over Widmerpool, as if in literal application of her theory that he " needed sweetening," because she picked up this receptacle and shook it over him. For some reason, perhaps because it was so full, no sugar at first sprayed out. Barbara now tipped the castor so that it was poised vertically over Widmerpool's head, holding it there like the sword of Damocles above the tyrant. However, unlike the merely minatory quiescence of that normally inactive weapon, a state of dispensation was not in this case maintained, and suddenly, without the slightest warning, the massive silver apex of the castor dropped from its base, as if severed by the slash of some invisible machinery, and crashed heavily to the floor: the sugar pouring out on to Widmerpool's head in a dense and overwhelming cascade.

More from surprise than because she wished additionally to torment him, Barbara did not remove her hand before the whole contents of the vessel—which voided itself in an instant of time—had descended upon his head and shoulders, covering him with sugar more completely than might have been thought possible in so brief a space. Widmerpool's rather sparse hair had been liberally greased with a dressing—the sweetish smell of which I remembered as somewhat disagreeable when applied in France—this lubricant retaining the grains of sugar, which, as they adhered thickly to his skull, gave him the appearance of having turned white with shock at a single stroke; which, judging by what could be seen of his expression, he might very well in reality have done underneath the glittering incrustations that enveloped his head and shoulders. He had writhed sideways to avoid the downpour, and a cataract of sugar had entered the space between neck and collar; yet another jet streaming between eyes and spectacles.

Barbara was, without doubt, dismayed by the consequences of what she had done; not, I think, because she cared in the least about covering Widmerpool with sugar, an occurrence, however deplorable, that was hard to regard, with the best will in the world, as anything other than funny at that moment. This was the kind of incident, however, to get a girl a bad name; a reputation for horse-play having, naturally, a detrimental effect on invitations. So far as everyone else, among those sitting near us, were concerned, there was a great deal of laughter. Even if some of the people who laughed may also have felt sorry for Widmerpool in his predicament, there was no escape from the fact that he looked beyond words grotesque. The sugar sparkled on him like hoar-frost, and, when he moved, there was a faint rustle as of snow falling gently from leaves of a tree in some wintry forest.

It was a hard situation for anyone to carry off with dignity and good temper. Widmerpool did not exactly attempt to conform to either of these two ideal standards; though in a rather specialised sense—to the eye of an attentive observer—he displayed elements of both qualities. His reaction to circumstances was, in its way, peculiarly characteristic of his nature. He stood up, shook himself like an animal, sending out specks of sugar over many persons in the immediate vicinity, and, smiling slightly, almost apologetically, to himself, took off his spectacles and began to rub their lenses with his handkerchief.

For the second time that night I recalled Stringham's story of Budd and the banana. It must have been, I could now appreciate, just such a moment as this one. I remembered Stringham's exact phrase: "Do you know, an absolutely *slavish* look came into Widmerpool's face." There could have been no better description of his countenance as he shook off the sugar on to the carpet beneath him. Once again the same situation had arisen; parallel acceptance of public humiliation; almost the identically explicit satisfaction derived from grovelling before someone he admired; for this last element seemed to show itself unmistakably—though only for a flash—when he glanced reproachfully towards Barbara: and then looked away. This self-immolation, if indeed to be recorded as such, was displayed for so curtailed a second that any substance possessed by that almost immediately shifting mood was to be appreciated only by someone, like myself, cognisant already of the banana incident; so that when Widmerpool pushed his way between the chairs, disappearing a minute later through the doors of the supper-room, he seemed to the world at large, perhaps correctly, to be merely a man in a towering rage.

However, reaction took place so soon as he was gone. There fell all at once a general public dejection similar in every respect, as recorded by Stringham, to that evoked by Widmerpool's former supposedly glad acceptance of the jolt from Budd's over-ripe fruit. This frightful despondency appeared to affect everyone near enough the scene of action to share a sense of being more or less closely concerned in the affair. For my own part, oddly enough, I was able to identify this sudden sensation of discomfort, comparable to being dowsed with icy water, an instantaneous realisation—simultaneously and most emphatically conveyed in so objective a form—that I had made an egregious mistake in falling in love with Barbara. Up to that moment the situation between us had seemed to be on the way to resolving itself, on my side at least, rather sadly, perhaps not irretrievably, with excusably romantic melancholy. Now I felt quite certain that Barbara, if capable of an act of this sort, was not—and had never been—for me. This may have been a priggish or cowardly decision. Certainly I had had plenty of opportunity to draw similar conclusions from less dramatic occasions. It was, however, final. The note struck by that conclusion was a disagreeable one; totally unlike the comparatively acceptable sentiments of which it took the place.

Barbara herself at first made no serious effort to repair, morally or physically, any of the damage she had caused. Indeed, it was not easy to see what she could do. Now she went so far as to pick up the top of the sugar-castor, and, before she sat down again, returned, in their separate states, the upper and lower halves of this object to the sideboard.

"It really wasn't my fault," she said. "How on earth was I to know that the top of the wretched thing would fall off like that? People ought to screw everything of that sort on tight before they give a party."

She abandoned her project of going to sit with Pardoe, who was still very red in the face from laughter, changing her topic of conversation from racing to that of good works of some kind or other, with which she was, as I already knew, irregularly occupied in Bermondsey. There was no reason whatever to doubt the truth of her own account of the generous proportion of her time spent at the girls' club, or some similar institution, situated there; nor her popularity with those thereby brought within her orbit. All the same, this did not seem to be the ideal moment to hear about her philanthropic activities. Barbara herself may have felt this transition of mood to have been effected with too much suddenness, because quite soon she said: " I'm going to rescue Aunt Daisy now. It isn't fair to keep her up all night. Besides, Eleanor must have been longing to go home for hours. No—no—don't dream of coming too. Good night to both of you. See you soon."

She ran off before either Tompsitt or I could even rise or say good night. We sat for a minute or two together, finishing our wine: Tompsitt smiling rather acidly to himself, as if aware of the answer to a great many questions, some of them important questions at that.

" Do you know the chap Barbara poured sugar on?" he asked, at last.

" I was at school with him."

" What was he like?"

" Rather the kind of man people pour sugar on."

Tompsitt looked disapproving and rather contemptuous. I thought at the time that his glance had reference to Widmerpool. I can now see that it was directed, almost certainly, towards my own remark, which he must have regarded, in some respects justly, as an answer inadequate to his question. Looking back on this exchange, I have no doubt that Tompsitt had already recognised as existing in Widmerpool some potential to which I was myself still almost totally blind; and, although he may neither have liked nor admired Widmerpool, he was at the same time aware of a shared approach to life which supplied a kind of bond between them. My own feeling that it would have been unjustifiable to mention the story of the banana, because I felt myself out of sympathy with Tompsitt, and, although often irritated by his behaviour, was conscious of a kind of uncertain loyalty, even mild liking, for Widmerpool, probably represented a far less instinctive and more artificial or unreal understanding between two individuals.

It would, indeed, be hard to over-estimate the extent to which persons with similar tastes can often, in fact almost always, observe these responses in others : women : money : power : whatever it is they seek; while this awareness remains a mystery to those in whom such tendencies are less highly, or not at all, developed. Accordingly, Tompsitt's acceptance of Widmerpool, and indifference, even rudeness, to many other persons of apparently greater outward consideration—in so much as I reflected on it—seemed to me odd; but this merely because, at that time, I did not understand the foundations required to win Tompsitt's approval. In any case, I saw no advantage in inquiring further into the matter at that hour, having myself already decided to go home to bed as soon as possible. Tompsitt, too, had no doubt had enough of the *tête-à-tête*. He rose, as a matter of fact, before I did, and we walked out together, separating as soon as we had passed through the door, Tompsitt strolling upstairs again towards the ballroom, while I made for the cloak-room. Eleanor was crossing the hall.

"Off to get my bonnet and shawl," she remarked, delighted that for her, at least, another dance was at an end.

I handed in the ticket, and was waiting while they looked for my hat, when Widmerpool himself appeared from the back regions of the house. He, and no doubt others too, had engaged in a thorough scouring of his person and clothes, most of the sugar having been by now removed, though a few grains still glistened round the button-hole of his silk lapel. He appeared also to have recovered his normal self-possession, such as it was. One of the servants handed him an opera hat, which he opened with a sharp crepitation, placing it on his head at a tilt as we went down the steps together. The night was a little cooler, though still mild enough.

" Which way do you go?" he asked.

" Piccadilly."

" Are you taxi-ing?"

" I thought I might walk."

" It sounds as if you lived in a rather expensive area," said Widmerpool, assuming that judicial air which I remembered from France.

" Shepherd's Market. Quite cheap, but rather noisy."

" A flat?"

" Rooms—just beside an all-night garage and opposite a block of flats inhabited almost exclusively by tarts."

" How convenient," said Widmerpool; rather insincerely, I suspected.

" One of them threw a lamp out of her window the other night."

" I go towards Victoria," said Widmerpool.

He had evidently heard enough of a subject that might reasonably be regarded as an unpleasant one, because the local prostitutes were rowdy and aggressive: quite unlike the sad sisterhood of innumerable novels, whose members, by speaking of the days of their innocence, bring peace to lonely men, themselves compromised only to unburden their hearts. My neighbours quarrelled and shouted all night long; and, when business was bad, were not above tapping on the ground-floor window in the small hours.

" My mother's flat is near the Roman Catholic Cathedral," Widmerpool added. " We usually let it for a month or two later on in the summer, if we can find a tenant, and take a cottage in the country. Last year we went quite near the Walpole-Wilsons at Hinton Hoo. We are going to do the same next month. I take my holiday then, and, if working, come up every day."

We strolled towards Grosvenor Place. I hardly knew whether or not to condole with him on the sugar incident. Widmerpool marched along, breathing heavily, rather as if he were taking part in some contest.

"Are you going to the Whitneys' on Thursday?" he asked suddenly.

"No."

"Neither am I."

He spoke with resignation; perhaps with slight relief that he had met another who remained uninvited to the Whitneys' dance.

"What about Mrs. Soundness?"

"I can't think why, but I haven't been asked to Mrs. Soundness's," said Widmerpool, almost petulantly. "I was taken to dinner there not so long ago—at rather short notice, I agree. But I expect I shall see you at Bertha, Lady Drum's and Mrs. Arthur Clinton's."

"Probably."

"I am dining with Lady Augusta Cutts for the Drum-Clinton dance," said Widmerpool. "One eats well at Lady Augusta's. But I feel annoyed—even a little hurt—about Mrs. Soundness. I don't think I could possibly have done or said anything at dinner to which exception might have been taken."

"The card may have gone astray in the post."

"As a matter of fact," said Widmerpool, "one gets very tired of these dances."

Everyone used to say that dances bored them; especially

those young men—with the honourable exception of Archie Gilbert—who never failed to respond to an invitation, and stayed, night after night, to the bitter end. Such complaints were made rather in the spirit of people who grumble at the inconvenience they suffer from others falling in love with them. There was, of course, nothing out of the way in Widmerpool, who had apparently been attending dances for several years, showing by that time signs of disillusionment, especially in the light of his experience at the Huntercombes'; although the way he was talking suggested that he was still keen enough to receive invitations. This projection of himself as a " dancing man," to use his own phrase, was an intimation—many more were necessary before the lesson was learnt—of how inadequate, as a rule, is one's own grasp of another's assessment of his particular rôle in life. Widmerpool's presence at the Walpole-Wilsons' had at first struck me, rather inexcusably perhaps, as just another proof of the insurmountable difficulties experienced by hostesses in their untiring search for young men at almost any price. It had never occurred to me, when at La Grenadière he had spoken of London dances, that Widmerpool regarded himself as belonging to the backbone of the system.

" You must come and lunch with me in the City," he said. " Have you an office in that part of the world?"

Thinking it unlikely that he would ring up, I gave him the telephone number, explaining that my work did not take place in the City. He made some formal inquiries about the firm, and seemed rather disapproving of the nature of the business.

" Who exactly buys ' art books '?"

His questions became more searching when I tried to give an account of that side of publishing, and of my own part in it. After further explanations, he said : " It doesn't sound to me a very serious job."

" Why not?"

" I can't see it leading to much."

" What ought it to lead to?"

" You should look for something more promising. From what you say, you do not even seem to keep very regular hours."

" That's its great advantage."

Widmerpool shook his head, and was silent for a time. I supposed him to be pondering my affairs—trying to find a way in which my daily occupation could be directed into more ambitious avenues—and I felt grateful, indeed rather touched, at any such interest. However, it turned out that he had either dismissed my future momentarily from his mind when he spoke again, or the train of thought must somehow have led him back to his own problems, because his words were quite unexpected.

" To tell the truth," he said, " I was upset—very upset—by what happened to-night."

" It was silly of Barbara."

" It was more than silly," said Widmerpool, speaking with unusual intensity, his voice rising in tone. " It was a cruel thing to do. I shall stop seeing her."

" I shouldn't take it all too seriously."

" I shall certainly take it seriously. You are probably not aware of the situation."

" What situation?"

" As I think I told you before dinner, Barbara and I used to live near each other in the country. She knows well what my feelings are for her, even though I may not have expressed them in so many words. Of course I see now that it was wrong to take hold of her as I did."

This disclosure was more than a little embarrassing, both for its unexpectedness and also in the light of my own sentiments, or at least former sentiments, on the subject of Barbara. At that stage of life all sorts of things were going on round about that only later took on any meaning or pattern. Thus some people enjoyed distinctly public love affairs, often quickly forgotten, while others fell in love without anyone, perhaps even including the object of their love, knowing or caring anything about these covert affections. Only years later, if at all, could the consequences of such bottled-up emotions sometimes be estimated : more often, of course, they remained entirely unknown. In Widmerpool's case, for example, I had no idea, and could, I suppose, have had no idea, that he had been in love with Barbara all the time that I myself had adored her. Moreover, in those days, as I have already indicated, I used to think that people who looked and behaved like Widmerpool had really no right to fall in love at all, far less have any success with girls—least of all a girl like Barbara—a point of view that in due course had, generally speaking, to be revised : sometimes in mortifying circumstances. This failure to recognise Widmerpool's passion had, of course, restricted any understanding of his conduct, when at the supper table he had appeared so irritable from the mere consequence of the loss of a dance. I could now guess that, while we sat there, he had been burning in the fires of hell:

" Of course I appreciate that the Gorings are a family of a certain distinction," said Widmerpool. " But without the Gwatkin money they would never be able to keep up Pembringham Woodhouse as they do."

" What was the Gwatkin money ? "

" Gwatkin was Lord Aberavon's family name. The peerage was one of the last created by Queen Victoria. As a matter of fact the Gwatkins were perfectly respectable landed stock, I believe. And, of course, the Gorings have not produced a statesman of the first rank since their eighteenth-century ancestor—and he is entirely forgotten. As you probably know, they have no connection whatever with the baronets of the same name."

He produced these expository facts as if the history of the Gorings and the Gwatkins offered in some manner a key to his problem.

"What about Barbara's father?"

"As a young man he was thought to show promise of a future in the House of Lords," said Widmerpool. "But promise in that Chamber has become of late years increasingly difficult to develop to any satisfactory end. He performed, I have been told, a lot of useful work in committee, but he never held office, and sank into political obscurity. As I heard Sir Horrocks Rusby, K.C., remark at dinner the other night: 'It's no good being useful if you don't achieve recognition.' Sir Horrocks added that this maxim was a natural corollary of the appearance of sin being as bad as sin itself. On the other hand the farming at Pembringham is some of the most up-to-date in the country, and that is well known."

"Were you going to propose to Barbara?"

"You don't suppose I have the money to marry, do you?" he said violently. "That is why I am telling you all this."

He spoke as if everyone ought already to be familiar with his emotional predicament; indeed, as if it were not only unobservant, but also rather heartless on my part, to have failed to comprehend the implications of his earlier ill-humour. By some curious manipulation of our respective positions—a trick of his I remembered from our time together at the Leroys'—his manner contrived also to suggest that I was being at once callous and at the same time unnecessarily inquisitive about his private affairs. Such aspects of this sudden revelation about himself and Barbara occurred to me only after I had thought things over the following day. At that moment I was not even particularly struck by the surprising fact that Widmerpool should suddenly decide to unburden himself on the subject of a love affair to someone whose relationship to him was neither that of an intimate friend, nor yet sufficiently remote to justify the man-to-man methods of imparting confidences employed by the total stranger who unfolds his life story in a railway carriage or bar. However, I was impressed at that point chiefly by the fact that Widmerpool had described so closely my own recently passed dilemma : a problem formerly seeming to admit of no solution, from which I had now, however, been freed as abruptly and absolutely as its heavy obligation had so mysteriously arisen in the months before.

By this time we had come to Grosvenor Place, in sight of the triumphal arch, across the summit of which, like a vast paper-weight or capital ornament of an Empire clock, the Quadriga's horses, against a sky of indigo and silver, pranced desperately towards the abyss. Here our ways divided. It was on the tip of my tongue to say something of my own position regarding Barbara; for it is always difficult to hear anyone lay claim to having endured the agonies of love without putting forward pretensions to similar experience : especially when the same woman is in question. Whether or not some such reciprocal confidence, advisable or the contrary, would finally have passed between us is hard to say. Probably any material I could have contributed to the subject would have proved all but meaningless, or at best merely irritating, to Widmerpool in his current mood. That is my opinion in face of subsequent dealings with him. However, at that stage in the walk one of those curious changes took place in circumstances of mutual intercourse that might almost be compared, scientifically speaking, with the addition in the laboratory of one chemical to another, by which the whole nature of the experiment is altered: perhaps even an explosion brought about.

For a minute or two we had been standing by the edge of the pavement. Widmerpool was no doubt preparing to say good night, because he took a sudden step backward. Like so many of his movements, this one was effected awkwardly, so that he managed to precipitate himself into the path of two persons proceeding, side by side, in the direction of Hyde Park Corner. There was, in fact, a minor collision of some force, in which the other parties were at once established as a comparatively elderly man, unusually tall, and a small woman, or girl. Upon the last of these Widmerpool had apparently trodden heavily, because she exclaimed in a raucous voice: "Hi, you, why the bloody hell can't you go where you're looking!"

So aggressive was the manner in which this question was put that at first I thought the pair of them were probably drunk: a state which, in addition, the discrepancy between their respective heights for some reason quite illogically helped to suggest. Widmerpool began to apologise, and the man now answered at once in a deep tone: "No, no. Of course it was an accident. Gypsy, I have told you before that you must control yourself when you are out with me. I will not tolerate gratuitous rudeness."

There was something strangely familiar about these words. He was grey-haired and hatless, carrying a fairly bulky parcel of newspapers, or so they appeared, under his left arm. His voice bore with it memories of time long past. Its tone was, indeed, laden with forgotten associations of childhood; those curious, rather fearful responses weighted with a sense of restriction and misgiving. Even so, there was also something about the stranger that seemed to belong to the immediate present; something that made me feel that a matter which had to do with him, even on that very evening, had already been brought to my notice. Yet his presence conveyed, too, an instant and vertiginous sense of being "abroad," this last impression suddenly taking shape as that of a far-off visit to Paris. The same scattered records of sight and sound that *Boyhood of Cyrus* had suggested when first seen at the Walpole-Wilsons'. I had another look at the whitening hairs, and saw that they were Mr. Deacon's, last surveyed, years before, on that day in the Louvre among the Peruginos.

He looked much the same, except that there was now something wilder—even a trifle sinister—in his aspect; a representation of Lear on the heath, or Peter the Hermit, in some nineteenth-century historical picture, preaching a crusade. Sandals worn over black socks gave an authentically medieval air to his extremities. The former rôle was additionally suggested by the undeniably boyish exterior of his companion, whose hair was cut short : barbered, in fact, in a most rough-and-ready fashion in the style then known as an "Eton crop." This young woman might, so far as outward appearances were concerned, have passed easily on the stage for the aged king's retainer, for, although her manner was more actively combative than the Fool's, the shortness of her skirt, and bare knees, made her seem to be clad in a smock, or tunic, of the kind in which the part is sometimes played.

When I think of that encounter in Grosvenor Place,

my attempt to reintroduce myself to Mr. Deacon in such circumstances seems to me strange, foolhardy even, and the fact still more extraordinary that he should almost immediately have succeeded in grasping my own identity. It was an occasion that undoubtedly did more credit to Mr. Deacon's social adroitness than to my own, because I was still young enough to be only dimly aware that there are moments when mutual acquaintance may be allowed more wisely to pass unrecognised. For example, to find a white-haired gentleman wandering about the streets in the small hours in the company of a young woman wearing an ample smear of lipstick across her face, and with stockings rolled to the knee, might easily prove a juncture when former meetings in irreproachable surroundings could, without offence, have been tactfully disregarded; although, as it turned out, there was not the smallest breath of scandal at that moment encompassing either of them.

" I had dinner at a house where one of your pictures hangs," I told him, when inquiries about my family had been made and answered.

" Good gracious," said Mr. Deacon. " Which one?"

" *Boyhood of Cyrus.*"

" Was that Aberavon's? I thought he was dead these twenty years."

" One of his daughters became Lady Walpole-Wilson. The picture is at her house in Eaton Square."

" Well, I'm glad to know its whereabouts," said Mr. Deacon. " I always make bold to consider it rather a successful achievement of mine, within the limits of the size of the canvas. It is unusual for people of that sort to have much taste in art. Aberavon was the exception. He was a man with vision. I expect his descendants have hung it in some quite incongruous place."

I thought it wiser to supply no further details on the subject of the hanging of *Boyhood of Cyrus*. " Skyed " in the hall was a position even the most modest of painters could hardly regard as complimentary; though I was impressed by Mr. Deacon's perspicacity in guessing this fate. It is, indeed, strange how often persons, living in other respects quite unobjectively, can suddenly become acutely objective about some specific concern of their own. However, no answer was required, because at that moment Widmerpool suddenly stepped in.

At first, after making some sort of an apology for his earlier clumsiness, he had stood staring at Mr. Deacon and the girl as if exhibits at a freak show—which it would hardly be going too far to say they somewhat resembled— but now he seemed disposed to dispute certain matters raised by Mr. Deacon's remarks. I had felt, immediately after making this plunge of recognition, that Widmerpool, especially in his existing mood, would scarcely be inclined to relish this company. In fact, I could not understand why he did not at once make for home, leaving us in peace to wind up the reunion, a duty that my own eagerness, perhaps misplaced, had imposed mutually upon Mr. Deacon and myself. Now to my surprise Widmerpool suddenly said : " I think, if you meet her, you will find Lady Walpole-Wilson most appreciative of art. She was talking to me about the Academy only this evening—in connection with the question of the Haig statue—and her comments were illuminating."

Mr. Deacon was delighted by this frank expression of opinion. There was, naturally, no reason why he should possess any knowledge of Widmerpool, whom I discovered in due course to be—in Mr. Deacon's pre-determined view and own words—" a typical empty-headed young fellow

with more money than is good for him" who was now
preparing to tell an older man, and an artist, "what was
what in the field of painting." This was, indeed, the kind
of situation in which Mr. Deacon had all his life taken
pleasure, and such eminence as he had, in fact, achieved
he owed largely to making a habit of speaking in an
overbearing and sarcastic, sometimes almost insulting,
manner to the race thus generically described as having
"more money than was good for them." He looked upon
himself as the appointed scourge of all such persons,
amongst whom he had immediately classed Widmerpool.
The mistake was perhaps inevitable in the circumstances.
In fairness to Mr. Deacon it should be added that these on-
slaughts were almost without exception accepted by the
victims themselves—a fact borne out by Barnby—as in some
eclectic manner complimentary, so that no harm was done;
even good, if the sale of Mr. Deacon's pictures could be so
regarded.

"Should I ever have the honour of meeting her Lady-
ship," said Mr. Deacon, with the suggestion of a flourish,
"I shall much look forward to a discussion on the subject
of that *interesting* institution, the Royal Academy. When
in need of mirth, I should be lost without it. I expect
Isbister, R.A., is one of her special favourites."

"I have not heard her mention his name," said Widmerpool, forgoing none of his seriousness. "But, for my own
part, I was not displeased with Isbister's portrait of Cardinal
Whelan at Burlington House last year. I preferred it to—
was it the wife of the Solicitor-General—that was so much
praised?"

It showed a rather remarkable effort of will on the part
of Widmerpool, whose interest in such matters was not

profound, to have been able to quote these examples on the spur of the moment; and there is no knowing into what inextricable tangle this subject would have led them both, if their conversation had not been mercifully interrupted by the girl, who now said: "Are we going to stand here all night? My feet hurt."

"But how shameful," said Mr. Deacon, with all his earlier formality. "I have not introduced you yet. This is Miss Gypsy Jones. Perhaps you have already met. She goes about a great deal."

I mentioned Widmerpool's name in return, and Miss Jones nodded to us, without showing much sign of friendliness. Her face was pale, and she possessed an almost absurdly impudent expression, in part natural outcome of her cast of features, but also, as almost immediately became apparent, in an even greater degree product of her temperament. She looked like a thoroughly ill-conditioned errand-boy. Her forehead had acquired a smudge of coal-dust or lamp-black, darker and denser than, though otherwise comparable to, the smudge on Tompsitt's shirt-front. It seemed to have been put there deliberately to offset her crimson mouth. Like Mr. Deacon, she too clutched a pile of papers under her arm, somehow suggesting in doing so the appearance of one of those insects who carry burdens as large, or even larger, than their own puny frame.

"You must wonder why we are on our way home at this late hour," said Mr. Deacon. "We have been attempting in our poor way to aid the cause of disarmament at Victoria Station."

Mr. Deacon's purpose had not, in fact, occurred to me— it is later in life that one begins to wonder about other people's activities—nor was it immediately made clear by Gypsy Jones extracting a kind of broadsheet from the sheaf under her arm, and holding it towards Widmerpool.

"Penny, *War Never Pays!*" she said.

Widmerpool, almost counterfeiting the secretive gesture of Lady Walpole-Wilson pressing money on Archie Gilbert in the taxi, fumbled in his trouser pocket, and in due course passed across a coin to her. In return she gave him the sheet, which, folding it without examination, he transferred to an inner pocket on his hip or in his tails. Scarcely knowing how to comment on the dealings in which Mr. Deacon and his companion were engaged. I inquired whether night-time was the best season to dispose of this publication.

"There is the depot," said Mr. Deacon. "And then some of the late trains from the Continent. It's not too bad a pitch, you know."

"And now you are going home?"

"We decided to have a cup of coffee at the stall by Hyde Park Corner," said Mr. Deacon, adding with what could only be described as a deep giggle : "I felt I could venture there chaperoned by Gypsy. Coffee can be very grateful at this hour. Why not join us in a cup?"

While he was speaking a taxi cruised near the kerb on the far side of the road. Widmerpool was still staring rather wildly at Gypsy Jones, apparently regarding her much as a doctor, suspecting a malignant growth, might examine a diseased organism under the microscope; although I found later than any such diagnosis of his attitude was far from the true one. Thinking that physical removal might put him out of his supposed misery, I asked if he wanted to hail the passing cab. He glanced uncertainly across the street. For a second he seemed seriously to contemplate the taxi; and then, finally, to come to a decision important to himself.

" I'll join you in some coffee, if I may," he said. " On thinking things over, coffee is just what I need myself."

This resolution was unexpected, to say the least. However, if he wanted to prolong the night in such company, I felt that determination to be his own affair. So far as I was myself concerned, I was not unwilling to discover more of someone like Mr. Deacon who had loomed as a mysterious figure in my mind in the manner of all persons discussed by grown-ups in the presence of a child.

We set off up the hill together, four abreast: Widmerpool and Gypsy Jones on the flanks. Across the road the coffee-stall came into sight, a spot of light round which the scarlet tunics and white equipment of one or two Guardsmen still flickered like the bright wings of moths attracted from nocturnal shadows by a flame. From the park rose the heavy scent of London on a summer night. Here, too, bands could be heard distantly throbbing. We crossed the road at the island and joined a knot of people round the stall, at the side of which, as if killing time while he waited for a friend late in arrival, an elderly person in a dinner-jacket was very slowly practising the Charleston, swaying his weight from one side of his patent leather shoes to the other, while he kept the tips of his fingers delicately in his coat pockets. Mr. Deacon glanced at him with disapproval, but acknowledged, though without warmth, the smirk proffered by a young man in a bright green suit, the uncomfortable colour of which was emphasised by auburn hair, erratically dyed. This was perhaps not a spot one might have chosen to soothe Widmerpool after his unfortunate experience with Barbara and the sugar. All the same, at the far end of the stall's little counter, he seemed already to have found something to discuss with Gypsy Jones—aspects of the question of the Haig statue, possibly, or the merits of

Isbister's portrait-painting—and both of them seemed fairly happy. Mr. Deacon began to explain to me how contemporary Paris had become " altogether too rackety " for his taste.

" The Left Bank was all right when I met you in the Louvre with your family," he said. " Wasn't the Peace Conference in progress then? I didn't take much interest in such things in those days. Now I know better. The truth is one gets too intimate with too many people if one stays in Montparnasse too long. I have come back to England for a little quiet. Besides, the French can be very interfering in their own particular way."

Purveying *War Never Pays!* at midnight in the company of Gypsy Jones seemed, on the face of it, a capricious manner of seeking tranquillity; but—as I knew nothing of the life abandoned by Mr. Deacon to which such an undertaking was alternative—the extent of its potentially less tempting contrasts was impossible to gauge. Regarded from a conventional standpoint, Mr. Deacon gave the impression of having gone down-hill since the days when he had been accustomed to visit my parents, to whom he made little or no reference beyond expression of pious hopes that both of them enjoyed good health. It appeared that he was himself now running a curiosity-shop in the neighbourhood of Charlotte Street. He pressed me to " look him up " there at the earliest opportunity, writing the address on the back of an envelope. In spite of his air of being set apart from worldly things, Mr. Deacon discoursed with what at least sounded like a good deal of practical common sense regarding the antique business, hours spent in the shop, time given to buying, closing arrangements, and such material points. I did not know what his financial position might be, but the shop was evidently providing, for the time being, an adequate livelihood.

"There are still a few people who are prepared to pay for nice things," he remarked.

When given coffee, he had handed back his cup, after examination, in objection to the alleged existence on the rim of the china of cracks and chips "in which poison might collect."

"I am always worried as to whether or not the crockery is properly washed up in places like this," he said.

Reflectively, he turned in his hand the cup that had replaced the earlier one, and continued to digress on the general inadequacy of sanitary precautions in shops and restaurants.

"It's just as bad in London as in Paris cafés—worse in some ways," he said.

He had just returned the second cup as equally unsatisfactory, when someone at my elbow asked: "Can one get matches here?" I was standing half-turned away from the counter, listening to Mr. Deacon, and did not see this new arrival. For some reason the voice made me glance towards Widmerpool; not because its tone bore any resemblance to his own thick utterance, but because the words suggested, oddly enough, Widmerpool's almost perpetual presence as an unvaried component of everyday life rather than as an unexpected element of an evening like this one. A moment later someone touched my arm, and the same voice said: "Where are you off to, may I ask, in all those fine clothes?" A tall, pale young man, also in evening dress, though without a hat, was standing beside me.

At first sight Stringham looked just the same; indeed, the fact that on the former occasion, as now, he had been wearing a white tie somehow conveyed the illusion that he had been in a tail-coat for all the years since we had last met. He looked tired, perhaps rather irritable, though evidently pleased to fall in like this with someone known to him. I was conscious of that peculiar feeling of restraint in meeting someone, of whom I had once seen so much, now dropped altogether from everyday life : an extension— and refinement, perhaps—of the sensation no doubt mutually experienced between my parents and Mr. Deacon on that day in the Louvre : more acute, because I had been far more closely associated with Stringham than ever they with Mr. Deacon. The presence of Widmerpool at the stall added a touch of fantasy to Stringham's appearance at that spot; for it was as if Widmerpool's own antics had now called his mimic into being as inexorable accessory to any real existence to which Widmerpool himself might aspire. I introduced Mr. Deacon and Gypsy Jones.

"Why, hallo, Stringham," said Widmerpool, putting down his coffee-cup with a clatter and puffing out his cheeks in a great demonstration of heartiness. "We haven't met since we were at Le Bas's."

He thought, no doubt—if he thought of the matter at all—that Stringham and I were friends who continued to see each other often, inevitably unaware that this was, in fact, our first meeting for so long. Stringham, on his side, clearly supposed that all four of us—Widmerpool, Mr. Deacon, Gypsy Jones, and myself—had been spending an evening together; though it was obvious that he could determine no easy explanation for finding me in Widmerpool's company, and judged our companionship immensely funny. He laughed a lot when I explained that Widmerpool and I had been to the Huntercombes' dance.

"Well, well," he said. "It's a long time since I went to a dance. How my poor mother used to hate them when my sister was first issued to an ungrateful public. Was it agony?"

"May one inquire why you should suppose a splendid society ball to have been agony?" asked Mr. Deacon, rather archly.

There could be no doubt that, at first sight, he had taken a great fancy to Stringham. He spoke in his ironically humorous voice from deep down in his throat.

"In the first place," said Stringham, "I rather dislike being crowded and uncomfortable—though, heaven knows, dances are not the only places where that happens. A most serious criticism I put forward is that one is expected, when attending them, to keep at least moderately sober."

When he said this, it struck me that Stringham had already, perhaps, consumed a few drinks before meeting us.

"And otherwise behave with comparative rectitude?" said Mr. Deacon, charmed by this answer. "I believe I understand you perfectly."

"Exactly," said Stringham. "For that reason I am now on my way—as I expect you are too—to Milly Andriadis's. I expect that will be crowded and uncomfortable too, but at least one can behave as one wishes there."

"Is that woman still extorting her toll from life?" asked Mr. Deacon.

"Giving a party in Hill Street this very night. I assumed you were all going there."

"This coffee tastes of glue," said Gypsy Jones, in her small, rasping, though not entirely unattractive voice.

She was dissatisfied, no doubt, with the lack of attention paid to her; though possibly also stimulated by the way events were shaping.

"One heard a lot of Mrs. Andriadis in Paris," said Mr.

Deacon, taking no notice of this interruption. " In fact, I went to a party of hers once—at least I think she was joint hostess with one of the Murats. A deplorable influence she is, if one may say so."

" One certainly may," said Stringham. " She couldn't be worse. As a matter of fact, my name is rather intimately linked with hers at the moment—though naturally we are unfaithful to each other in our fashion, when opportunity arises, which in my case, I have to confess, is not any too often."

I really had no very clear idea what all this talk was about, and I had never heard of Mrs. Andriadis. I was also uncertain whether Stringham truly supposed that we might all be on our way to this party, or if he were talking completely at random. Mr. Deacon, however, seemed to grasp the situation perfectly, continuing to laugh out a series of deep chuckles.

" Where do you come from now?" I asked.

" I've a flat just round the corner," said Stringham. " At first I couldn't make up my mind whether I was in the vein for a party, and thought a short walk would help me decide. To tell the truth, I have only just risen from my couch. There had, for one reason and another, been a number of rather late nights last week, and, as I didn't want to miss poor Milly's party in case she felt hurt—she is too touchy for words—I went straight home to bed this afternoon so that I might be in tolerable form for the festivities—instead of the limp rag one feels most of the time. It seemed about the hour to stroll across. Why not come, all of you? Milly would be delighted."

" Is it near?"

" Just past those Sassoon houses. Do come. That is, if none of you mind low parties."

TWO

Uncle Giles's standard of values was, in most matters, ill-adapted to employment by anyone except himself. At the same time, I can now perceive that by unhesitating contempt for all human conduct but his own—judged among his immediate relatives as far from irreproachable—he held up a mirror to emphasise latent imperfections of almost any situation that momentary enthusiasm might, in the first instance, have overlooked. His views, in fact, provided a kind of yardstick to the proportions of which no earthly yard could possibly measure up. This unquestioning condemnation of everyone, and everything, had no doubt supplied armour against some of the disappointments of life; although any philosophical satisfaction derived from reliance on these sentiments had certainly not at all diminished my uncle's capacity for grumbling, in and out of season, at anomalies of social behaviour to be found, especially since the war, on all sides. To look at things through Uncle Giles's eyes would never have occurred to me; but—simply as an exceptional expedient for attempting to preserve a sense of proportion, a state of mind, for that matter, neither always acceptable nor immediately advantageous—there may have been something to be said for borrowing, once in a way, something from Uncle Giles's method of approach. This concept of regarding one's own affairs through the medium of a friend or relative is not, of course, a specially profound one; but, in the case of my uncle, the field of vision surveyed was always likely to be

so individual to himself that almost any scene contemplated
from this point of vantage required, on the part of another
observer, more than ordinarily drastic refocusing.

He would, for example, have dismissed the Huntercombes' dance as one of those formal occasions that he himself, as it were by definition, found wholly unsympathetic.
Uncle Giles disapproved on principle of anyone who could
afford to live in Belgrave Square (for he echoed almost the
identical words of Mr. Deacon regarding people " with
more money than was good for them "), especially when
they were, in addition, bearers of what he called " handles
to their names "; though he would sometimes, in this same
connection, refer with conversational familiarity, more in
sorrow than anger, to a few members of his own generation, known to him in a greater or lesser degree in years
gone by, who had been brought by inheritance to this unhappy condition. He had, for some reason, nothing like so
strong an aversion for recently acquired wealth—from
holders of which, it is true, he had from time to time even
profited to a small degree—provided the money had been
amassed by owners safely to be despised, at least in private,
by himself or anyone else; and by methods commonly
acknowledged to be indefensible. It was to any form of
long-established affluence that he took the gravest exception,
particularly if the ownership of land was combined with
any suggestion of public service, even when such exertions
were performed in some quite unspectacular, and apparently harmless, manner, like sitting on a borough council,
of helping at a school-treat. " Interfering beggars," he used
to remark of those concerned.

My uncle's dislike for the incidence of Mrs. Andriadis's
party—equally, as a matter of course, overwhelming—would
have required, in order to avoid involving himself as an

auxiliary of more than negative kind in some warring faction, the selection of a more careful approach on his part than that adopted to display potential disapproval of the Huntercombes; for, by taking sides too actively, he might easily find himself in the position of defending one or another of the systems of conducting human existence which he was normally to be found attacking in another sector of the battlefield. At the same time, it would hardly be true to say that Uncle Giles was deeply concerned with the question of consistency in argument. On the contrary, inconsistency in his own line of thought worried him scarcely at all. As a matter of fact, if absolutely compelled to make a pronouncement on the subject, he—or, so far as that went, anyone else investigating the matter—might have taken a fairly firm stand on the fact that immediate impressions at Mrs. Andriadis's were not, after all, greatly different from those conveyed on first arrival at Belgrave Square.

The house, which had the air of being rented furnished only for a month or two, was bare; somewhat unattractively decorated in an anonymous style which, at least in the upholstery, combined touches of the Italian Renaissance with stripped panelling and furniture of "modernistic" design, these square, metallic pieces on the whole suggesting Berlin rather than Paris. Although smaller than the Huntercombes', my uncle would have detected there a decided suggestion of wealth, and also—something to which his objection was, if possible, even more deeply ingrained—an atmosphere of frivolity. Like many people whose days are passed largely in a state of inanition, when not of crisis, Uncle Giles prided himself on his serious approach to life, deprecating nothing so much as what he called "trying to laugh things off"; and it was true that a lifetime of laughter would scarcely have sufficed to exorcise some of his own fiascos.

On the whole, Mrs. Andriadis's guests belonged to a generation older than that attending the dance, and their voices swelled more loudly throughout the rooms. The men were in white ties and the ladies' dresses were carried in general with a greater flourish than at the Huntercombes': some of the wearers distinctly to be classed as "beauties." A minute sprinkling of persons from both sexes still in day clothes absolved Mr. Deacon and Gypsy Jones from looking quite so out of place as might otherwise have been apprehended; and, during the course of that night, I was surprised to notice how easily these two (who had deposited their unsold copies of *War Never Pays!* in the hall, under a high-backed crimson-and-gold chair, designed in an uneasy compromise between *avant garde* motifs and seventeenth-century Spanish tradition) faded unobtrusively into the general background of the party. There were, indeed, many girls present not at all dissimilar in face and figure to Gypsy Jones; while Mr. Deacon, too, could have found several prototypes of himself among a contingent of sardonic, moderately distinguished, grey-haired men, some of whom smelt of bath-salts, dispersed here and there throughout the gathering. The comparative formality of the scene to be observed on our arrival had cast a certain blight on my own—it now seemed too ready—acceptance of Stringham's assurance that invitation was wholly unnecessary; for the note of "frivolity," to which Uncle Giles might so undeniably have taken exception, was, I could not help feeling, infused with an undercurrent of extreme coolness, a chilly consciousness of conflicting egoisms, far more intimidating than anything normally to be met with at Walpole-Wilsons', Huntercombes', or, indeed, anywhere else of " that sort."

However, as the eye separated individuals from the mass, marks of a certain exoticism were here revealed, notably absent from the scene at Belgrave Square: such deviations from a more conventional standard alleviating, so far as they went, earlier implications of stiffness; although these intermittent patches of singularity—if they were to be regarded as singular—were, on the whole, not necessarily predisposed to put an uninvited newcomer any more at his ease; except perhaps in the sense that one act of informality in such surroundings might, roughly speaking, be held tacitly to excuse another.

For example, an elderly gentleman with a neat white moustache and eye-glass, evidently come from some official assemblage—perhaps the reception at the Spanish Embassy —because he wore miniatures, and the cross of some order in white enamel and gold under the points of his collar, was conversing with a Negro, almost tawny in pigmentation, rigged out in an elaborately waisted and square-shouldered tail-coat with exaggeratedly pointed lapels. It was really this couple that had made me think of Uncle Giles, who, in spite of advocacy of the urgent dissolution of the British Empire on grounds of its despotic treatment of backward races, did not greatly care for coloured people, whatever their origin; and, unless some quite exceptional circumstance sanctioned the admixture, he would certainly not have approved of guests of African descent being invited to a party to which he himself had been bidden. In this particular case, however, he would undoubtedly have directed the earlier momentum of his disparagement against the man with the eye-glass, since my uncle could not abide the wearing of medals. " Won 'em in Piccadilly, I shouldn't wonder," he was always accustomed to comment, when his eye fell on these outward and visible awards, whoever the recipient, and whatever the occasion.

Not far from the two persons just described existed further material no less vulnerable to my uncle's censure, for a heavily-built man, with a greying beard and the air of a person of consequence, was unsuccessfully striving, to the accompaniment of much laughter on both sides, to wrest a magnum of champagne from the hands of an ancient dame, black-browed, and wearing a tiara, or jewelled head-dress of some sort, who was struggling manfully to retain possession of the bottle. Here, therefore, were assembled in a single group—as it were of baroque sculpture come all at once to life—three classes of object all equally abhorrent to Uncle Giles; that is to say, champagne, beards, and tiaras : each in its different way representing sides of life for which he could find no good to say; beards implying to him Bohemianism's avoidance of those practical responsibilities with which he always felt himself burdened : tiaras and champagne unavoidably conjuring up images of guilty opulence of a kind naturally inimical to " radical " principles.

Although these relatively exotic embellishments to the scene occurred within a framework on the whole commonplace enough, the shifting groups of the party created, as a spectacle, illusion of moving within the actual confines of a picture or tapestry, into the depths of which the personality of each new arrival had to be automatically amalgamated; even in the case of apparently unassimilable material such as Mr. Deacon or Gyspy Jones, both of whom, as I have said, were immediately absorbed, at least to the eye, almost as soon as they had crossed the threshold of Mrs. Andriadis.

" Who is this extraordinary old puss you have in tow?"
Stringham had asked, while he and I had walked a little
ahead of the other three, after we had left the coffee-stall.

" A friend of my parents."

" Mine know the oddest people too—especially my father.
And Miss Jones? Also a friend—or a cousin?"

He only laughed when I attempted to describe the circumstances that had led to my finding myself with Mr.
Deacon, who certainly seemed to require some explanation
at the stage of life, and of behaviour, that he had now
reached. Stringham pretended to think—or was at least
unwilling to disbelieve—that Gypsy Jones was my own
chosen companion, rather than Mr. Deacon's. However,
he had shown no sign of regarding either of them as noticeably more strange than anyone else, encountered on a
summer night, who might seem eligible to be asked to a
party given by a friend. It was, indeed, clear to me that
strangeness was what Stringham now expected, indeed, demanded from life: a need already become hard to satisfy.
The detachment he had always seemed to possess was now
more marked than ever before. At the same time he had
become in some manner different from the person I had
known at school, so that, in spite of the air almost of relief
that he had shown at falling in with us, I began to feel
uncertain whether, in fact, Anne Stepney had not used the
term " pompous " in the usual, and not some specialised,
sense. Peter Templer, too, I remembered had employed the
same word years before at school when he had inquired
about Stringham's family. " Well, I imagine it was all
rather pompous even at lunch, wasn't it?" he had asked. At
that time I associated pomposity with Le Bas, or even with
Widmerpool, both of whom habitually indulged in
mannerisms unthinkable in Stringham. Yet there could

be no doubt that he now possessed a personal remoteness, a kind of preoccupation with his own affairs, that gave at least some *prima facie* excuse for using the epithet. All the rather elaborate friendliness, and apparent gratitude for the meeting—almost as if it might offer means of escape from some burdensome commitment—was unquestionably part of a barrier set up against the rest of the world. Trying to disregard the gap, of which I felt so well aware, as it yawned between us, I asked about his family.

"My father sits in Kenya, quarrelling with his French wife."

"And your mother?"

"Similarly occupied with Buster over here."

"At Glimber?"

"Glimber—as arranged by Buster—is let to an Armenian. They now live in a house of more reasonable proportions at Sunningdale. You must come there one day—if only to see dawn breaking over the rock garden. I once arrived there in the small hours and had that unforgettable experience."

"Is Buster still in the Navy?"

"Not he."

"A gentleman of leisure?"

"But much humbled. No longer expects one to remember every individual stroke he made during the polo season."

"So you both rub along all right?"

"Like a house on fire," said Stringham. "All the same, you know parents—especially step-parents—are sometimes a bit of a disappointment to their children. They don't fulfil the promise of their early years. As a matter of fact, Buster may come to the party if he can get away."

"And Miss Weedon?"

"Tuffy has left. I see her sometimes. She came into a little money. My mother changes her secretary every week now. She can't get along with anyone since Tuffy resigned."

"What about Peggy Stepney?"

"What, indeed?"

"I sat next to her sister, Anne, at dinner to-night."

"Poor Anne, I hope you were kind to her."

He gave no hint as to whether or not he was still involved with Peggy Stepney. I presumed that there was at least no longer any question of an engagement.

"Are you still secretary to Sir Magnus Donners?"

"Still to be seen passing from time to time through the Donners-Brebner Buildings," said Stringham, laughing again. "It might be hard to establish my precise status there."

"Nice work if you can get it!"

"'A transient and embarrassed spectre'," as Le Bas used to say, when one tried to slip past him in the passage without attracting undue attention. As a matter of fact I saw Le Bas not so long ago. He turned up at Cowes last year. Not my favourite place at the best of times, but Buster seems to like the life."

"Was Le Bas sailing?"

"Got up rather like a park-keeper. It is extraordinary how schoolmasters never get any older. In early life they settle on a cruising speed and just stick to it. Le Bas confused me with a Kenya friend of my father's called Dicky Umfraville—you probably know the name as a gentleman-rider—who left the school—sacked as a matter of fact—some fifteen or twenty years earlier than myself."

It was true that Le Bas, like most of his profession, was accustomed to behave as if never particularly clear as to the actual decade in which he might, at any given moment, be existing; but once assuming that recognition had not been immediate, his supposition that Stringham was something more than twenty-three or twenty-four—whatever his age at their meeting at Cowes—was not altogether surprising, because he looked, so it seemed to me by then, at least ten years older than when we had last seen each other. At the same time, it was no doubt unreasonable to mistake Stringham for Dicky Umfraville, of whose activities in Kenya I remember Sillery speaking a word of warning towards the end of my first year at the university. However, *tête-à-tête* conversation between Stringham and myself had now to come to an end, because by this time we had been admitted to the house, and the presence of a surrounding crowd of people put a stop to that kind of talk.

In one room the carpet had been rolled back, and a hunchback wearing a velvet smoking-jacket was playing an accordion, writhing backwards and forwards as he attacked his instrument with demiurgic frenzy.

> " I took one look at you——
> That's all I meant to do——
> And then my heart—stood still . . ."

To this music, cheek to cheek, two or three couples were dancing. Elsewhere the party, again resembling the Huntercombes', had spread over the entire building, its density as thick on landings and in passages as among the rooms. There were people everywhere, and voices sounded from the upper levels of bedroom floors. Stringham pushed his way through this swarming herd, the rest of us following. There was a buffet in the drawing-room, where hired butlers were serving drinks. Moving through the closely packed mob, from which a powerful aroma of tobacco, alcohol, and cosmetics arose, like the scent of plants and flowers in some monstrous garden, we came suddenly upon Mrs. Andriadis herself, when a further, and enormous, field of speculation was immediately projected into being. Stringham took her hand.

" Milly . . ."

" Darling . . ." she said, throwing an arm round his neck and kissing him energetically. " Why so disgustingly late?"

" Overslept."

" Milly ought to have been there."

" Why wasn't she?"

" Milly thought this was going to be a horrible party and she was going to hate it."

" Not now?"

" Couldn't be."

I did not remember exactly what outward appearance I had planned before arrival for Mrs. Andriadis. A suspicion may not have been altogether suppressed that she might turn out to resemble, in physiognomy and dress, one of those formalised classical figures from bronze or ceramic art, posed as Le Bas would sometimes contort himself; but my invention, though perhaps in one aspect ancient Greek, was certainly modern Greek in another. However, the shape any imaginary portrait may have taken was quite unlike this small woman with powder-grey hair, whose faint touch of a Cockney accent, like her coiffure, was evidently retained deliberately as a considered attraction. She was certainly pretty, though the effect was obtained in some indirect and unobtrusive manner. Her dark eyebrows were strongly marked.

She stood clinging to Stringham's arm, while, as if danc-

ing, she twitched her body this way and that. Her eyes
were brown and very bright, and the jewels she wore, in
rather defiant profusion, looked as if they might have cost
a good deal of money. She could have been about thirty-
five; perhaps a year or two more. At first it seemed to me
that she must have been a great beauty ten or fifteen years
earlier; but I discovered, in due course, from those who
had known Mrs. Andriadis for a long time that, on the
contrary, the epoch of this party represented perhaps the
peak of her good looks—that is, if her looks (or anyone
else's) could be admitted as open to objective judgment by
some purely hypothetical standard; for, as Barnby used
to say: " It's no good being a beauty alone on a desert
island." Barnby himself adhered to the theory that Mrs.
Andriadis's appearance had been greatly improved after her
hair had turned grey; being accustomed to add to this
opinion the statement that the change of shade had taken
place " After her first night with The Royal Personage,
as Edgar always calls him." I was strongly reminded by
her appearance—so it seemed to me—of another woman;
though of whom I could not decide.

" I brought some friends along, Milly," said Stringham.
" You don't mind?"

" You darlings," said Mrs. Andriadis. " It is going to be
a lovely party now. All arranged on the spur of the
moment. Come with me, Charles. We are making Deauville plans."

Although obviously in the habit of having her own way
in most matters, she showed no surprise at all at the sight
of Widmerpool, Mr. Deacon, Gypsy Jones, and myself.
Indeed, it seemed probable that, as newly-arrived entities,
she took cognisance, so far as our self-contained group was
concerned, of no more than Mr. Deacon and me, since

Widmerpool and Gypsy Jones, threading their way across
the room, had been left some little way behind the rest of
us. Even Mr. Deacon, in spite of strenuous efforts on his
own part, scarcely managed to shake hands with Mrs.
Andriadis, although, as he bent almost double, the tips of
their fingers may have touched. It was at that instant of
tenuous contact that Mr. Deacon attempted to explain
the matter, mentioned already by him at the coffee-stall, to
the effect that he thought they had met once before " in
Paris with the Murats." An assertion of which Mrs.
Andriadis herself took no notice whatsoever.

As it turned out, neither Widmerpool nor Gyspy Jones
ever reached her at that—nor, as far as I know, any other—
stage of the party, because, evidently deciding to spend
no more time on her welcome of such miscellaneous guests,
she took Stringham by the arm, and bore him away. Widmerpool, with a set expression on his face, passed obliquely
through the crowd, still filled, as I supposed, with an un-
quenchable determination, even stronger, if possible, than
Mr. Deacon's, to make himself at all costs known to his
hostess. Gypsy Jones also disappeared from sight at the
same moment, though not, it might be presumed, with the
same aim. Their effacement was effected rather to my
relief, because I had feared from Widmerpool a stream of
comment of a kind for which I felt not at all in the mood;
while at the same time, rather snobbishly, I did not wish
to appear too closely responsible for being the cause, however indirect, of having brought Mr. Deacon and Gypsy
Jones to the house. This was the moment when the surrounding tableaux formed by the guests began to take
coherent shape in my eyes, when viewed from the corner
by the grand piano, where I had been left beside Mr.
Deacon, who now accepted with a somewhat roguish

glance, a beaker of champagne from the tray of one of the men-servants.

"I cannot say I altogether like these parties," he said. "A great many of them seem to be given these days. Paris was just the same. I really should not have accepted your nice-looking friend's invitation if we had not had such a very indifferent evening with *War Never Pays!* As it was, I felt some recreation was deserved—though I fear I shall not find much here. Not, at least, in any form likely to appeal to my present mood. By the way, I don't know whether you would ever care to lend a hand with *War Never Pays!*, a penny, one of these days? We are always glad to enlist new helpers."

I excused myself decisively from any such undertaking on grounds of lacking aptitude for any kind of salesmanship.

"Not everyone feels it a bounden duty," said Mr. Deacon. "I need not tell you that Gypsy is scarcely a colleague I should choose, if I were a free agent, but she is so keen I cannot very well raise objection. Her political motives are not identical with my own, but Pacifism is ally of all who desire this country's disarmament. Do you know, I even put her up at my place? After all, you can't expect her to get all the way back to Hendon Central at this time of night. It wouldn't be right."

He spoke almost with unction at the nobility of such self-sacrifice, and, finishing his champagne at a gulp, wiped the corners of his mouth carefully with a silk handkerchief. On the wall opposite us, one of the panels of the room had been replaced—possibly with the object of increasing the rather "daring" effect at which decoration of the house evidently aimed—with squares of looking-glass, in the reflections of which could be observed the changing pattern made by the occupants of the room.

The lady with the tiara had at last reluctantly abandoned the magnum to her bearded opponent (now accommodated with a younger, though less conspicuous, woman), and, apparently much flattered by the attention, she was accepting a cigarette from the Negro's long case, which he was holding out towards her, the metal seeming delicately matched in tone with the skin of its owner's hand, also the tint of old gold. Beyond this couple, the gentleman with the eye-glass and medals was now talking to a figure whose back-view—for some reason familiar—showed an immensely time-worn suit of evening clothes, the crumpled tails of which hung down almost to its wearer's heels, giving him the appearance of a musical-hall comedian, or conjuror of burlesque, whose baggy Charlie Chaplin trousers, threatening descent to the ground at any moment, would probably reveal red flannel, grotesquely spotted, or some otherwise traditionally comic, underclothes, or lack of them, beneath. Matted white hair protruded over the back of this person's collar, and he was alternately rubbing together his hands and replacing them in the pockets of these elephantine trousers, while he stood nodding his head, and sagging slightly at the knees. I suddenly became aware, with some surprise, that the man with the medals was Colonel Budd—Margaret Budd's father—who held some minor appointment at Court. He had also perhaps, " come on " from the Huntercombes'.

" She reposes herself at the back of the shop," said Mr. Deacon, pursuing the topic of his connection with Gypsy Jones. " I make up the bed—a divan—myself, with some rather fine Cashmere shawls a former patron of mine left

me in his will. However, I don't expect she will need them
on a warm night like this. Just as well, if they are not
to be worn to shreds. As a matter of fact they are going for
a mere song if you happen to know anyone interested in
Oriental textiles. I can always find something else to put
over Gypsy. Of course Barnby doesn't much like her being
there."

I did not at that time know who Barnby might be,
though I felt sure that I had heard of him; connecting the
name—as it turned out, correctly—with painting.

" I see his point," said Mr. Deacon, " even though I
know little of such things. Gypsy's attitude naturally—perhaps Barnby would prefer me to say ' unnaturally '—offends
his *amour propre*. In some ways he is not an ideal tenant
himself. I don't want women running up and down stairs
all day long—and all night long too, for that matter—just
because I have to put up with Gypsy in a good cause."

He spoke complainingly, and paused for breath, coughing
throatily, as if he might be suffering from asthma. Both of
us helped ourselves to another drink. Meanwhile, seen
in the looking-glass, Colonel Budd and the wearer of the
Charlie Chaplin trousers now began to edge their way
round the wall to where a plump youth with a hooked nose
and black curly hair, perhaps an Oriental, was talking to
a couple of strikingly pretty girls. For a minute or two
I had already been conscious of something capable of
recognition about the old clothes and assured carriage of
the baggy-trousered personage, whose face, until that
moment, had been hidden from me. When he turned towards the room, I found that the features were Sillery's,
not seen since I had come down from the university.

To happen upon Sillery in London at that season of the
year was surprising. Usually, by the time the first few

weeks of the Long Vacation had passed, he was already
abroad, in Austria or Italy, with a reading party of picked
undergraduates : or even a fellow don or two, chosen with
equal care, always twenty or thirty years younger than himself. Sillery, probably with wisdom, always considered
himself at a disadvantage outside his own academical
strongholds. He was accordingly accustomed, on the whole,
to emphasise the corruption of metropolitan life as such,
in spite of almost febrile interest in the affairs of those
who found themselves habitually engaged in London's
social activities; but, on the other hand, if passing through
on his way to the Continent, he would naturally welcome
opportunity to be present, as if by accident, at a party of
this kind, when luck put such a chance in his way. The
accumulated gossip there obtainable could be secreted, and
eked out for weeks and months—even years—at his own
tea-parties; or injected in judiciously homeopathic doses
to rebut and subdue refractory colleagues at High Table.
Possibly, with a view to enjoying such potential benefits, he
might even have delayed departure to the lakes and moun-
tains where his summers were chiefly spent; but if he had
come to London specially to be present, there could be no
doubt that it was to pursue here some negotiation judged
by himself to be of first-rate importance.

As they skirted the wall, Sillery and his companion, by
contrast remarkably spruce, had almost the appearance of
a pair of desperadoes on their way to commit an act of
violence, and, on reaching the place where the dark young
man was standing, the Colonel certainly seemed to get rid
of the women without much ceremony, treating them almost as a policeman might peremptorily " move on " from
the corner of the street female loiterers of dubious complexion. The taller of the two girls was largely built, with

china-blue eyes and yellow hair, holding herself in a some-what conventionally languorous style: the other, dark, with small, pointed breasts and a neat, supple figure. The combined effect of their beauty was irresistible, causing a kind of involuntary pang, as if for a split-second I loved both of them passionately; though a further survey con-vinced me that nothing so disturbing had taken place. The girls composedly allowed themselves to be dislodged by Colonel Budd and Sillery: at the same time remaining on guard in a strategic position at a short distance, talking and laughing with each other, and with people in the immedi-ate neighbourhood: evidently unwilling to abandon en-tirely their original stations *vis-à-vis* the young man.

The Colonel, imperceptibly inclining his neck in an abrupt gesture suggesting almost the sudden suppression of an unexpected eructation, presented Sillery, not without deference to this rather mysterious figure, regarding whom I had begun to feel a decided curiosity. The young man, smiling graciously, though rather shyly, held out a hand. Sillery, grinning broadly in return, made a deep bow that seemed, by its mixture of farce and formality, to accord perfectly with the cut of his evening clothes, in their impli-cation of pantomime or charade. However, fearing that absorption in this scene, as reflected in the looking-glass, might have made me seem inattentive to Mr. Deacon's exposition of difficulties experienced in contending with his household, I made further inquiries regarding Barnby's status as a painter. Mr. Deacon did not warm to this sub-ject. I found when I knew him better that this luke-warm attitude was not to be attributed entirely to jealousy he might feel towards Barnby's success, but rather because, finding his own views on the subject so opposed to con-temporary opinion as to be in practice untenable, he preferred to close his eyes to the existence of modern painting, just as formerly he had closed his eyes to politics and war. Accordingly, I asked about the nature of Barnby's objections to Gypsy Jones.

"When Gypsy and I were first acquainted," said Mr. Deacon, lowering his voice, "I was given to understand—well, hasn't Swinburne got some lines about 'wandering watery sighs where the sea sobs round Lesbian promontories'? In fact restriction to such a coastline was almost a condition of our association."

"Did Barnby object?"

"I think he undoubtedly felt resentment," said Mr. Deacon. "But, as a very dear friend of mine once remarked when I was a young man—for I was a young man once, whatever you may think to the contrary—'Gothic manners don't mix with Greek morals.' Gypsy would never learn that."

Mr. Deacon stopped speaking. He seemed to be deliberating within himself whether or not to ask some question, in the wording of which he found perhaps a certain embarrassment. After a few seconds he said: "As a matter of fact I am rather worried about Gypsy. I suppose you don't happen to know the address of any medicos—I don't mean the usual general practitioner with the restricted views of his profession—no, I didn't for a moment suppose that you did. And of course one does not wish to get mixed up. I feel just the same as yourself. But you were inquiring about Barnby. I really must arrange for you to meet. I think you would like each other."

When such scraps of gossip are committed to paper, the words bear a heavier weight than when the same information is imparted huskily between draughts of champagne, in the noise of a crowded room; besides which, my thoughts hovering still on the two girls who had been displaced by Sillery and Colonel Budd, I had not been giving very full attention to what Mr. Deacon had been saying. However, if I had at that moment considered Gypsy Jones's difficulties with any seriousness, I should probably have decided, rightly or wrongly, that she was well able to look after herself. Even in the quietest forms of life the untoward is rarely far from the surface, and in the intemperate circles to which she seemed to belong nothing was surprising. I felt at the time absolutely no inclination to pursue the matter further. Mr. Deacon himself became temporarily lost in thought.

Our attention was at that moment violently reorientated by the return to the room of Mrs. Andriadis, who now shouted—a less forcible word would have been inadequate to describe her manner of announcing the news—that "darling Max" was going to sing: a statement creating a small upheaval in our immediate surroundings, owing to the proximity of the piano, upon which a bottle of champagne was now placed. A mild-looking young man in spectacles was thrust through the crowd, who seating himself on the music-stool, protested: "Must I really tickle the dominoes?" A number of voices at once encouraged him to embark upon his musical activity, and, after winding round the seat once or twice, apparently more as a ritual than for practical reasons, he struck a few chords.

"Really," said Mr. Deacon, as if entitled to feel honest disgust at this development, "Mrs. Andriadis does not seem to care in the least whom she makes friends with."

"Who is he?"

"Max Pilgrim—a public performer of some sort."

The young man now began to sing in a tremulous, quavering voice, like that of an immensely ancient lady, though at the same time the words filled the room with a considerable volume of sound :

> " I'm Tess of Le Touquet,
>   My morals are flukey,
>   Tossed on the foam, I couldn't be busier;
>   Permanent waves
>   Splash me into the caves;
>   Everyone loves me as much as Delysia.
>   When it's wet on the Links, I know where to
>   have a beau
>   Down in the club-house—next door to the
>   lavabo."

There was muffled laughter and some fragmentary applause, though a hum of conversation continued to be heard round about us.

" I don't care for this at all," said Mr. Deacon. " To begin with, I do not entirely understand the meaning of the words—if they have any meaning—and, in the second place, the singer once behaved to me in what I consider an objectionable manner. I can't think how Mrs. Andriadis can have him in the house. It can't do her reputation any good."

The appearance of Max Pilgrim at the piano had thoroughly put out Mr. Deacon. In an attempt to relieve the gloom that had fallen on him I inquired about Mrs. Andriadis's past.

" Barnby knows more about her than I do," he said, rather resentfully. " She is said to have been mistress of a Royal Personage for a time. Personally I am not greatly stimulated by such revelations."

" Is she still kept?"

" My dear boy, you have the crudest way of putting things," said Mr. Deacon, smiling at this, and showing signs of cheering up a little. " No—so far as I am aware —our hostess is no longer ' kept,' as you are pleased to term the former state of life to which she was called by Providence. A client of mine told me that her present husband —there have been several—possessed comprehensive business interests in Manchester, or that region. My friend's description suggested at least a sufficient competence on the latest husband's part for the condition of dependence you mention to be, financially speaking, no longer necessary for his lady—even, perhaps, undesirable. Apart from this, I know little of Mr. Andriadis, though I imagine him to be a man of almost infinite tolerance. You are, I expect, familiar, with Barnby's story of the necklace?"

" What necklace?"

" Milly," said Mr. Deacon, pronouncing Mrs. Andriadis's name with affected delicacy, " Milly saw a diamond-and-emerald necklace in Cartier's. It cost, shall we say, two million francs. She approached the Royal Personage, who happened to be staying at the Crillon at that moment, and asked for the money to buy herself the necklace as a birthday present. The Royal Personage handed her the banknotes—which he was no doubt accustomed to keep in his pocket—and Milly curtsied her way out. She went round the corner to the apartment of a well-known French industrialist—I cannot remember which, but you would know the name—who was also interested in her welfare, and requested him to drive there and then to Cartier's and buy the necklace on the spot. This the industrialist was obliging enough to do. Milly, was, therefore, two million francs to the good, and could, at the same time, give pleasure to both her protectors by wearing the necklace in the company of either. Simple—like all great ideas."

Mr. Deacon paused. He seemed all at once to regret this sudden, and uncharacteristic, outburst of sophistication on so mundane a subject. The anecdote had certainly been told in a manner entirely foreign to his accustomed tone in dealing with worldly matters; discussed by him in general, at least publicly—as I found at a later date, as if all practical transactions were wrapped in mystery impenetrable for one of his simple outlook. Such an approach had been, indeed, habitual with him at all times, and, even so far back as the days when my parents used to speak of him, I could recall banter about Mr. Deacon's repeatedly expressed ignorance of the world. This attitude did not, of course, repudiate on his part a certain insistence on his own knowingness in minor, and more "human," affairs, such as the running of his shop, described so precisely by him a short time earlier at the coffee-stall. The story of the necklace was, I thought, in some way vaguely familiar to me. It had possibly figured in the repertoire of Peter Templer at school, the heroine of Templer's anecdote, so I believed, represented as a well-known actress rather than Mrs. Andriadis herself.

"Not that I know anything of such gallivanting," said Mr. Deacon, as if by now ashamed of his momentary abandonment of the unassailable position vouchsafed to him by reliance, in all circumstances, on an artist's traditional innocence of heart. "Personally I should be delighted for kings, priests, armament manufacturers, *poules de luxe,* and *hoc genus omne* to be swept into the dust-bin —and I might add all the nonsense we find about us tonight."

As he stopped speaking, the words of the song, which had been proceeding through a number of verses, now became once more audible :

> " Even the fairies
> Say how sweet my hair is;
> They mess my mascara and pinch the peroxide.
> I know a coward
> Would be overpowered,
> When they all offer to be orthodox. I'd
> Like to be kind but say : ' Some other day, dears;
> Pansies for thoughts remains still the best way,
>   dears.' "

This verse gave great offence to Mr. Deacon. Indeed, its effect was almost electric in the suddenness of the ferment it caused within him. He brushed away a lock of grey hair fallen over his forehead, and clenched his fist until the knuckles were white. He was evidently very angry. " Insufferable!" he said. " And from such a person."

He had gone quite pale with irritation. The Negro, too, perhaps himself a vocalist, or performer upon some instrument, had also been watching Max Pilgrim with a look of mounting, though silent, hatred that had contracted the whole of his face into a scowl of self-righteous rage. This look seemed by then to have dramatised his bearing into the character of Othello. But the pianist, taking occasional nips at his champagne, showed no sign of observing any of the odium aroused by him in these or other quarters. Mr. Deacon sighed. There was a moment when I thought he might, there and then, have decided to leave the house. His chest heaved. However, he evidently made up his mind to dismiss unpleasant reflections.

"Your young friend appears to hold the place of honour here," he said, in a more restrained voice. "Is he rich? Who are his parents—if I am not being inquisitive?"

"They are divorced. His father married a Frenchwoman and lives in Kenya. His mother was a South African, also remarried—to a sailor called Foxe."

"Buster Foxe?"

"Yes."

"Rather a chic sailor," said Mr. Deacon. "If I mistake not, I used to hear about him in Paris. And she started life as wife of some belted earl or other."

He was again showing recklessness in giving voice to these spasmodic outbursts of worldly knowledge. The champagne perhaps caused this intermittent pulling aside of the curtain that concealed some, apparently considerable, volume of practical information about unlikely people: a little storehouse, the existence of which he was normally unwilling to admit, yet preserved safely at the back of his mind in case of need.

"What was the name?" he went on. "She is a very handsome woman—or was."

"Warrington."

"The Beautiful Lady Warrington!" said Mr. Deacon. "I remember seeing a photograph of her in *The Queen*. There was some nonsense there, too, about a fancy-dress ball she had given. When will people learn better? And Warrington himself was much older than she, and died soon after their marriage. He probably drank."

"So far as I know, he was a respectable brigadier-general. It is Charles Stringham's father who likes the bottle."

"They are all the same," said Mr. Deacon, decisively. Whether this condemnation was aimed at all husbands of Stringham's mother, or, more probably, intended, in principle, to embrace members of the entire social stratum from which these husbands had, up to date, been drawn, was not made clear. Once more he fell into silence, as if thinking things over. Max Pilgrim continued to hammer and strum and take gulps of champagne, while against an ever-increasing buzz of conversation, he chanted his song continuously, as if it were a narrative poem or saga recording the heroic, legendary deeds of some primitive race:

"I do hope Tallulah
Now feels a shade cooler,
But why does she pout, as she wanders so far off
From Monsieur Citröen,
Who says something knowin'
To Lady Cunard and Sir Basil Zaharoff?
Has someone guessed who was having a beano
At Milly's last party behind the Casino?"

This verse turned out to be the climax. Max Pilgrim, removing his spectacles, rose and bowed. Since the beginning of the song, many people, among them Mrs. Andriadis herself, had drifted away, and the room was now half empty, though a small group of enthusiasts still hovered round the piano. This residuum now clapped and applauded heartily. Pilgrim was almost immediately led away by two ladies, neither of them young. What remained of the crowd began to shift and rearrange its component parts, so that in the movement following the song's termination Mr. Deacon was swept away from his corner. I watched him betake himself by easy stages to the door, no doubt with the object of further exploration. While I was looking, someone grasped my arm, and I found that Sillery was standing beside me.

By employment of a successful disengaging movement, the dark young man had by then managed to extract himself from the encirclement that had cut him off from the two girls, to whom he had now successfully returned; an operation made easier by the fact that the girls themselves had remained conveniently near, chattering and tittering together. At this development Sillery, who seemed to be enjoying himself hugely, must have pottered away from Colonel Budd, with whom his association was no doubt on a purely business footing. He had paused by me, as if to take breath, apparently unable to decide where best to make his next important descent, puffing out his still dark walrus moustache, and leaning forward, as he swayed slightly. This faint oscillation was not, of course, due to drink, which he touched in no circumstances, but sustained himself through hour after hour of social adventure on a cup or two of *café au lait*, with perhaps an occasional sandwich or biscuit. His white tie was knotted so loosely that it formed a kind of four-in-hand under the huge wings of his collar, itself limp from want of starch.

" Why so thoughtful?" he asked, grinning widely. " Did Charles Stringham bring you here? Such a friend of our hostess is Charles, isn't he? I heard that you and Charles had not been seeing so much of each other as you used in the old days when you were both undergraduates."

He was obviously well aware that Stringham's life had changed greatly from the period of which he spoke, and he probably knew, too, as his words implied, that Stringham and I had not met for years. On such stray pieces of information, the cumulative effect not to be despised, Sillery's intelligence system was built up. As to the effectiveness of this system, opinion, as I have said before, differed greatly. At any rate, Sillery himself believed implicitly in his own

powers, ceaselessly collecting, sorting, and collating small
items in connection with the personal relationships of the
people he knew; or, at least, knew about. No doubt a
few of these units of information turned out to be of value
in prosecuting schemes in which, for one reason or another,
he might himself become suddenly interested.

I admitted that I had not seen Stringham for some little
time before that evening, but I did not feel it necessary to
reveal in detail to Sillery the circumstances that had brought
me to the house of Mrs. Andriadis.

"You stayed too long in the company of that gentleman
with the equivocal reputation," said Sillery, giving my arm
a pinch. "People have to be careful about such things.
They do, indeed. Can't think how he got to this very respectable party—but don't let's talk about such matters. I
have just been having a most enlightening chat with Prince
Theodoric."

"The Levantine young man?"

"A dark young prince with curly hair," said Sillery,
chuckling. "That's quite a Tennysonian line, isn't it?
Handsome, if it were not for that rather too obtrusive nose.
One would never guess him descended from Queen Victoria. Perhaps he isn't. But we mustn't be scandalous. A
very clever family, his Royal House—and well connected,
too."

I remembered that there had been some talk of Prince
Theodoric at the Walpole-Wilsons'. Although aware that
his visit was in progress, I could not recall much about the
Prince himself, nor the problems that he was called upon
to discuss. Remarks made by Widmerpool and Tompsitt
on the subject earlier that evening had become somewhat
confused in my mind with the substance of an article in
one of the "weeklies," skimmed through recently in a club,

in which the writer associated " the question of industrial development of base metals "—the phrase that had caught Archie Gilbert's ear at dinner—with " a final settlement in Macedonia." The same periodical, in its editorial notes, had spoken, rather slightingly, of " the part Prince Theodoric might be hoped to play on the Balkan chess-board," adding that " informed circles in Belgrade, Bucharest, and Athens are watching this young man's movements closely; while scarcely less interest has been evoked in Sofia and Tirana, in spite of a certain parade of aloofness in the latter capital. Only in Ankara is scepticism freely expressed as to the likelihood of the links of an acceptable solution being welded upon the, by now happily obsolescent, anvil of throne- room diplomacy," Sillery's description of the Prince as " well connected " made me think again, involuntarily, of Uncle Giles, who would no doubt, within the same reference, also have commented on Prince Theodoric's employment of " influence " in the advancement of his own or his country's interests.

" Mrs. Andriadis must be at least a tiny bit flattered to find H.R.H. here to-night," said Sillery. " Although, of course, our hostess, as you are probably aware, is no stranger to Royalty in its lighter moments. I expect it is the first time, too, that the good Theodoric has been at the same party as one of our coloured cousins. However, he is broad-minded. It is that touch of Coburgh blood."

" Is he over here for long?"

" Perhaps a month or two. Is it aluminium? Something like that. Hope we are paying a fair price. Some of us try and organise public opinion, but there are always people who think we should have our own way, no matter what, aren't there? However, I expect all that is safe in the hands of such a great and good man as Sir Magnus Donners—

with two such great and good assistants as Charles Stringham and Bill Truscott."

He chuckled again heartily at his last comment.

"Was Prince Theodoric educated over here?"

Sillery shook his head and sighed.

"Tried to get him," he said. "But it couldn't be did.
All the same, I think we may be going to have something
almost as good."

"Another brother?"

"Better than that. Theodoric is interested in the proposed Donners-Brebner Fellowships. Picked students to
come to the university at the Donners-Brebner Company's
expense. After all, we have to do something for them, if
we take away their metal, don't we?"

"Will you organise the Fellowships, Sillers?"

"The Prince was good enough to ask my advice on
certain academical points."

"And you told him how it should be done?"

"Said I would help him as much as he liked, if he
promised not to give me one of those great gawdy decora-
tions that I hate so much, because I never know how to put
them on right when I have to go out all dressed up to
grand parties."

"Did he agree to that?"

"Also said a few words 'bout de political sitchivashun,"
remarked Sillery, ignoring the question and grinning more
broadly than ever. "Dull things for de poor Prince, I'm
'fraid. 'Spect he's 'joying hisself more now."

He gave no explanation of this sudden metamorphosis
into confused memories of Uncle Remus and the diction
of the old plantations, aroused perhaps at that moment by
sight of the Negro, who passed by, now in friendly conversation with Pilgrim. Possibly the impersonation was merely

some Dickensian old fogey. It was impossible to say with certainty. Probably the act had, in truth, no meaning at all. These sudden character parts were a recognised element in Sillery's technique of attacking life. There could be no doubt that he was delighted with the result of his recent conversation, whatever the ground covered; though he was probably correct in his suggestion that the Prince was more happily occupied at that moment with the girls than in earlier discussion of economic or diplomatic problems.

However, apart from the fact that he had presumably initiated the counter-move that had finally displaced Sillery, Prince Theodoric, as it happened, was showing little, if any, outward sign of this presumed partiality. He was gravely watching the two young women between whom he stood, as if attempting to make up his mind which of this couple had more to offer. I could not help feeling some envy at his monopoly of the companionship of such an attractive pair, each in her contrasted looks seeming to personify a style of beauty both exquisite and notably fashionable at that moment: the latter perhaps a minor, even irrelevant, consideration, but one hard to resist. I inquired the names of these friends of Prince Theodoric.

"Well-known nymphs," said Sillery, sniggering. "The smaller one is Mrs. Wentworth—quite a famous person in her way—sister of Jack Vowchurch. Mixed up in the divorce of Charles's sister. I seem to remember her name was also mentioned in the Derwentwater case, though not culpably. The tall and statuesque is Lady Ardglass. She was, I believe, a mannequin before her marriage."

He began to move off, nodding, and rubbing his hands together, deriving too much pleasure from the party to waste any more valuable time from the necessarily limited period of its prolongation. I should have liked to make the acquaintance of one or both ladies, or at least to hear more of them, but I could tell from Sillery's manner that he knew neither personally, or was, at best, far from being at ease with them, so that to apply for an introduction—should they ever leave Prince Theodoric's side—would, therefore, be quite useless. Mrs. Wentworth was, outwardly, the more remarkable of the pair, on account of the conspicuous force of her personality: a characteristic accentuated by the simplicity of her dress, short curly hair, and look of infinite slyness. Lady Ardglass was more like a caryatid, or ship's figurehead, though for that reason no less superb. Seeing no immediate prospect of achieving a meeting with either, I found my way to another room, where I suddenly came upon Gypsy Jones, who appeared to have taken a good deal to drink since her arrival.

"What's happened to Edgar?" she asked clamorously.

She was more untidy than ever, and appeared to be in a great state of excitement: even near to tears.

"Who is Edgar?"

"Thought you said you'd known him since you were a kid!"

"Do you mean Mr. Deacon?"

She began to laugh uproariously at this question.

"And your other friend," she said. "Where did you pick that up?"

Laughter was at that moment modified by a slight, and quickly mastered, attack of hiccups. Her demeanour was becoming more noticeably hysterical. The state she was in might easily lead to an awkward incident. I was so accustomed to the general principle of people finding Widmerpool odd that I could hardly regard her question as even hypercritical. It was, in any case, no more arbitrary an inquiry, so far as it went, than Stringham's on the subject of Mr. Deacon; although long-standing friendship made Stringham's form of words more permissible. However, Gypsy Jones's comment, when thought of later, brought home the impossibility of explaining Widmerpool's personality at all briefly, even to a sympathetic audience. His case was not, of course, unique. He was merely one single instance among many, of the fact that certain acquaintances remain firmly fixed within this or that person's particular orbit; a law which seems to lead inexorably to the conclusion that the often repeated saying that people can " choose their friends " is true only in a most strictly limited degree.

However, Gypsy Jones was the last person to be expected to relish discussion upon so hypothetical a subject, even if the proposition had then occurred to me, or she been in a fit state to argue its points. Although she seemed to be enjoying the party, even to the extent of being in sight of hysteria, she had evidently also reached the stage when moving to another spot had become an absolute necessity to her; not because she was in any way dissatisfied with the surroundings in which she found herself, but on account of the coercive dictation of her own nerves, not to be denied in their insistence that a change of scene must take place. I was familiar with a similar spirit of unrest that sometimes haunted Barbara.

" I want to find Edgar and go to The Merry Thought." She clung on to me desperately, whether as an affectionate gesture, a means of encouraging sympathy, or merely to maintain her balance, I was uncertain. The condition of excitement which she had reached to some extent communicated itself to me, for her flushed face rather improved her appearance, and she had lost all her earlier ill-humour.

"Why don't you come to The Merry Thought?" she said. "I got a bit worked up a moment ago. I'm feeling better now."

Just for a second I wondered whether I would not fall in with this suggestion, but the implications seemed so many, and so varied, that I decided against accompanying her. I felt also that there might be yet more to experience in Mrs. Andriadis's house; and I was not uninfluenced by the fact that I had, so far as I could remember, only a pound on me.

"Well, if Edgar can't be found, I shall go without him," said Gypsy Jones, speaking as if such a deplorable lack of gallantry was unexpected in Mr. Deacon.

She seemed to have recovered her composure. While she proceeded down the stairs, somewhat unsteadily, I called after her, over the banisters, a reminder that her copies of *War Never Pays!* should preferably not be allowed to lie forgotten under the chair in the hall, as I had no wish to share, even to a small degree, any responsibility for having imported that publication into Mrs. Andriadis's establishment. Gypsy Jones disappeared from sight. It was doubtful whether she had heard this admonition. I felt, perhaps rather ignobly, that she were better out of the house.

Returning through one of the doorways a minute or two later, I collided with Widmerpool, also red in the face, and with hair, from which customary grease had perhaps been dried out by sugar, ruffled into a kind of cone at the top of his head. He, too, seemed to have drunk more than he was accustomed.

"Have you seen Miss Jones?" he asked, in his most breathless manner.

Even though I had been speaking with her so recently, I could not immediately grasp, under this style, the identity of the person sought.

" The girl we came in with," he muttered impatiently.

" She has just gone off to a night-club."

" Is someone taking her there?"

" Not that I know of."

" Do you mean she has gone by herself?"

" That was what she said."

Widmerpool seemed more fussed than ever. I could not understand his concern.

" I don't feel she should have set off like that alone," he said. " She had had rather a lot to drink—more than she is used to, I should imagine—and she is in some sort of difficulty, too. She was telling me about it."

There could be no doubt at all that Widmerpool himself had been equally indiscreet in taking more champagne than usual.

" We were having rather an intimate talk together," he went on. " And then I saw a man I had been wanting to speak to for weeks. Of course, I could have rung him up, but I preferred to wait for a chance meeting. One can often achieve so much more at such moments than at an interview. I crossed the room to have a word with him—explaining to her, as I supposed quite clearly, that I was going to return after a short business discussion—and when I came back she had vanished."

" Too bad."

" That was very foolish of me," said Widmerpool, in a tone almost as if he were apologising abjectly for some grave error of taste. " Rather bad-mannered, too. . . ."

He paused, seemingly thoroughly upset: much as he had looked—I called to mind—on the day when he had witnessed Le Bas's arrest when we had been at school together. At the moment when he spoke those words, if I could have laid claim to a more discerning state of mind, I might have taken greater notice of the overwhelming change that had momentarily come over him. As it was, I attributed his excitement simply to drink: an entirely superficial view that even brief reflection could have corrected. For example—to illustrate how little excuse there was for my own lack of grasp—I had never before, so far as I can now recollect, heard Widmerpool suggest that anything he had ever done could be classed as foolish, or bad-mannered; and even then, on that evening, I suppose I ought to have been dimly aware that Gyspy Jones must have aroused his interest fairly keenly, as it were " on the rebound " from having sugar poured over his head by Barbara.

" There really are moments when one should forget about business," said Widmerpool. "After all, getting on isn't everything."

This precept, so far as I was myself concerned in those days, was one that required no specially vigorous inculcation.

" Pleasure before Business has always been my motto," I remembered Bill Truscott stating at one of Sillery's tea-parties when I was an undergraduate; and, although it would have been misleading to suppose that, for Truscott himself, any such label was in the least—in the smallest degree—applicable, the maxim seemed to me such a truism at the moment when I heard it quoted that I could not imagine why Truscott should seem to consider the phrase, on his part, something of an epigram or paradox. Pleasure still seemed to me a natural enough aim in life; and I certainly did not, on that night in Hill Street, appreciate at all how unusually disturbed Widmerpool must have been to have uttered aloud so profane a repudiation of his own deep-rooted system of opinion. However, he was pre-

vented from further particularising of the factors that had
impelled him to this revolutionary conclusion, by the
arrival beside us of the man whose practical importance had
seemed sufficient to cause abandonment of emotional pre-
occupations. That person had, so it appeared additional
dealings to negotiate. I was interested to discover the
identity of this figure who had proved, in the circumstances, so powerful a counter-attraction to the matter in
hand. The disclosure was, in a quiet way, sufficiently
dramatic. The " man " turned out to be Bill Truscott himself, who seemed, through another's pursuance of his own
loudly proclaimed precept, to have been, at least to some
degree, temporarily victimised.

When I had last seen him, earlier in the year, at a Roths-
child dance chatting with the chaperones, there could be
no doubt that Truscott was still a general favourite: a
" spare man " treated by everyone with respect and in quite
a different, and distinctly higher, category in the hierarchy
of male guests from, say, Archie Gilbert. It was, indeed,
impossible to deny Truscott's good looks, and the dignity
of his wavy, youthfully grey hair and broad shoulders. All
the same, the final form of his great career remained still,
so far as I knew, undecided. It was not that he was showing signs of turning out less capable—certainly not less reliable—than his elders had supposed; nor, as had been
evident on the night when I had seen him, was he growing
any less popular with dowagers. On the contrary, many
persons, if not all, continued to speak of Truscott's brilliance almost as a matter of course, and it was generally
agreed that he was contriving most successfully to retain
the delicate balance required to remain a promising young
man who still survived in exactly the same place—and a
very good place, too—that he had taken on coming down

from the university; rather than preferring to make his mark as an innovator in breaking new, and possibly unfruitful, ground in forwarding ambitions that seemed, whatever they were, fated to remain long masked from friends and admirers. At least outwardly, he had neither improved nor worsened his position, so it was said, at least, by Short, who, upon such subjects, could be relied upon to take the entirely unimaginative view of the world in general. In fact, Truscott might still be expected to make name and fortune before he was thirty, though the new decade must be perilously near, and he would have to be quick about it. The promised volume of poems (or possibly *belles lettres*) had never appeared; though there were still those who firmly declared that Truscott would " write something " one day. Meanwhile he was on excellent terms with most people, especially, for some reason, elderly bankers, both married and unmarried, with whom he was, almost without exception, a great favourite.

On that earlier occasion when I had seen him at the dance, Truscott, although he might excusably have forgotten our two or three meetings with Sillery in days past, had dispensed one of those exhausted, engaging smiles for which he was noted; while his eyes wandered round the ballroom " ear-marking duchesses," as Stringham—years later—once called that wistful, haunted intensity that Truscott's eyes took on, from time to time, among any large concourse of people that might include individuals of either sex potentially important to an ambitious young man's career. As he came through the door at that moment, he gave his weary smile again, to show that he still remembered me, saying at the same time to Widmerpool : " You went away so quickly that I had no time to tell you that the Chief will very likely be here to-night. He is an old friend of Milly's. Besides, I happen to know that he told Baby Wentworth he would look in—so it's a virtual certainty."

Truscott was still, so far as I knew, one of the secretaries of Sir Magnus Donners, to whom it was to be presumed he referred as " the Chief." Stringham's vagueness in speaking of his own employment had left me uncertain whether or not he and Truscott remained such close colleagues as formerly, though Sillery's remarks certainly suggested that they were still working together.

"Well, of course, that would be splendid," said Widmerpool slowly.

But, although unquestionably interested in the information just given him, he spoke rather forlornly. His mind seemed to be on other things: unable to concentrate fully on the comings and goings even of so portentous a figure as Sir Magnus Donners.

" He could meet you," Truscott said dryly. " And then we could talk things over next week."

Widmerpool, trying to collect himself, seemed still uncertain in his own mind. He smoothed down his hair, the disarrangement of which he must have observed in the mural looking-glass in front of us.

" The Chief is the most unconventional man in the world," said Truscott, more encouragingly. " He loves informality."

He stood there, smiling down at Widmerpool, for, although not more than an inch or two taller, he managed to give an impression of height. His thick and glossy hair had grown perceptibly more grey round the ears. I wondered how Truscott and Widmerpool had been brought together, since it was clear that arrangements projected for that night must have been the result of earlier, possibly even laborious, negotiation between them. There could be no doubt, whatever my own opinion of Widmerpool's natural endowments, that he managed to make a decidedly good impression on people primarily interested in "getting on." For example, neither Tompsitt nor Truscott had much in common except concentration on "the main chance," and yet both had apparently been struck—in Tompsitt's case, almost immediately—by some inner belief in Widmerpool's fundamental ability. This matter of making headway in life was one to which I felt perhaps I, too, ought to devote greater consideration in future, if I were myself not to remain inextricably fixed in a monotonous, even sometimes dreary, groove.

"You don't think I had better ring you up in the morning?" said Widmerpool, rather anxiously. "My brain is a bit confused to-night. I don't want to make a poor impression on Sir Magnus. To tell the truth, I was thinking of going home. I don't usually stay up as late as this."

"All right," said Truscott, not attempting to repress a polite smile at the idea of anyone being so weak in spirit as to limit their chances of advancement by reluctance to keep late hours. "Perhaps that might be best. Donners-Brebner, Extension 5, any time after ten o'clock."

"I don't expect it would be much use looking for my hostess to say good-bye," said Widmerpool, gazing about him wildly as if by now tired out. "You know, I haven't managed to meet her properly the whole time I have been here."

"Not the slightest use," said Truscott, smiling again at such naïveté.

He regarded Widmerpool as if he thought—now that a decision to retire to bed had been finally taken—that the sooner Widmerpool embarked upon a good night's rest, the better, if he were to be fit for the plans Truscott had in store for him in the near future.

"Then I'll bid you good night," said Widmerpool, turning to me and speaking in a voice of great exhaustion.

"Sweet dreams."

"Tell Stringham I was sorry not to see him before I left the party."

"I will."

"Thank him for bringing us. It was kind. He must lunch with me in the City."

He made his way from the room. I wondered whether or not it had indeed been kind of Stringham to bring him to the party. Kind or the reverse, I felt pretty sure that Stringham would not lunch with Widmerpool in the City. Truscott showed more surprise at Widmerpool's mention of Stringham than he usually allowed himself, at least in public.

"Does he know Charles, then?" he asked, as Widmerpool disappeared through the door.

"We were all at the same house at school."

"Indeed?"

"Widmerpool was a shade senior."

"He really might be quite useful in our new politico-legal branch," said Truscott. "Not necessarily full time—anyway at first—and the Chief always insists on hand-picking everyone himself. He'll grow out of that rather unfortunate manner, of course."

I thought it improbable that Widmerpool would ever change his manner at the mandate of Sir Magnus Donners, Truscott, Stringham, or anyone else, though the projected employment—an aspect of those rather mysterious business activities, so different from those of my own small firm—

sounded normal enough. In fact the job, as such, did not at the time make any strong impression on me. I felt more interest in trying to learn something of Stringham's life. This seemed an opportunity to make some inquiries.

"Oh, yes," said Truscott, almost with enthusiasm. "Of course Charles is still with us. He can really be quite an asset at times. Such charm, you know. But I see my Chief has arrived. If you will forgive me . . ."

He was gone instantaneously, stepping quickly across the floor to meet, and intercept, a tallish man, who, with Mrs. Wentworth at his side, had just entered the room. At first I was uncertain whether this outwardly unemphatic figure could indeed be Sir Magnus Donners, the person addressed by Truscott being so unlike my pre-conceived idea of what might be expected from the exterior of a public character of that particular kind. Hesitation on this point was justifiable. The name of Sir Magnus Donners, both in capacity of well-known industrialist and former member of the Government (in which he had never reached Cabinet rank) attached to the imagination, almost automatically, one of those paraphrases—on the whole uncomplimentary—presented by the cartoonist; representations that serve, more or less effectually, to supply the mind on easy terms with the supposedly salient traits, personal, social, or political, of individuals or types: such delineations being naturally concerned for the most part with men, or categories of men, to be thought of as important in exercising power in one form or another.

In the first place, it was unexpected that Sir Magnus Donners should look at least ten years younger than might reasonably have been supposed; so that, although well into his middle fifties—where he stood beneath an unsatisfying picture executed in the manner of Derain—he seemed scarcely middle-aged. Clean-shaven, good-looking, rather than the reverse, possibly there was something odd, even a trifle disturbing, about the set of his mouth. Something that perhaps conveyed interior ferment kept in severe repression. Apart from that his features had been reduced, no doubt by laborious mental discipline, to a state of almost unnatural ordinariness. He possessed, however, a suggestion about him that was decidedly parsonic: a lay-reader, or clerical headmaster: even some distinguished athlete, of almost uncomfortably rigid moral convictions, of whose good work at the boys' club in some East End settlement his own close friends were quite unaware. The complexion was of a man whose life appeared to have been lived, on the whole, out of doors. He seemed, indeed, too used to the open air to be altogether at ease in evening clothes, which were carelessly worn, as if only assumed under protest, though he shared that appearance of almost chemical cleanliness characteristic, in another form, of Archie Gilbert. At the same time, in spite of these intimations of higher things, the heavy, purposeful walk implied the professional politician. A touch of sadness about his face was not unprepossessing.

That ponderous tread was also the only faint hint of the side expressed by common gossip, for example, at Sillery's —where Bill Truscott's connection with Donners-Brebner made Sir Magnus's name a relatively familiar one in the twilight world of undergraduate conversation—that is to say, of a kind of stage "profiteer" or "tycoon": a man of Big Business and professionally strong will. Such, indeed, I had previously pictured him. Now the matter, like so many others, had to be reconsidered. Equally, he showed still less of that aspect called up by the remark once let fall by Stringham: "He is always trying to get in with my

mother." Everything about Sir Magnus seemed far too
quiet and correct for any of his elements even to insinu-
ate that there could be in his conduct, or nature, anything
that might urge him to push his way into a world where
welcome admission might be questionable—even deliberately withheld. Indeed, much later, when I came to hear
more about him, there could be no doubt that whatever
efforts Sir Magnus may have made to ingratiate himself
with Mrs. Foxe, through her son, or otherwise—and there
was reason to suppose such efforts had in truth been made—
must have been accountable to one of those whims to which
men of his sort are particularly subject; that is to say, desire
to cut a figure somewhere outside the circle familiar to
themselves; because Sir Magnus was, after all, in a position,
so far as that went, to " go " pretty well anywhere he might
happen to wish. The social process he elected to follow was
rather like that of mountaineers who chose deliberately the
sheer ascent of the cliff face; for it was true I found
particular difficulty in associating him with Stringham, or,
so far as I knew of them, with Stringham's family. Widmerpool, on the other hand, though this was by the way,
was a victim easily imaginable; no doubt, as I guessed,
fated to be captivated irrevocably at his pending interview
by that colourless, respectable, dominating exterior of
" the Chief."

What part Mrs. Wentworth played in Sir Magnus's life
was, of course, a question that at once suggested itself. He
was not married. Truscott's words: " He told Baby Wentworth he would look in—so it's a virtual certainty,"
seemed to imply a fairly firm influence, or attachment, of
one kind or another, probably temporary. However, as Sir
Magnus and Mrs. Wentworth came through the door, side
by side, there was nothing in their outward appearance to

denote pleasure in each other's company. On the contrary, they had entered the room together, both of them, with an almost hang-dog air, and Mrs. Wentworth's features had lost all the gaiety and animation assumed earlier to charm Prince Theodoric. She now appeared sulky, and, if the word could be used at all of someone so self-possessed, and of such pleasing face and figure, almost awkward. It was rather as if they were walking away together from some excessively embarrassing scene in which they had been taking joint part: some incident for which the two of them felt both equally to blame, and heartily ashamed. I could not help thinking of one of those pictures—neither traditional, nor in Mr. Deacon's vernacular, but in " modern dress " a pictorial method of treating Biblical subjects then somewhat in vogue—of Adam and Eve leaving the Garden of Eden after the Fall: this impression being so vivid that I almost expected them to be followed through the door by a well-tailored angel, pointing in their direction a flaming sword.

Any such view of them was not only entirely fanciful, but perhaps also without any foundation in fact, because Truscott seemed to regard their bearing as perfectly normal. He came up to them buoyantly, and talked for a minute or two in his accustomed easy style. Mrs. Wentworth lit a cigarette, and, without smiling, watched him, her eyebrows slightly raised. Then she spoke to Sir Magnus, at which he nodded his head heavily several times. Perhaps arrangements were being made for sending her home in his car, because he looked at his watch before saying good night, and asked Truscott some questions. Then Mrs. Wentworth, after giving Sir Magnus little more than a nod, went off with Truscott; who returned a minute or two later, and settled down with his employer on the sofa. They began to talk gravely, looking rather like father and son, though, strangely enough, it might have been Truscott who was playing the paternal rôle.

By now the crowd had thinned considerably, and the music of the hunchback's accordion had ceased. I was beginning to feel more than a little exhausted, yet, unable to make up my mind to go home, I wandered rather aimlessly round the house, throughout which the remaining guests were now sitting about in pairs, or larger groups. Chronological sequence of events pertaining to this interlude of the party became afterwards somewhat confused in my head. I can recall a brief conversation with a woman— not pretty, though possessing excellent legs—on the subject of cheese, which she alleged to be unprocurable, at the buffet. Prince Theodoric and Sillery had disappeared, and already there was the impression, given by most parties, sooner or later, that the residue still assembled under Mrs. Andriadis's roof was gradually, inexorably, sinking to a small band of those hard cases who can never tear themselves away from what still remains, for an hour or so longer, if not of gaiety, then at least some sort of mellow companionship, and protection from the austerities of the outer world.

Two young men strolled by, and I heard one of them say: "Poor Milly really got together quite an elegant crowd to-night."

The other, who wore an orchid in his button-hole, replied: "I felt that Sillery imparted a faintly bourgeois note—and there were one or two extraordinary figures from the lofts of Chelsea."

He added that, personally, he proposed to have "one more drink" before leaving, while the other murmured something about an invitation to "bacon and eggs at the

Kit-Cat." They parted company at this, and when the young man with the orchid returned from the bar, he set down his glass near me, and without further introduction, began to discuss, at large, the house's style of decoration, of which he appeared strongly to disapprove.

"Of course it must have cost a fortune to have had all those carpets cut right up to the walls," he said. "But why go and spoil everything by these appalling Italianate fittings—and the pictures—my God, the pictures."

I asked if the house belonged to Mrs. Andriadis.

"Good heavens, no," he said. "Milly has only taken it for a few months from a man named Duport."

"Bob Duport?"

"Not an intimate friend of yours, I hope?"

"On the contrary."

"Because his manners don't attract me."

"Nor me."

"Not that I ever see him these days, but we were at the same college—before he was sent down."

I commented to the effect that, however unsatisfactory its decoration might be, I found the house an unexpectedly sumptuous place for Duport to inhabit. The young man with the orchid immediately assured me that Duport was not short of money.

"He came into quite a bit," he said. "And then he is one of those men money likes. He is in the Balkans at the moment—doing well there, too, I have no doubt. He is, I regret to say, that sort of man."

He sighed.

"Is he married?"

"Rather a nice wife."

Although I scarcely knew Bob Duport, he had always remained in my mind on account of his having been one

of the company when Peter Templer, in a recently purchased car, had driven Stringham and myself into the
ditch, together with a couple of shop-girls and another unprepossessing friend of Templer's called Brent. That
episode had been during the single term that Stringham had
remained in residence at the university. The incident
seemed absurd enough when looked back upon, but I had
not greatly liked Duport. Now I felt, for some reason,
inexplicably annoyed that he should own a house like this
one, however ineptly decorated, and also be the possessor of
a wife whom my informant—whose manner suggested
absolute infallibility on such matters—regarded as attractive; while I myself, at the same time, lived a comparative
hand-to-mouth existence in rooms, in my own case, there
had never been any serious prospect of getting married.
This seemed, on examination, a contrast from which I came
out rather poorly.

Since living in London, I had seen Peter Templer several
times, but, in the course of an interminable chain of anecdotes about his ever-changing circle of cronies, I could not
remember the name of Duport figuring, so that I did
not know whether or not the two of them continued to see
each other. Peter himself had taken to the city like a duck
to water. He now talked unendingly of " cleaning up a
packet " and " making a killing "; money, with its multi-
farious imagery and restrictive mystique, holding a place in
his mind only seriously rivalled by preoccupation with the
pursuit of women : the latter interest having proportion-
ately increased with opportunity to experiment in a wider
field than formerly.

When we had lunched or dined together, the occasions
had been enjoyable, although there had hardly been any
renewal of the friendship that had existed between us at

school. Peter did not frequent the world of dances because —like Stringham—he was bored by their unduly respectable environment.

"At least," he said once, when discussing the matter, "I don't go as a habit to the sort of dance you see reported in *The Morning Post* or *The Times*. I don't say I have never attended similar entertainments in some huge and gloomy house in Bayswater or Holland Park—probably Jewish— if I happened to take a fancy to a girl who moves in those circles. There is more fun to be found amongst all that mahogany furniture and Moorish brasswork than you might think."

In business, at least in a small way, he had begun to "make a bit " on his own, and there seemed no reason to disbelieve his account of himself as looked upon in his firm as a promising young man. In fact, it appeared that Peter, so far from becoming the outcast from society prophesied by our housemaster, Le Bas, now showed every sign of being about to prove himself a notable success in life: an outcome that seemed to demand another of those revisions of opinion, made every day more necessary, in relation to such an enormous amount of material, accepted as incontrovertible at an earlier period of practical experience.

Thinking that if the young man with the orchid knew Duport, he might also know Peter, whom I had not by then seen for about a year, I asked if the two of them had ever met.

"I've never run across Templer," he said. "But I've heard tell of him. As a matter of fact, I believe Duport married Templer's sister, didn't he? What was her name?"

"Jean."

"That was it. A thin girl with blue eyes. I think they

got married abroad—South America or somewhere, was it?"

The sudden awareness of displeasure felt a second earlier at the apparent prosperity of Duport's general state was nothing to the pang I suffered on hearing this piece of news: the former sense of grievance caused, perhaps, by premonition that worse was to come. I had not, it was true, thought much of Jean Templer for years, having relegated any question of being, as I had once supposed, "in love" with her to a comparatively humble position in memory; indeed, regarding the incident as dating from a time when any such feelings were, in my own eyes, hopelessly immature, in comparison, for example, with sentiments felt for Barbara. However, I now found, rather to my own surprise, deep vexation in the discovery that Jean was the wife of someone so unsympathetic as Bob Duport.

Such emotions, sudden bursts of sexual jealousy that pursue us through life, sometimes without the smallest justification that memory or affection might provide, are like wounds, unknown and quiescent, that suddenly break out to give pain, or at least irritation, at a later season of the year, or in an unfamiliar climate. The party, and the young man with the orchid, supplied perfect setting for an attack of that kind. I was about to return to the subject of Duport, with a view to relieving this sense of annoyance by further unfavourable comment regarding his personality (as it had appeared to me in the past) in the hope that my views would find ready agreement, when I became suddenly aware that Stringham and Mrs. Andriadis were together engaged in vehement argument just beside the place we sat.

"But, sweetie," Mrs. Andriadis was saying, "you can't possibly want to go to the Embassy *now*."

"But the odd thing is," said Stringham, speaking slowly and deliberately, " the odd thing is that is just what I do want to do. I want to go to the Embassy *at once*. Without further delay."

"But it will be closed."

"I am rather glad to hear that. I never really liked the Embassy. I shall go somewhere else."

"But you said it was just the Embassy you wanted to go to."

"I can't think why. I really want to go somewhere quite different."

"You really are being too boring for words, Charles."

"I quite agree," said Stringham, suddenly changing his tone. "The fact is I am much too boring to stay at a party. That is exactly how I feel myself. Especially one of your parties, Milly—one of your charming, gay, exquisite, un-rivalled parties. I cast a gloom over the merry scene. 'Who is that corpse at the feast?' people ask, and the reply is 'Poor old Stringham'."

"But you wouldn't feel any better at the Embassy, darling, even if it were open."

"You are probably right. In fact, I should certainly feel no better at the Embassy. I should feel worse. That is why I am going somewhere much lower than that. Somewhere really frightful."

"You are being very silly."

"The Forty-Three would be too stuffy—in all senses—for my present mood."

"You can't want to go to the Forty-Three."

"I repeat that I do not want to go to the Forty-Three. I am at the moment looking into my soul to examine the interesting question of where exactly I do want to go."

"Wherever it is, I shall come too."

" As you wish, Milly. As you wish. As a matter of fact I was turning over the possibilities of a visit to Mrs. Fitz."

" Charles, you are impossible."

I suppose he had had a good deal to drink, though this was, in a way, beside the point, for I knew from past experience that he could be just as perverse in his behaviour when there had been no question of drinking. If he were a little drunk, apart from making a slight bow, he showed no physical sign of such a condition. Mrs. Andriadis, who was evidently determined to master the situation—and who still, in her own particular style, managed to remain rather dazzling, in spite of being obviously put out by this altercation—turned to one of the men-servants who happened to be passing at that moment, carrying a tray laden with glasses, and said: " Go and get my coat—and be quick about it."

The man, an old fellow with a blotched face, who had perhaps taken the opportunity to sample the champagne himself more freely than had been wise, stared at her, and, setting down the tray, ambled slowly off. Stringham caught sight of us sitting near-by. He took a step towards me.

" At least I can rely on you, Nick, as an old friend," he said, " to accompany me to a haunt of vice. Somewhere where the stains on the table-cloth make the flesh creep— some cellar far below the level of the street, where ageing harlots caper cheerlessly to the discordant strains of jazz."

Mrs. Andriadis grasped at once that we had known each other for a long time, because she smiled with one of those looks of captivating and whole-hearted sincerity that must have contributed in no small degree to her adventurous career. I was conscious that heavy artillery was now ranged upon my position. At the same time she managed to present herself—as it were, stood before me—in her weakness, threatened by Stringham's behaviour certainly aggravating enough, remarking softly: " Do tell him not to be such an ass."

Stringham, too, perfectly took in the situation, evidently deciding immediately, and probably correctly, that if any kind of discussion were allowed to develop between the three of us, Mrs. Andriadis would, in some manner, bring him to heel. There had been, presumably, some collision of wills between them in the course of the evening; probably the consequence of mutual irritation extending over weeks, or even months. Perhaps he had deliberately intended to provoke a quarrel when he had arrived at the house that evening. The situation had rather the appearance of something of the sort. It was equally possible that he was suffering merely from the same kind of restlessness that had earlier afflicted Gypsy Jones. I did not know. In any case, though no business of mine, a break between them might be for the best. However, no time remained to weigh such question in the balance, because Stringham did not wait. He laughed loudly, and went off through the door. Mrs. Andriadis took my arm.

" Will you persuade him to stay!" she said, with that trace of Cockney which—as Barnby would have remarked —had once " come near to breaking a royal heart."

At that moment the young man with the orchid, who had risen with dignity from the sofa where he had been silently contemplating the world, came towards us, breaking into the conversation with the words: " My dear Milly, I simply must tell you the story about Theodoric and the Prince of Wales . . ."

" Another time, darling."

Mrs. Andriadis gave him a slight push with her left hand, so that he collapsed quietly, and apparently quite happily, into an easy-chair. Almost simultaneously an enormous, purple-faced man with a decided air of authority about him, whose features were for some reason familiar to me, accompanied by a small woman, much younger than himself, came up, mumbling and faintly swaying, as he attempted to thank Mrs. Andriadis for entertaining them. She brushed him aside, clearly to his immense, rather intoxicated surprise, with the same ruthlessness she had shown to the young man with the orchid: at the same time saying to another servant, whom I took, this time, to be her own butler: "I told one of those bloody hired men to fetch my coat. Go and see where he's got to."

All these minor incidents inevitably caused delay, giving Stringham a start on the journey down the stairs, towards which we now set off, Mrs. Andriadis still grasping my arm, along which, from second to second, she convulsively altered the grip of her hand. As we reached the foot of the last flight together, the front door slammed. Three or four people were chatting, or putting on wraps, in the hall, in preparation to leave. The elderly lady with the black eyebrows and tiara was sitting on one of the crimson and gold high-backed chairs, beneath which I could see a pile of *War Never Pays!* : Mr. Deacon's, or those forgotten by Gypsy Jones. She had removed her right shoe and was examining the heel intently, to observe if it were still intact. Mrs. Andriadis let go my arm, and ran swiftly towards the door, which she wrenched open violently, just in time to see a taxi drive away from the front of the house. She made use of an expletive that I had never before—in those distant days—heard a woman employ. The phrase left no doubt in the mind that she was extremely provoked. The door swung on its hinge. In silence Mrs. Andriadis watched it shut with a bang. It was hard to know what comment, if any, was required. At that moment the butler arrived with her coat.

"Will you wear it, madam?"

"Take the damned thing away," she said. "Are you and the rest of them a lot of bloody cripples? Do I have to wait half an hour every time I want to go out just because I haven't a rag to put round me?"

The butler, accustomed no doubt to such reproaches as all in the day's work—and possibly remunerated on a scale to allow a generous margin for hard words—seemed entirely undisturbed by these strictures on his own agility, and that of his fellows. He agreed at once that his temporary colleague "did not appear to have his wits about him at all." In the second's pause during which Mrs. Andriadis seemed to consider this statement, I prepared to say good-bye, partly from conviction that the occasion for doing so, once missed, might not easily recur; even more, because immediate farewell would be a convenient method of bringing to an end the distressing period of tension that had come into existence ever since Stringham's departure, while Mrs. Andriadis contemplated her next move. However, before there was time, on my own part, to take any step in the direction of leave-taking, a loud noise from the stairs behind distracted my attention. Mrs. Andriadis, too, was brought by this sudden disturbance out of the state of suspended animation into which she appeared momentarily to have fallen.

The cause of the commotion now became manifest. Mr. Deacon and the singer, Max Pilgrim, followed by the Negro, were descending the stairs rapidly, side by side, jerking down from step to step in the tumult of a frantic quarrel. At first I supposed, improbable as such a thing would be, that some kind of practical joke or "rag" was taking place in which all three were engaged; but looking closer, it became plain that Mr. Deacon was angry with Pilgrim, while the Negro was more or less a spectator, not greatly involved except by his obvious enjoyment of the row. The loose lock of Mr. Deacon's hair had once more fallen across his forehead: his voice had taken on a deep and mordant note. Pilgrim was red in the face and sweating, though keeping his temper with difficulty, and attempting to steer the dispute, whatever its subject, into channels more facetious than polemical.

"There are always leering eyes on the look-out," Mr. Deacon was saying. "Besides, your song puts a weapon in the hands of the puritans."

"I don't expect there were many puritans present——" began Pilgrim.

Mr. Deacon cut him short.

"It is a matter of *principle*," he said. "If you have any."

"What do you know about my principles?" said Pilgrim. "I don't expect your own principles bear much examination when the lights are out."

"I can give you an assurance that *you* have no cause to worry about *my* principles," Mr. Deacon almost screamed. "Such a situation could never arise—I can assure you of that. This is not the first time, to my knowledge, that you have presumed on such a thing."

This comment seemed to annoy Pilgrim a great deal, so that he now became scarcely less enraged than Mr. Deacon himself. His quavering voice rose in protest, while Mr. Deacon's sank to a scathing growl: the most offensive tone I have ever heard him employ.

"You person," he said.

Turning fiercely away from Pilgrim, he strode across the hall in the direction of the chair under which he had stored

away *War Never Pays!* Together with his own copies, he
gathered up those brought by Gypsy Jones—forgotten by
her, as I had foreseen—and, tucking a sheaf under each
arm, he made towards the front door. He ignored the
figure of Mrs. Andriadis, of whose presence he was no
doubt, in his rage, entirely unaware. The catch of the door
must have jammed, for that, or some other cause, prevented the hinge from opening freely. Mr. Deacon's first
intention was evidently to hold all the papers, his own and
those belonging to Gypsy Jones, under his left arm for the
brief second during which he opened the door with his
right hand to sweep for ever from the obnoxious presence
of Max Pilgrim. However, the two combined packets of
War Never Pays! made quite a considerable bundle, and he
must have found himself compelled to bring his left hand
also into play, while he hugged most of the copies of the
publication—by then rather crumpled—by pressure from his
left elbow against his side. The door swung open suddenly. Mr. Deacon was taken by surprise. All at once there
was a sound as of the rending of silk, and the papers, like
a waterfall—or sugar on Widmerpool's head—began to
tumble, one after another, to the ground from under Mr.
Deacon's arm. He made a violent effort to check their
descent, contriving only to increase the area over which
they were freely shed; an unexpected current of air blowing through the open door at that moment into the house
helped to scatter sheets of *War Never Pays!* far and wide
throughout the hall, even up to the threshold of the room
beyond. There was a loud, stagey laugh from the stairs in
the background. "Ha! Ha! Ha!"

It was the Negro. He was grinning from ear to ear, now
more like a nigger minstrel—a coon with bones and tam-
bourine from some old-fashioned show on the pier at

a seaside resort of the Victorian era—than his former dignified, well-groomed self. The sound of his wild, African laughter must have caused Mrs. Andriadis to emerge unequivocally from her coma. She turned on Mr. Deacon.

"You awful old creature," she said, "get out of my house."

He stared at her, and then burst into a fearful fit of coughing, clutching at his chest. My hat stood on a table not far away. While Mrs. Andriadis was still turned from me, I took it up without further delay, and passed through the open door. Mr. Deacon had proved himself a graver responsibility than I, for one, by then felt myself prepared to sustain. They could, all of them, arrange matters between themselves without my help. It would, indeed, be better so. Whatever solution was, in fact, found to terminate the complexities of that moment, Mr. Deacon's immediate expulsion from the house at the command of Mrs. Andriadis was not one of them; because, when I looked back—after proceeding nearly a hundred yards up the road—there was still no sign of his egress, violent or otherwise, from the house.

It was already quite light in the street, and although the air was fresh, almost breezy, after the atmosphere of the party, there was a hint, even at this early hour, of another sultry day on the way. Narrow streaks of blue were already beginning to appear across the flat surface of a livid sky. The dawn had a kind of heaviness, perhaps of thundery weather in the offing. No one was about, though the hum of an occasional car driving up Park Lane from time to time broke the silence for a few seconds, the sound, mournful as the huntsman's horn echoing in the forest, dying away quickly in the distance. Early morning bears with it a sense of pressure, a kind of threat of what the day will bring forth. I felt unsettled and dissatisfied though not in the least drunk. On the contrary, my brain seemed to be working all at once with quite unusual clarity. Indeed, I found myself almost deciding to sit down, as soon as I reached my room, and attempt to compose a series of essays on human life and character in the manner of, say, Montaigne, so icily etched in my mind at that moment appeared the actions and nature of those with whom that night I had been spending my time. However, second thoughts convinced me that any such efforts at composition would be inadvisable at such an hour. The first thing to do on reaching home would be to try and achieve some sleep. In the morning, literary matters might be reconsidered. I was conscious of having travelled a long way since the Walpole-Wilsons' dinner-party. I was, in fact, very tired.

Attempting to sort out and classify the events of the night, as I walked home between the grey Mayfair houses, I found myself unable to enjoy in retrospect the pleasure reasonably to be expected from the sense of having broken fresh ground. Mrs. Andriadis's party had certainly been something new. Its strangeness and fascination had not escaped me. But there appeared now, so far as I could foresee, no prospect of setting foot again within those unaccustomed regions; even temporary connection with them, tenuously supplied by Stringham in his latest avatar, seeming uncompromisingly removed by the drift of circumstance.

Apart from these reflections, I was also painfully aware that I had, so it appeared to me, prodigally wasted my time at the party. Instead, for example, of finding a girl to take the place of Barbara—she, at least had been finally swept away by Mrs. Andriadis—I had squandered the hours of opportunity with Mr. Deacon, or with Sillery. I thought suddenly of Sunny Farebrother, and the pleasure he had described himself as deriving from meeting "interesting people" in the course of his work at the Peace Conference. No such "interesting" contacts, so far as I myself had been concerned that evening, could possibly have been said to have taken place. For a moment I regretted having refused Gypsy Jones's invitation to accompany her to The Merry Thought. From the point of view of either sentiment or snobbery, giving both terms their widest connotation, the night had been an empty one. I had, so it appeared, merely stayed up until the small hours—no doubt relatively incapacitating myself for serious work on the day following—with nothing better to show for it than the certainty, now absolute, that I was no longer in love with Barbara Goring; though this emancipation would include, of course, relief also from such minor irritations as Tompsitt and his fellows. I remembered now, all at once, Widmerpool's apprehensions at what had seemed to him the "unserious" nature of my employment.

As I reached the outskirts of Shepherd Market, at that period scarcely touched by rebuilding, I regained once more some small sense of exultation, enjoyed whenever crossing the perimeter of that sinister little village, that I lived within an enchanted precinct. Inconvenient, at moments, as a locality: noisy and uncomfortable: stuffy, depressing, unsavoury: yet the ancient houses still retained some vestige of the dignity of another age; while the inhabitants, many of them existing precariously on their bridge earnings, or hire of their bodies, were—as more than one novelist had, even in those days, already remarked—not without their own seedy glory.

Now, touched almost mystically, like another Stonehenge,

by the first rays of the morning sun, the spot seemed one
of those clusters of tumble-down dwellings depicted by
Canaletto or Piranesi, habitations from amongst which
arches, obelisks and viaducts, ruined and overgrown with
ivy, arise from the mean houses huddled together below
them. Here, too, such massive structures might, one
felt, at any moment come into existence by some latent
sorcery, for the place was scarcely of this world, and anything was to be surmised. As I penetrated farther into the
heart of that rookery, in the direction of my own door,
there even stood, as if waiting to greet a friend, one of
those indeterminate figures that occur so frequently in
the pictures of the kind suggested—Hubert Robert or
Pannini—in which the architectural subject predominates.
This materialisation took clearer shape as a man, middle-
aged to elderly, wearing a bowler hat and discreetly horsy
overcoat, the collar turned-up round a claret-coloured scarf
with white spots. He leant a little to one side on a rolled
umbrella, just as those single figures in romantic landscape are apt to pose; as if the painter, in dealing with so
much static matter, were determined to emphasise " movement " in the almost infinitesimal human side of his composition.

" Where are you off to?" this person suddenly called
across the street.

The voice, grating on the morning air, was somewhat
accusing in tone. I saw, as a kind of instantaneous revelation, that it was Uncle Giles who stood on the corner in
front of the public-house. He seemed undecided which
road to take. It was plain that, a minute or two earlier,
he had emerged from one of the three main centres of
nocturnal activity in the immediate neighbourhood, represented by the garage, the sandwich bar, and the block of

flats of dubious repute. There was not a shred of evidence pointing to one of these starting points in preference to another, though other alternatives seemed excluded by his position. I crossed the road.

" Just up from the country," he said, gruffly.

" By car?"

" By car? Yes, of course."

" Is it a new one?"

" Yes," said Uncle Giles. " It's a new one."

He spoke as if he had only just thought of that aspect of the vehicle, supposedly his property, that was stated to have brought him to London. One of those pauses followed for which my uncle's conversation was noted within the family circle. I explained that I was returning from a dance, a half-truth that seemed to cover whatever information was required, then and there, to define my circumstances in as compact and easily intelligible a form as possible. Uncle Giles was not practised in following any narrative at all involved in its nature. His mind was inclined to stray back to his own affairs if a story's duration was of anything but the briefest. My words proved redundant, however. He was not in the least interested.

" I am here on business," he said. " I don't want to waste a lot of time. Never was keen on remaining too long in London. Your hand is never out of your pocket."

" Where are you staying?"

My uncle thought for a moment.

" Bayswater," he said, slowly and rather thoughtfully.

I must have looked surprised at finding him so comparatively far afield from his *pied-à-terre*, because Uncle Giles added :

" I mean, of course, that Bayswater is where I am going to stay—at the Ufford, as usual. There is a lot to be said for a place where they know you. Get some civility. At the moment I am on my way to my club, only round the corner."

" My rooms are just by here."

" Where?" he asked, suspiciously.

" Opposite."

" Can't you find anywhere better to live—I mean it's rather a disreputable part of the world, isn't it?"

As if in confirmation of my uncle's misgivings, a prostitute, small, almost a dwarf, with a stumpy umbrella tucked under her arm, came hurrying home, late off her beat—tap-tap-tap-tap-tap-tap-tap-tap—along the pavement, her extravagant heels making a noise like a woodpecker attacking a tree. She wore a kind of felt helmet pulled low over her face, which looked exceedingly bad-tempered. Some instinct must have told her that neither my uncle nor I were to be regarded in the circumstances as potential clients; for altering her expression no more than to bare a fang at the side of her mouth like an angry animal, she sped along the street at a furious pace—tap-tap-tap-tap-tap-tap—and up the steps of the entrance to the flats, when she disappeared from sight. Uncle Giles averted his eyes. He still showed no sign of wishing to move from the spot, almost as if he feared even the smallest change of posture might in some unforeseen manner prejudice the veil of secrecy that so utterly cloaked his immediate point of departure.

" I have been with friends in Surrey," he said grudgingly, as if the admission were unwillingly drawn from him. " It's a favourite county of mine. Lovely in the autumn. I'm connected with the paper business now."

I hoped sincerely that this connection took, as was probable, remote and esoteric form, and that he was not associated with some normal branch of the industry with which my own firm might be expected to open an account. However, he showed no desire to pursue this matter of his new employment. Instead, he produced from his overcoat pocket a handful of documents, looking like company reports, and glanced swiftly through them. I thought he was going to begin discussing the Trust—by now the Trust remained practically the only unsevered link between himself and his relations—in spite of the earliness of the hour. If his original idea had been to make the Trust subject of comment, he must have changed his mind, finding these memoranda, if such they were, in some way wanting, because he replaced the papers carefully in order and stuffed them back into his coat.

" Tell your father to try and get some San Pedro Warehouses Deferred," he said, shortly. " I have had reliable advice about them."

" I'll say you said so."

" Do you always stay up as late as this?"

" No—it was a specially good party."

I could see from my uncle's face that not only did he not accept this as an excuse, but that he had also chosen to consider the words as intended deliberately to disconcert him.

" Take a bit of advice from one who has knocked about the world for a good many years," he said. " Don't get in the habit of sitting up till all hours. It never did anyone any good."

" I'll bear it in mind."

" Parents well?"

" Very well."

" I've been having trouble with my teeth."

" I'm sorry."

" Well, I must be off. Good-bye to you."

He made a stiff gesture, rather as if motioning some-one away from him, and moved off suddenly in the direc-tion of Hertford Street, striding along very serious, with his umbrella shouldered, as if once more at the head of his troops, drums beating and colours flying, as the column, conceded all honours of war, marched out of the capitulated town. Just as I opened the door of my house, he turned to wave. I raised my hand in return. Within, the bedroom remained unaltered, just as it had appeared when I had set out for the Walpole-Wilsons', the suit I had worn the day before hanging dejectedly over the back of a chair. While I undressed I reflected on the difficulty of believing in the existence of certain human beings, my uncle among them, even in the face of unquestionable evidence—indica-tions sometimes even wanting in the case of persons for some reason more substantial to the mind—that each had dreams and desires like other men. Was it possible to take Uncle Giles seriously? And yet he was, no doubt, serious enough to himself. If a clue to that problem could be found, other mysteries of life might be revealed. I was still pondering Uncle Giles and his ways when I dropped into an uneasy sleep.

THREE

I used to imagine life divided into separate compartments, consisting, for example, of such dual abstractions as pleasure and pain, love and hate, friendship and enmity; and more material classifications like work and play: a profession or calling being, according to that concept—one that seemed, at least on the surface, unequivocally assumed by persons so

dissimilar from one another as Widmerpool and Archie
Gilbert, something entirely different from "spare time."
That illusion, as such a point of view was, in due course,
to appear—was closely related to another belief : that existence fans out indefinitely into new areas of experience,
and that almost every additional acquaintance offers some
supplementary world with its own hazards and enchant-
ments. As time goes on, of course, these supposedly
different worlds, in fact, draw closer, if not to each other,
then to some pattern common to all; so that, at last,
diversity between them, if in truth existent, seems to be
almost imperceptible except in a few crude and exterior
ways : unthinkable, as formerly appeared, any single con-
summation of cause and effect. In other words, nearly all
the inhabitants of these outwardly disconnected empires
turn out at last to be tenaciously inter-related; love and
hate, friendship and enmity, too, becoming themselves
much less clearly defined, more often than not showing
signs of possessing characteristics that could claim, to say
the least, not a little in common; while work and play
merge indistinguishably into a complex tissue of pleasure
and tedium.

All the same, although still far from appreciating many
of the finer points of Mrs. Andriadis's party—for there
were, of course, finer points to be appreciated in retrospect
—and, on the whole, no less ignorant of what the elements
there present had consisted, I was at the same time more
than half aware that such latitudes are entered by a door
through which there is, in a sense, no return. The lack
of ceremony that had attended our arrival, and the fact
of being so much in the dark as to the terms upon which
the party was being given, had been both, in themselves, a
trifle embarrassing; but, looking back on the occasion,

armed with later knowledge of individual affiliations among the guests, there is no reason to suppose that mere awareness of everyone's identity would have been calculated to promote any greater feeling of ease : if anything, rather the reverse. The impact of entertainments given by people like Mrs. Andriadis, as I learnt in due course, depends upon rapidly changing personal relationships; so that to be apprised suddenly of the almost infinite complication of such associations—if any such omniscience could, by some magical means, have been imparted—without being oneself, even at a distance, at all involved, might have been a positive handicap, perhaps a humiliating one, to enjoyment.

To begin with, there was the unanswered question of Stringham's entanglement with Mrs. Andriadis herself. I did not know how long in duration of time the affair had already extended, nor how seriously it was to be regarded. Their connection, on his part at least, seemed no more than a whim : a fancy for an older woman, of which, for example, in a Latin country nothing whatever would be thought. On the other hand, Mrs. Andriadis herself evidently accepted the fact that, so far as things went, she was fairly deeply concerned. I thought of the casual adventure with the woman in Nairobi that he had described to me, and of the days when he and Peter Templer had been accustomed to discuss " girls " together at school.

I could now recognise in Stringham's attitude a kind of reticence, never apparent at the time when such talks had taken place. This reticence, when I thought it over, was not in what Stringham said, or did not say, so much as in what, I suppose, he felt; and, when he used to sweep aside objections raised by myself to Templer's often cavalier treatment of the subject, I saw—at this later date—his attitude was assumed to conceal a lack of confidence at least comparable with my own. I did not, of course, come to these conclusions immediately. They were largely the result of similar talks pursued later over a long period with Barnby, of whom Mr. Deacon, congenitally unappreciative in that sphere, used to say: "I can stand almost anything from Barnby except his untidiness and generalisations about women." However, personally I used to enjoy Barnby's pronouncements on the subject of feminine psychology, and, when I came to know him well, we used to have endless discussions on that matter.

This—as Barnby himself liked to believe—almost scientific approach to the subject of " women " was in complete contrast to Peter Templer's, and, I think, to Stringham's too, both of whom were incurious regarding questions of theory. Templer, certainly, would have viewed these relatively objective investigations as fearful waste of time. In a different context, the antithesis of approach could be illustrated by quoting a remark of Stringham's made a dozen or more years later, when we met during the war. " You know, Nick," he said, " I used to think all that was necessary to fire a rifle was to get your eye, sights, and target in line, and press the trigger. Now I find the Army have written a whole book about it." Both he and Templer would have felt a similar superfluity attached to these digressions with Barnby, with whom, as it happened, my first words exchanged led, as if logically, to a preliminary examination of the subject: to be followed, I must admit, by a lifetime of debate on the same theme.

The circumstances of our initial encounter to some extent explain this early emphasis. It had been the end of August, or beginning of September, in days when that desolate season of late summer had fallen like a pall on excavated streets, over which the fumes of tar hung heavy in used-up air, echoing to the sound of electric drills. After two or three weeks away from London, there was nothing to be enjoyed in anticipation except an invitation to spend a week-end at Hinton with the Walpole-Wilsons: a visit arranged months ahead, and still comparatively distant, so it seemed, in point of time. Every soul appeared to be away. A sense of isolation, at least when out of the office, had become oppressive, and I began to feel myself a kind of hermit, threading his way eternally through deserted and sultry streets, never again to know a friend. It was in this state of mind that I found myself wondering whether some alleviation of solitude could be provided by " looking up " Mr. Deacon, as he had suggested at the coffee-stall; although it had to be admitted that I felt no particular desire to see him after the closing scenes of the party, when his be-haviour had struck me as intolerable. However, there appeared to exist no other single acquaintance remaining within a familiar orbit, and the Walpole-Wilson week-end still seemed lost in the future. As a consequence of pro-longed, indeed wholly disproportionate, speculation on the matter, I set out one afternoon, after work, for the address Mr. Deacon had scrawled on an envelope.

Charlotte Street, as it stretches northward towards Fitz-roy Square, retains a certain unprincipled integrity of character, though its tributaries reach out to the east, where, in Tottenham Court Road, structural anomalies pass all bounds of reason, and west, into a nondescript ocean of bricks and mortar from which hospitals, tenements and warehouses gloomily manifest themselves in shapeless bulk above mean shops. Mr. Deacon's " place " was situated in a narrow by-street in this westerly direction: an alley-way, not easy to find, of modest eighteenth-century—per-haps even late seventeenth-century—houses, of a kind still

to be seen in London, though growing rarer, the fronts of
some turned to commercial purposes, others bearing the
brass plate of dentist or midwife. Here and there a dusty
creeper trailed from window to window. Those that remained private dwellings had three or four bells, one
above the other, set beside the door at a height from the
ground effectively removed from children's runaway rings.
Mr. Deacon's premises stood between a French polisher's
and the offices of the Vox Populi Press. It was a sordid
spot, though one from which a certain implication of expectancy was to be derived. Indeed, the façade was not
unlike that row of shops that form a backcloth for the
harlequinade; and, as I approached the window, I was
almost prepared for Mr. Deacon, with mask and spangles
and magic wand, suddenly to pirouette along the pavement,
tapping, with disastrous consequence, all the passers-by.

However, the shop was shut. Through the plate glass,
obscured in watery depths, dark green like the interior of
an aquarium's compartments, Victorian work-tables, *papier-
mâché* trays, Staffordshire figures, and a varnished scrap
screen—upon the sombrely coloured *montage* of which
could faintly be discerned shiny versions of *Bubbles* and
For He Had Spoken Lightly Of A Woman's Name—swam
gently into further aqueous recesses that eddied back into
yet more remote alcoves of the double room : additional
subterranean grottoes, hidden from view, in which, like a
grubby naiad, Gypsy Jones, as described so vividly by Mr.
Deacon, was accustomed, from time to time, to sleep, or at
least to recline, beneath the monotonous, conventionalised
arabesques of rare, if dilapidated, Oriental draperies. For
some reason, the thought roused a faint sense of desire. The
exoticism of the place as a bedroom was undeniable. I had
to ring the bell of the side door twice before anyone

answered the summons. Then, after a long pause, the door was half opened by a young man in shirt-sleeves, carrying a dustpan and brush.

"Yes?" he asked abruptly.

My first estimate of Barnby, whom I immediately guessed this to be, the *raisonneur* so often quoted at the party by Mr. Deacon as inhabiting the top floor of the house, was not wholly favourable; nor, as I learnt later, was his own assessment of myself. He looked about twenty-six or twenty-seven, dark, thick-set, and rather puffed under the eyes. There was the impression of someone who knew how to look after his own interests, though in a balanced and leisurely manner. I explained that I had come to see Mr. Deacon.

"Have you an appointment?"

"No."

"Business?"

"No."

"Mr. Deacon is not here."

"Where is he?"

"Cornwall."

"For long?"

"No idea."

This allegedly absolute ignorance of the duration of a landlord's retirement to the country seemed scarcely credible in a tenant whose life, at least as presented in Mr. Deacon's anecdotes, was lived at such close range to the other members of the household. However, the question, put in a somewhat different form, achieved no greater success. Barnby stared hard, and without much friendliness. I saw that I should get no further with him at this rate, and requested that he would inform Mr. Deacon, on his return, of my call.

" What name?"

" Jenkins."

At this, Barnby became on the spot more accommodating. He opened the door wider and came out on to the step.

" Didn't you take Edgar to Milly Andriadis's party?" he asked, in a different tone.

" In a manner of speaking."

" He was in an awful state the next day," Barnby said. " Worried, too, about losing so many copies of that rag he hawks round. I believe he had to pay for them out of his own pocket. Anyway, Edgar is too old for that kind of thing."

He spoke this last comment sadly, though without implication of disapproval. I mentioned the unusual circumstances that had brought Mr. Deacon and myself to the party. Barnby listened in a somewhat absent manner, and then made two or three inquiries regarding the names of other guests. He seemed, in fact, more interested in finding out who had attended the party than in hearing a more specific account of how Mr. Deacon had received his invitation, or had behaved while he was there.

" Did you run across a Mrs. Wentworth?" he asked. " Rather a handsome girl."

" She was pointed out to me. We didn't meet."

" Was she with Donners?"

" Later in the evening. She was talking to a Balkan royalty when I first saw her."

" Theodoric?"

" Yes."

" Had Theodoric collected anyone else?"

" Lady Ardglass."

" I thought as much," said Barnby. " I wish I'd managed

to get there. I've met Mrs. Andriadis—but I can't say I really know her."

He nodded gravely, more to himself than in further comment to me, seeming to admit by this movement the justice of his own absence from the party. For a moment or two there was silence between us. Then he said: "Why not come in for a minute? You know, all sorts of people ask for Edgar. He likes some blackmailers admitted, but by no means all of them. One has to be careful."

I explained that I had not come to blackmail Mr. Deacon.

"Oh, I guessed that almost at once," said Barnby. "But I was doing a bit of cleaning when you rang—the studio gets filthy—and the dust must have confused my powers of differentiation."

All this was evidently intended as some apology for earlier gruffness. As I followed up a narrow staircase, I assured him that I had no difficulty in grasping that caution might be prudent where Mr. Deacon's friends were concerned. In answer to this Barnby expressed himself very plainly regarding the majority of Mr. Deacon's circle of acquaintance. By this time we had reached the top of the house, and entered a fairly large, bare room, with a north light, used as a studio. Barnby pointed to a rickety arm-chair, and throwing dustpan and brush in the corner by the stove, sat down on a kind of divan that stood against one wall.

"You've known Edgar for a long time?"

"Since I was a child. But the other night was the first time I ever heard him called that."

"He doesn't let everyone use the name," said Barnby. "In fact, he likes to keep it as quiet as he can. As it happens, my father was at the Slade with him."

"He has given up painting, hasn't he?"

" Entirely."

" Is that just as well?"

" Some people hold that as a bad painter Edgar carries all before him," said Barnby. " I know good judges who think there is literally no worse one. I can't say I care for his work myself—but I'm told Sickert once found a good word to say for some of them, so there may have been something there once."

" Is he making a success of the antique business?"

" He says people are very kind. He marks the prices up a bit. Still, there always seems someone ready to pay—and I know he is glad to be back in London."

" But I thought he liked Paris so much."

" Only for a holiday, I think. He had to retire there for a number of years. There was a bit of trouble in the park, you know."

This hint of a former contretemps explained many things about Mr. Deacon's demeanour. For example, the reason for his evasive manner in the Louvre was now made plain; and I recalled Sillery's words at Mrs. Andriadis's party. They provided an illustration of the scope and nature of Sillery's stock of gossip. Mr. Deacon's decided air of having " gone downhill " was now also to be understood. I began to review his circumstances against a more positive perspective.

" What about *War Never Pays!*, and Gypsy Jones?"

" The pacifism came on gradually," said Barnby. " I think it followed the period when he used to pretend the war had not taken place at all. Jones's interests are more political—world revolution, at least."

" Is she in residence at the moment?"

" Returned to the bosom of her family. Her father is a

schoolmaster in the neighbourhood of Hendon. But may I ask if you, too, are pursuing her?"

After the remarks, largely incoherent, though apparently pointed enough, made by Mr. Deacon at the party, to the effect that Barnby's disapproval of Gypsy Jones's presence in the house was radically vested in his own lack of success in making himself acceptable to her, I assumed this question to be intended to ascertain whether or not I was myself to be considered a rival in that quarter. I therefore assured him at once that he could set his mind at rest upon that point, explaining that my inquiry had been prompted by the merest curiosity.

The inference on my part may have been a legitimate one in the light of what Mr. Deacon had said, but it proved to be a long way wide of the mark. Barnby appeared much annoyed at the suggestion that his own feelings for Gypsy Jones could be coloured by any sentiment short of the heartiest dislike : stating in the most formidable terms at hand his ineradicable unwillingness for that matter actual physical incapacity, to be inveigled into any situation that might threaten intimacy with her. These protests struck me at the time as perhaps a shade exaggerated, since I had to admit that, for my own part, I had found Gypsy Jones, sluttish though she might be, less obnoxious than the impression of her conveyed by Barnby's words. However, I tried to make amends for the unjust imputation laid upon him, although, owing to their somewhat uncomplimentary nature, I was naturally unable to explain in precise terms the form taken by Mr. Deacon's misleading comments.

"I meant the chap with spectacles," said Barnby. "Isn't he a friend of yours? He always seems to be round here when Jones is about. I thought she might have made a conquest of you as well."

The second that passed before I was able to grasp that Barnby referred to Widmerpool was to be attributed to that deep-seated reluctance that still remained in my heart, in the face of a volume of evidence to the contrary, to believe Widmerpool capable of possessing a vigorous emotional life of his own. He was a person outwardly unprepossessing, and therefore, according to a totally misleading doctrine, confined to an inescapable predicament that allowed no love affairs : or, at best, love affairs of so obscure and colourless a kind as to be of no possible interest to the world at large. Apart from its many other flaws, this approach was entirely subjective in its assumption that Widmerpool must of necessity appear, even to persons of the opposite sex, as physically unattractive as he seemed to me; though there could probably be counted on my side, in support of this misapprehension, the opinion of most, perhaps all, of our contemporaries at school. On the other hand, I could claim a certain degree of vindication regarding this particular point at issue by insisting, with some justice, that Gypsy Jones, on the face of it, was the last girl on earth who might be expected to occupy Widmerpool's attention; which, on his own comparatively recent showing, seemed so unhesitatingly concentrated on making a success, in the most conventional manner, of his own social life.

At least that was how matters struck me when I was talking to Barnby; though I remembered then how the two of them—Gypsy Jones and Widmerpool—had apparently found each other's company congenial at the party. It was a matter to which I had given no thought at the time. Now I considered some of the facts. Although the theory that, in love, human beings like to choose an " opposite " may be genetically unsound, there is also, so it seems, a basic validity in such emotional situations as Montague and

Capulet, Cavalier and Roundhead. If certain individuals fall in love from motives of convenience, they can be contrasted with plenty of others in whom passion seems principally aroused by the intensity of administrative difficulty in procuring its satisfaction. In fact, history is full of examples of hard-headed personages—to be expected to choose partners in love for reasons helpful to their own career—who were, as often as not, the very people most to embarrass themselves, even to the extent of marriage, in unions that proved subsequently formidable obstacles to advancement.

This digression records, naturally, a later judgment; although even at the time, thinking things over, I could appreciate that there was nothing to be regarded as utterly unexpected in Widmerpool, after the sugar incident, taking a fancy to someone, " on the rebound," however surprisingly in contrast with Barbara the next girl might be. When I began to weigh the characteristics of Gypsy Jones, in so far as I knew them, I wondered whether, on examination, they made, indeed, so violent an antithesis to Barbara's qualities as might at first sight have appeared. Arguments could unquestionably be brought forward to show that these two girls possessed a good deal in common. Perhaps, after all, Barbara Goring and Gypsy Jones, so far from being irreconcilably different, were in fact notably alike; Barbara's girls' club, or whatever it was, in Bermondsey even pointing to a kind of sociological preoccupation in which there was—at least debatably—some common ground.

These speculations did not, of course, occur to me all at once. Still less did I think of a general law enclosing, even in some slight degree, all who share an interest in the same woman. It was not until years later that the course matters took in this direction became more or less explicable to me along such lines—that is to say, the irresistible pressure in certain emotional affairs of the most positive circumstantial inconvenience to be found at hand. Barnby, satisfied that I was clear regarding his own standpoint, was now prepared to make concessions.

"Jones has her admirers, you know," he said. "In fact, Edgar swears that she is the toast of the 1917 Club. It's my belief that in a perverted sort of way he rather fancies her himself—though, of course, he would never admit as much."

"He talked a lot about her at the party."

"What did he say?"

"He was deploring that she found herself in rather an awkward spot."

"You know about that, do you?"

"Mr. Deacon seemed very concerned."

"You make me laugh when you call Edgar 'Mr. Deacon'," said Barnby. "It certainly makes a new man of him. As a matter of fact, I rather think Jones has solved her problem. You know, she is older than you'd think—too old to get into that sort of difficulty. What do you say to going across the road for a drink?"

On the way out of the studio I asked if one of the unframed portraits standing against the easel could be a likeness of Mrs. Wentworth. Barnby, after scarcely perceptible hesitation, agreed that the picture represented that lady.

"She is rather paintable," he explained.

"Yes?"

"But tricky at times."

The subject of Mrs. Wentworth seemed to dispirit him a little, and he remained silent until we were sitting in front of our drinks in the empty saloon bar of the pub on the corner.

" Do you have any dealings with Donners?" he asked at last.

" A friend of mine called Charles Stringham had some sort of a job with him."

" I've heard Baby speak of Stringham. Wasn't there something about a divorce?"

" His sister's."

" That was it," said Barnby. " But the point is—what is happening about Baby and Donners?"

" How do you mean?"

" They are seen about a lot together. Baby has been appearing with some rather nice diamond clips, and odds and ends of that sort, which seem to be recent acquisitions."

Barnby screwed up his face in thought.

" Of course," he said. " I realise that a poor man competing with a rich one for a woman should be in a relatively strong position if he plays his cards well. Even so, Donners possesses to a superlative degree the advantages of his handicaps—so that one cannot help feeling a bit agitated at times. Especially with Theodoric cutting in, though I don't think he carries many guns."

" What about Mrs. Wentworth's husband?"

" Divorced," said Barnby. " She may even want to marry Donners. The point is, in this—as, I believe, in business matters too—he is rather a man of mystery. From time to time he has a girl hanging about, but he never seems to settle down with anyone. The girls themselves are evasive. They admit to no more than accepting presents and giving nothing in return. That's innocent enough, after all."

Although he spoke of the matter as if not to be taken too

seriously, I suspected that he was, at least for the moment,
fairly deeply concerned in the matter of Baby Wentworth;
and when conversation turned to the supposed whims of
Sir Magnus, Barnby seemed to take a self-tormenting pleasure in the nature of the hypotheses he put forward. It
appeared that the position was additionally complicated
by the fact that he had sold a picture to Sir Magnus a
month or two before, and that there was even some question of his undertaking a mural in the entrance of the
Donners-Brebner building.

"Makes the situation rather delicate," said Barnby.

He was, so I discovered, a figure of the third generation
(perhaps the descent, if ascertainable, would have proved
even longer) in the world in which he moved: a fact that
seemed to give his judgment, based on easy terms of long
standing with the problems involved, a scope rather unusual among those who practise the arts, even when they
themselves perform with proficiency. His father—though
he had died comparatively young, and left no money to
speak of—had been, in his day, a fairly successful sculptor
of an academic sort; his grandfather, not unknown in the
'sixties and 'seventies, a book illustrator in the Tenniel
tradition.

There were those, as I found later, among Barnby's
acquaintances who would suggest that his too extensive
field of appreciation had to some degree inhibited his own
painting. This may have been true. He was himself fond
of saying that few painters, writers or musicians had anything but the vaguest idea of what had been thought by
their forerunners even a generation or two before; and
usually no idea at all, however much they might protest to
the contrary, regarding each other's particular branch of
æsthetic. His own work diffused that rather deceptive air

of emancipation that seemed in those years a kind of neo-classicism, suggesting essentially that same impact brought home to me by Paris in the days when we had met Mr. Deacon in the Louvre: an atmosphere I can still think of as excitingly peculiar to that time.

Sir Magnus's interest in him showed enterprise in a great industrialist, for Barnby was then still comparatively unknown as a painter. In some curious manner his pictures seemed to personify a substantial proportion of that wayward and melancholy, perhaps even rather spurious, content of the self-consciously disillusioned art of that epoch. I mention these general aspects of the period and its moods, not only because they serve to illustrate Barnby, considered, as it were, as a figure symbolic of the contemporary background, but also because our conversation, when later we had dinner together that night, drifted away from personalities into the region of painting and writing; so that, by the time I returned to my rooms, I had almost forgotten his earlier remarks about such individuals as Widmerpool and Gypsy Jones, or Mrs. Wentworth and Sir Magnus Donners.

As it turned out, some of the things Barnby had told me that night threw light, in due course, on matters that would otherwise have been scarcely intelligible; for I certainly did not expect that scattered elements of Mrs. Andriadis's party would recur so comparatively soon in my life; least of all supposing that their new appearance would take place through the medium of the Walpole-Wilsons, who were involved, it is true, only in a somewhat roundabout manner. All the same, their commitment was sufficient to draw attention once again to that extraordinary process that causes certain figures to appear and reappear in the performance of one or another sequence of a ritual dance.

Their summons to the country, although, as an invitation, acceptable to say the least at that time of year, was in itself, unless regarded from a somewhat oblique angle, not specially complimentary. This was because Eleanor herself looked upon house-parties at Hinton Hoo without enthusiasm, indeed with reluctance, classing them as a kind of extension of her " season," calculated on the whole to hinder her own chosen activities by bringing to her home people who had, in a greater or lesser degree, to be entertained; thereby obstructing what she herself regarded, perhaps with reason, as the natural life of the place. There was no doubt something to be said for this point of view; and her letter, painfully formulated, had made no secret of a sense of resignation, on her own part, to the inevitable, conveying by its spirit, rather than actual words, the hope that at least I, for one, as an old, if not particularly close, friend, might be expected to recognise the realities of the situation, and behave accordingly.

Eleanor's candour in this respect certainly did not preclude gratitude. On the other hand, it had equally to be admitted that some fundamental support sustaining the Walpole-Wilson family life had become at some stage of existence slightly displaced, so that a visit to Hinton, as to all households where something fundamental has gone obscurely wrong, was set against an atmosphere of tensity. Whether this lack of harmony had its roots in Sir Gavin's professional *faux pas* or in some unresolved imperfection in the relationship of husband and wife could only be conjectured. Hard up as I was at that moment for entertainment, I might even have thought twice about staying there —so formidable could this *ambience* sometimes prove— if I had not by then been wholly converted to Barbara's view that " Eleanor was not a bad old girl when you know her."

I was rather glad to think that Barbara herself was in Scotland, so that there would be no likelihood of meeting her at her uncle's house. I felt that, if we could avoid seeing each other for long enough, any questions of sentiment— so often deprecated by Barbara herself—could be allowed quietly to subside, and take their place in those niches of memory especially reserved for abortive emotional entanglements of that particular kind.

All the same, this sensation of starting life again, as it were, with a clean sheet, made me regret a little to find on arrival that the assembled house-party consisted only of Sir Gavin's unmarried sister, Miss Janet Walpole-Wilson, Rosie Manasch, and Johnny Pardoe. On the way down in the train I had felt that it would be enjoyable to meet some new girl, even at risk of becoming once more victim to the afflictions from which I had only recently emerged. However, it seemed that no such situation was on this occasion likely to arise. Miss Janet Walpole-Wilson I knew of only by name, though I had heard a great deal about her from time to time when talking to Eleanor, who, possessing a great admiration for her aunt, often described the many adventures for which she was noted within the family.

The other two guests, although in theory a perfectly suitable couple to invite together, were, I thought, not quite sure whether they liked one another. Barnby used to say that a small man was at more of a disadvantage with a small woman than with a big one, and it was certainly true that the short, squat, black figures of Rosie Manasch and Pardoe sometimes looked a little absurd side by side. " Johnny is so amusing," she used to say, and he had been heard to remark : " Rosie dances beautifully," but almost any other pair of Eleanor's acquaintances would have liked each other as well, if not better. As a matter of fact, Sir

Gavin, hardly concealed a certain *tendresse* for Rosie, which
may have accounted for her presence; and he certainly felt
strong approval of Pardoe's comfortable income. Eleanor's
own indifference to the matter might be held to excuse her
parents for asking to the house guests who at least appealed
in one way or another to their own tastes.

The red brick Queen Anne manor house stood back from
the road in a small park, if such an unpretentious setting of
trees and paddocks could be so called. A walled orchard on
the far side stretched down to the first few cottages of the
village. The general impression of the property was of an
estate neat and well superintended, rather than large. The
place possessed that quality, perhaps more characteristic
of country houses in England than in some other parts
of Europe, of house and grounds forming an essential part
of the landscape. The stables stood round three sides of a
courtyard a short way from the main buildings, and there
Eleanor was accustomed to spend a good deal of her time,
with animals of various kinds, housed about the loose-
boxes in hutches and wooden crates.

Within, there existed, rather unexpectedly, that somewhat
empty, insistently correct appearance of the private dwellings of those who have spent most of their lives in official
residences of one kind or another. A few mementoes of
posts abroad were scattered about. For example, an enormous lacquer cabinet in the drawing-room had been brought
from Pekin—some said Tokyo—by Sir Gavin, upon the
top of which stood several small, equivocal figures carved in
wood by the Indians of an obscure South American tribe.
The portraits in the dining-room were mostly of Wilson
forebears: one of them, an admiral, attributed to Zoffany.
There was also a large painting of Lady Walpole-Wilson's
father by the Academician, Isbister (spoken of with such

horror by Mr. Deacon), whose portrait of Peter Templer's father I remembered as the only picture in the Templer home. This canvas was in the painter's earlier manner, conveying the impression that at any moment Lord Aberavon, depicted in peer's robes, would step from the frame and join the company below him in the room.

The Wilsons had lived in the county for a number of generations, but Sir Gavin had bought Hinton (with which he possessed hereditary connections through a grandmother) only after retirement. This comparatively recent purchase of the house was a subject upon which Sir Gavin's mind was never wholly at rest; and he was always at pains to explain that its ownership was not to be looked upon as an entirely new departure so far as any hypothetical status might be concerned as a land-owner " in that part of the world."

" As a matter of fact, the Wilsons are, if anything, an older family than the Walpoles—well, perhaps not that, but at least as old," he used to say. " I expect you have heard of Beau Wilson, a young gentleman who spent a lot of money in the reign of William and Mary, and was killed in a duel. I have reason to suppose he was one of our lot. And then there was a Master of the Mint a bit earlier. The double-barrel, which I greatly regret, and would discard if I could, without putting myself and my own kith and kin to a great deal of inconvenience, was the work of a great-uncle—a most consequential ass, between you and me, and a bit of a snob, I'm afraid—and has really no basis whatever, beyond the surname of a remote ancestor in the female line."

He was accustomed to terminate this particular speech with a number of " m'ms," most of them interrogative, and some uneasy laughter. His sister, on this occasion, looked rather disapproving at these excursions into family history.

She was a small, defiant woman, some years younger than Sir Gavin, recently returned from a journey in Yugoslavia, where she had been staying with a friend married to a British consul in that country. Although spoken of as " not well off," Miss Janet Walpole-Wilson was also reported to maintain herself at a respectable level of existence by intermittent odd jobs that varied between acting as secretary, usually in a more or less specialised capacity, to some public figure, often a friend or relative of the family; alternatively, by undertaking, when they travelled abroad, the rôle of governess or duenna to children of relations, some of whom were rather rich.

" Aunt Janet says you must never mind asking," Eleanor had informed me, when speaking of the ease with which Miss Walpole-Wilson, apparently on account of her freedom from inhibition upon this point, always found employment. Her aunt certainly seemed to have enjoyed throughout her life a wide variety of confidences and experiences. She dressed usually in tones of brown and green, colours that gave her for some reason, possibly because her hats almost always conveyed the impression of being peaked, an air of belonging to some dedicated order of female officials, connected possibly with public service in the woods and forests, and bearing a load of responsibility, the extent of which was difficult for a lay person—even impossible if a male—to appreciate, or wholly to understand. The outlines of her good, though severe, features were emphasised by a somewhat reddish complexion.

Sir Gavin, though no doubt attached to his sister, was sometimes openly irritated by her frequent, and quite uncompromising, pronouncements on subjects that he must have felt himself, as a former diplomatist of some standing, possessing the right, at least in his own house, to speak of with authority. Lady Walpole-Wilson, on the other hand, scarcely made a secret of finding the presence of her sister-in-law something of a strain. A look of sadness would steal over her face when Miss Walpole-Wilson argued with Sir Gavin about ethnological problems in the Sanjak of Novi Bazar, or spoke of times when " the Ford's big end went in the Banat," or " officials made themselves so disagreeable at Nish : " geographical entities of that kind playing a great part in her conversation. Although seriously concerned with the general welfare of the human race, she sometimes displayed a certain capricious malignity towards individuals, taking, for example, a great dislike to Pardoe, though she showed a guarded friendship towards Rosie Manasch. I was relieved to find her attitude to myself suggested nothing more hostile than complete indifference.

One, perhaps the chief, bone of contention lying between herself and her brother was Miss Walpole-Wilson's conviction that the traditions of his service, by their very nature, must have rendered him impervious to anything in the way of new ideas or humanitarian concepts; so that much of Sir Gavin's time was taken up in attempting to demonstrate to his sister that, so far from lagging behind in the propagation of reforms of almost every kind, he was prepared to go, theoretically at least, not only as far as, but even farther than, herself. Both of them knew Sillery, who had recently stayed in the neighbourhood, and for once they were in agreement that he was " full of understanding." The subject of Sillery's visit came up at dinner on the night of my arrival.

" It was at Stourwater," said Lady Walpole-Wilson. " As a matter of fact we have been asked over there on Sunday. Prince Theodoric is staying there with Sir Magnus Donners."

I knew the castle by name, and was even aware in a vague kind of way that it had often changed hands during the previous fifty or hundred years; but I had never seen the place, nor had any idea that Sir Magnus Donners lived there.

"And I so much wanted that afternoon to see those two hound puppies Nokes is walking," said Eleanor. "Now it turns out we are being forced to go to this ghastly luncheon-party."

"Got to be civil to one's neighbours, my dear," said Sir Gavin. "Besides, Theodoric has particularly asked to see me."

"I don't know what you call 'neighbours'," said Eleanor. "Stourwater is twenty-five miles, at least."

"Nonsense," said Sir Gavin. "I doubt if it is twenty-three."

His attitude towards Eleanor varied between almost doting affection and an approach most easily suggested by the phrase "making the best of a bad job." There were times when she vexed him. Arguing with her father brought out the resemblance between the two of them, though features that, in Sir Gavin, seemed conventionalised to the point, almost, of stylisation took on a peculiar twist in his daughter. As she sat there at the table, I could recognise no similarity whatever to Barbara—of whom at times I still found myself thinking—except for their shared colouring.

"I explained to Donners that we should be quite a large party," said Sir Gavin, "but he would not hear of anyone being left behind. In any case, there is plenty of room there, and the castle itself is well worth seeing."

"I don't think I shall come after all, Gavin," said Miss Walpole-Wilson. "No one will want to see me there—least of all Prince Theodoric. Although I dare say he is too young to remember the misunderstanding that arose, when I stayed with you, regarding that remark about 'travesty of democratic government'—and you know I never care for people with too much money."

"Oh, come, Janet," said Sir Gavin. "Of course they will all want to see you—the Prince especially. He is a very go-ahead fellow, everyone who has met him agrees. As a matter of fact, you know as well as I do, the old King laughed heartily when I explained the circumstance of your remark. He made a rather broad joke about it. I've told you a thousand times. Besides, Donners is not a bad fellow at all."

"I can't get on with those people—ever."

"I don't know what you mean by 'those people'," said Sir Gavin, a trifle irritably. "Donners is no different from anyone else, except that he may be a bit richer. He didn't start life barefoot—not that I for one should have the least objection if he had, more power to his elbow—but his father was an eminently solid figure. He was knighted, I believe, for what that's worth. Donners went to some quite decent school. I think the family are of Scandinavian, or North German, extraction. No doubt very worthy people."

"Oh, I do hope he isn't German," said Lady Walpole-Wilson. "I never thought of that."

"Personally, I have a great admiration for the Germans— I do not, of course, mean the Junkers," said her sister-in-law. "They have been hardly treated. No one of liberal opinions could think otherwise. And I certainly do not object to Sir Magnus on snobbish grounds. You know me too well for that, Gavin. I have no doubt, as you say, that he has many good points. All the same, I think I had better stay at home. I can make a start on my article about the

Bosnian Moslems for the news-sheet of the Minority Problems League."

" If Aunt Janet doesn't go, I don't see why I should," said Eleanor. " I don't in the least want to meet Prince Theodoric."

" I do," said Rosie Manasch. " I thought he looked too fetching at Goodwood."

In the laugh that followed this certainly tactful expression of preference, earlier warnings of potential family difference died away. Sir Gavin began to describe, not for the first time, the occasion when, as a young secretary in some Oriental country, he had stained his face with coffee-grounds and, like Haroun-al-Raschid, " mingled " in the bazaar: with, so it appeared, useful results. The story carried dinner safely to the dessert, a stage when Pardoe brought conversation back once more to Sunday's expedition by asking whether Sir Magnus Donners had purchased Stourwater from the family with whom Barbara was staying in Scotland, for whose house he was himself bound on leaving Hinton.

" He bought it from a relation of mine," said Rosie Manasch. " Uncle Leopold always says he sold it—with due respect to you, Eleanor—because the hunting round here wasn't good enough. I think it was really because it cost too much to keep up."

" It is all very perfect now," said Sir Gavin. " Rather too perfect for my taste. In any case, I am no medievalist."

He looked round the table challengingly after saying this, rather as Uncle Giles was inclined to glare about him after making some more or less tendentious statement, whether because he suspected that one or other of us, in spite of this disavowal, would charge him with covert medievalism, or in momentary hesitation that, in taking so high a line on the subject of an era at once protracted and diversified, he ran risk of exposure to the impeachment of " missing something " thereby, was uncertain.

" There is the Holbein, too," said Lady Walpole-Wilson. " You really must come, Janet. I know you like pictures."

" The castle belongs, like Bodiam, to the later Middle Ages," said Sir Gavin, assuming all at once the sing-song tones of a guide or lecturer. " And, like Bodiam, Stourwater possesses little or no historical interest, as such, while remaining, so far as its exterior is concerned, architecturally one of the most complete, and comparatively unaltered, fortified buildings of its period. For some reason——"

"——for some reason the defences were not dismantled— ' sleighted,' I think you call it—at the time of the Civil Wars," cut in Lady Walpole-Wilson, as if answering the responses in church, or completing the quotation of a well-known poem to show apreciation of its aptness. " Though subsequent owners undertook certain improvements in connection with the structural fabric of the interior, with a view to increasing Stourwater's convenience as a private residence in more peaceful times."

" I have already read a great deal of what you have been saying in *Stourwater and Its Story*, a copy of which was kindly placed by my bed," said Miss Walpole-Wilson. " I doubt if all the information given there is very accurate."

For some reason a curious sense of excitement rose within me at prospect of this visit. I could not explain to myself this feeling, almost of suspense, that seemed to hang over the expedition. I was curious to see the castle, certainly, but that hardly explained an anxiety that Eleanor's hound puppies, or Miss Walpole-Wilson's humours, might prevent my going there. That night I lay awake thinking about

Stourwater as if it had been the sole motive for my coming
to Hinton: fearing all the time that some hitch would
occur. However, the day came and we set out, Miss Walpole-Wilson, in spite of her earlier displeasure, finally
agreeing to accompany the party, accommodated in two
cars, one of them driven by Sir Gavin himself. There was
perhaps a tacit suggestion that he would have liked Rosie
Manasch to travel with him, but, although as a rule not
unwilling to accept his company, and approval, she chose,
on this occasion, the car driven by the chauffeur.

When we came to Stourwater that Sunday morning, the
first sight was impressive. Set among oaks and beeches in
a green hollow of the land, the castle was approached by a
causeway crossing the remains of a moat, a broad expanse
of water through which, with great deliberation, a pair of
black swans, their passage sending ripples through the
pond weed, glided between rushes swaying gently in the
warm September air. Here was the Middle Age, from the
pages of Tennyson, or Scott, at its most elegant: all
sordid and painful elements subtly removed. Some such
thought must have struck Sir Gavin too, for I heard him
murmuring at the wheel:

> "'And sometimes thro' the mirror blue
> The knights come riding two and two . . .'"

There was, in fact, no one about at all; neither knights
nor hinds, this absence of human life increasing a sense of
unreality, as if we were travelling in a dream. The cars
passed under the portcullis, and across a cobbled quad-
rangle. Beyond this open space, reached by another arch-
way, was a courtyard of even larger dimensions, in the
centre of which a sunken lawn had been laid out, with a

fountain at the centre, and carved stone flower-pots, shaped like urns, at each of the four corners. The whole effect was not, perhaps, altogether in keeping with the rest of the place. Through a vaulted gateway on one side could be seen the high yew hedges of the garden. Steps led up to the main entrance of the castle's domestic wing, at which the cars drew up.

Mounted effigies in Gothic armour guarded either side of the door by which we entered the Great Hall; and these dramatic figures of man and horse struck a new and somewhat disturbing note; though one at which the sunken garden had already hinted. Such implications of an over-elaborate solicitude were followed up everywhere the eye rested, producing a result altogether different from the cool, detached vision manifested a minute or two earlier by grey walls and towers rising out of the green, static landscape. Something was decidedly amiss. The final consequence of the pains lavished on these halls and galleries was not precisely that of a Hollywood film set, the objects assembled being, in the first place, too genuine, too valuable; there was even a certain sense of fitness, of historical association more or less correctly assessed. The display was discomforting, not contemptible. The impression was of sensations that might precede one of those episodes in a fairy story, when, at a given moment, the appropriate spell is pronounced to cause domes and minarets, fountains and pleasure-gardens, to disappear into thin air; leaving the hero—in this case, Sir Magnus Donners—shivering in rags beneath the blasted oak of a grim forest, or scorched by rays of a blazing sun among the rocks and boulders of some desolate mountainside. In fact, Sir Gavin's strictures on Stourwater as "too perfect" were inadequate as a delineation to the extent of being almost beside the point.

I had supposed that, in common with most visits paid on these terms in the country, the Walpole-Wilson group might be left most of the time huddled in a cluster of their own, while the Donners house-party, drawn together as never before by the arrival of strangers, would discourse animatedly together at some distance off, the one faction scarcely mixing at all with the other. This not uncommon predicament could no doubt in a general way have been exemplified soon after we had been received by Sir Magnus —looking more healthily clerical than ever—in the Long Gallery (at the far end of which hung the Holbein, one of the portraits of Erasmus), had not various unforeseen circumstances contributed to modify what might be regarded as a more normal course of events. For example, among a number of faces in the room possessing a somewhat familiar appearance, I suddenly noticed Stringham and Bill Truscott, both of whom were conversing with an unusually pretty girl.

We were presented, one by one, to Prince Theodoric, who wore a grey flannel suit, unreservedly continental in cut, and appeared far more at his ease than at Mrs. Andriadis's party: smiling in a most engaging manner when he shook hands. He spoke that scrupulously correct English, characteristic of certain foreign royalties, that confers on the language a smoothness and flexibility quite alien to the manner in which English people themselves talk. There was a word from him for everyone. Sir Gavin seized his hand as if he were meeting a long lost son, while Prince Theodoric himself seemed, on his side, equally pleased at their reunion. Lady Walpole-Wilson, probably because she remembered Prince Theodoric only as a boy, showed in her eye apparent surprise at finding him so grown-up. Only

Eleanor's, and her aunt's firmly-clasped lips and stiff curtsey suggested entire disapproval.

Further introductions took place. The Huntercombes were there—Lord Huntercombe was Lord Lieutenant of the county—and there were a crowd of persons whose identities, as a whole, I failed to assimilate; though here and there was recognisable an occasional notability like Sir Horrocks Rusby, whose name I remembered Widmerpool mentioning on some occasions, who had not so long before achieved a good deal of prominence in the newspapers as counsel in the Derwentwater divorce case. I also noticed Mrs. Wentworth—whom Sir Horrocks had probably cross-questioned in the witness-box—still looking rather sulky, as she stood in one of the groups about us. When the formalities of these opening moves of the game had been completed, and we had been given cocktails, Stringham strolled across the room. His face was deeply burned by the sun. I wondered whether this was the result of the Deauville trip, of which Mrs. Andriadis had spoken, or if, on the contrary, division between them had been final. He had not wholly lost his appearance of fatigue.

" You must inspect my future wife," he said at once.

This announcement of imminent marriage was a complete surprise. Barnby had said, during the course of the evening we had spent together : " When people think they are never further from marriage, they are often, in reality, never nearer to it," but that kind of precept takes time to learn. I had certainly accepted the implication that nothing was more distant than marriage from Stringham's intentions when he had so violently abandoned Mrs. Andriadis's house; although now I even wondered whether he could have decided to repair matters by making Mrs. Andriadis herself his wife. To be able to consider this a possibility showed, I suppose, in its grasp of potentialities, an advance on my own part of which I should have been incapable earlier in the year. However, without further developing the news, he led me to the girl from whose side he had come, who was still talking to Truscott.

"Peggy," he said, "this is an old friend of mine."

Apart from former signs given by Stringham's behaviour, external evidence had been supplied, indirectly by Anne Stepney, and directly by Rosie Manasch, to the effect that anything like an engagement was "off." Peggy Stepney, whom I now recognised from pictures I had seen of her, was not unlike her sister, with hair of the same faintly-reddish shade, though here, instead of a suggestion of disorder, the elder sister looked as if she might just have stepped gracefully from the cover of a fashion magazine; "too perfect," indeed, as Sir Gavin might have said. She was, of course, a "beauty," and possessed a kind of cold symmetry, very taking, and at the same time a little alarming. However, this exterior was not accompanied by a parallel coolness of manner; on the contrary, she could in the circumstances scarcely have been more agreeable. While we talked, we were joined by Mrs. Wentworth, at whose arrival I was conscious of a slight stiffening in Stringham's bearing, an almost imperceptible acerbity, due possibly—though by no means certainly, I thought—to the part played by Mrs. Wentworth in his sister's divorce. In comparing the looks of the two young women, it was immediately clear that Peggy Stepney was more obviously the beauty; though there was something about Mrs. Wentworth that made the discord she had aroused in so many quarters easily understandable.

"How long have I got to go on sitting next to that

equerry of Theodoric's, Bill?" she asked. "I've been through his favourite dance tunes at dinner last night. I can't stand them at lunch again to-day. I'm not as young as I was."

"Talk to him about birds and beasts," said Stringham. "I've already tried that with great success—the flora and fauna of England and Wales."

Mrs. Wentworth seemed not greatly amused by this facetiousness. Her demeanour was less friendly than Peggy Stepney's, and she did no more than glance in my direction when we were introduced. I was impressed by Barnby's temerity in tackling so formidable an objective. Luncheon was announced at that moment, so that the four of us temporarily parted company.

The dining-room was hung with sixteenth-century tapestries. I supposed that they might be Gobelins from their general appearance, blue and crimson tints set against lemon yellow. They illustrated the Seven Deadly Sins. I found myself seated opposite *Luxuria*, a failing principally portrayed in terms of a winged and horned female figure, crowned with roses, holding between finger and thumb one of her plump, naked breasts, while she gazed into a looking-glass, supported on one side by Cupid and on the other by a goat of unreliable aspect. The four-footed beast of the Apocalypse, with his seven dragon-heads dragged her triumphal car, which was of great splendour. Hercules, bearing his club, stood by, somewhat gloomily watching this procession, his mind filled, no doubt, with disquieting recollections. In the background, the open doors of a pillared house revealed a four-poster bed, with hangings rising to an apex, under the canopy of which a couple lay clenched in a priapic grapple. Among trees, to the right of the composition, further couples and groups, three or four of them at least, were similarly occupied in smaller houses and Oriental tents; or, in one case, simply on the ground.

I had been placed next to Rosie Manasch, who was, at the moment of seating herself, engaged in talk with her neighbour on the far side; and—curious to investigate some of the by-products of indulgence depicted in this sequence of animated, and at times enigmatic, incidents—I found myself fully occupied in examining unobtrusively the scenes spread out on the tapestry. There had been, I was dimly aware, some rearrangement of places on my right-hand side, where a chair had remained empty for a moment or two. Now a girl sat down there, next to me, to whom I had not yet, so far as I knew, been introduced, with some muttered words from Truscott, who had instigated the change of position—possibly to relieve Mrs. Wentworth from further strain of making conversation with Prince Theodoric's equerry.

"I don't think you remember me," she said, almost at once, in a curiously harsh voice that brought back, in fact, that same sense of past years returning that Stringham's inquiry for matches had caused me at the coffee-stall. "I used to be called Jean Templer. You are a friend of Peter's, and you came to stay with us years ago."

It was true that I had not recognised her. I think we might even have exchanged words without my guessing her identity, so little had she been in my thoughts, so unexpected a place was this to find her. That was not because she had changed greatly. On the contrary, she still seemed slim, attenuated, perhaps not—like the two other girls with whom I had been talking, and round whom my thoughts, before the distraction of the tapestry, had been drifting—exactly a " beauty;" but all the same, mysterious and absorb-

ing: certainly pretty enough, so far as that went, just as
she had seemed when I had visited the Templers after
leaving school. There was perhaps a touch of the trim
secretary of musical comedy. I saw also, with a kind of
relief, that she seemed to express none of the qualities I had
liked in Barbara. There was a sense of restraint here, a re-
serve at present unpredictable. I tried to excuse my bad
manners in having failed at once to remember her. She
gave one of those quick, almost masculine laughs. I was
not at all sure how I felt about her, though conscious suddenly that being in love with Barbara, painful as some of
its moments had been, now seemed a rather amateurish
affair; just as my feelings for Barbara had once appeared
to me so much more mature than those previously possessed for Suzette; or, indeed, for Jean herself.

"You were so deep in the tapestry," she said.

"I was wondering about the couple in the little house on
the hill."

"They have a special devil—or is he a satyr?—to themselves."

"He seems to be collaborating, doesn't he?"

"Just lending a hand, I think."

"A guest, I suppose—or member of the staff?"

"Oh, a friend of the family," she said. "All newly-
married couples have someone of that sort about. Sometimes several. Didn't you know? I see you can't be married."

"But how do you know they are newly married?"

"They've got such a smart little house," she said. "They
must be newly married. And rather well off, too, I should
say."

I was left a trifle breathless by this exchange, not only
because it was quite unlike the kind of luncheon-table con-

versation I had expected to come my way in that particular place, but also on account of its contrast with Jean's former deportment, when we had met at her home. At that moment I hardly considered the difference that age had made, no doubt in both of us. She was, I thought, about a couple of years younger than myself. Feeling unable to maintain this show of detachment towards human—and, in especial, matrimonial—affairs, I asked whether it was not true that she had married Bob Duport. She nodded; not exactly conveying, it seemed to me, that by some happy chance their union had introduced her to an unexpected terrestrial paradise.

" Do you know Bob?"

" I just met him years ago with Peter."

" Have you seen Peter lately?"

"Not for about a year. He has been doing very well in the City, hasn't he? He always tells me so."

She laughed.

"Oh, yes," she said. " He has been making quite a lot of money, I think. That is always something. But I wish he would settle down, get married, for instance."

I was aware of an unexpected drift towards intimacy, although this sudden sense of knowing her all at once much better was not simultaneously accompanied by any clear portrayal in my own mind of the kind of person she might really be. Perhaps intimacy of any sort, love or friendship, impedes all exactness of definition. For example, Mr. Deacon's character was plainer to me than Barnby's, although by then I knew Barnby better than I knew Mr. Deacon. In short, the persons we see most clearly are not necessarily those we know best. In any case, to attempt to describe a woman in the broad terms employable for a man is perhaps irrational.

"I went to a party in your London house given by Mrs. Andriadis."

"How very grand," she said. "What was it like? We let the place almost as soon as we took it, because Bob had to go abroad. It's rather a horrid house, really. I hate it, and everything in it."

I did not know how to comment on this attitude towards her own home, which—as I had agreed upon that famous night with the young man with the orchid—certainly left, in spite of its expensive air, a good deal to be desired. I said that I wished she had been present at the party.

"Oh, us," she said laughing again, as if any such eventuality were utterly unthinkable. "Besides, we were away. Bob was arguing about nickel or aluminium or something for months on end. As a matter of fact, I think we shall have to sue Mrs. Andriadis when he comes back. She has raised absolute hell in the house. Burnt the boiler out and broken a huge looking-glass."

She reminded me immediately of her brother in this disavowal of being the kind of person asked to Mrs. Andriadis's parties; for the setting in which we found ourselves seemed, on the face of it to be perfectly conceivable as an extension of Mrs. Andriadis's sort of entertaining. Indeed, it appeared to me, in my inexperience, that almost exactly the same chilly undercurrent of conflict was here perceptible as that permeating the house in Hill Street a month or two before. Dialectical subtleties could no doubt be advanced—as Stringham had first suggested, and remarks at Sillery's had seemed to substantiate—to demolish Sir Magnus's pretensions, hierarchically speaking, to more than the possession of "a lot of money;" in spite of various testimonials paid to him, at

Hinton and elsewhere, on the score of his greatness in other directions. However, even allowing that Sir Magnus might be agreed to occupy a position only within this comparatively modest category of social differentiation, such assets as were his were not commonly disregarded, even in the world of Mrs. Andriadis. Her sphere might be looked upon, perhaps, as a more trenchant and mobile one, though it was doubtful if even this estimate were beyond question.

In fact, I was uncertain whether or not I might have misunderstood Jean, and that she had intended to imply that her existence was at a higher, rather than lower, plane. Some similar thought may have struck her too, because, as if in explanation of a matter that needed straightening out, she said: "Baby brought me here. She wanted someone to play for her side, and Bob's aluminium fitted in nicely for this week-end, as Theodoric knew Bob—had even met him."

The concept of "playing for her side" opened up in the imagination fascinating possibilities in connection with Mrs. Wentworth's position in the household. I remembered the phrase as one used by Stringham when enlisting my own support in connection with his project of "going down" from the university after a single term of residence —the time, in fact, when he had asked his mother to lunch to meet Sillery. However, the status of Mrs. Wentworth at the castle was obviously not a matter to be investigated there and then, while, in addition to any question of diffidence in inquiring about that particular affair, Jean's initial display of vivacity became suddenly exhausted, and she sank back into one of those silences that I remembered so well from the time when we had first met. For the rest of the meal she was occupied in fragmentary conversation with the man on her right, or I was myself talking with Rosie

Manasch; so that we hardly spoke to one another again while in the dining-room.

The rest of the members of the luncheon-party, on the whole, appeared to be enjoying themselves. Prince Theodoric, sitting at the other end of the long table between Lady Walpole-Wilson and Lady Huntercombe, was conversing manfully, though he looked a shade cast down. From time to time his eyes wandered, never for more than an instant, in the direction of Mrs. Wentworth, who had cheered up considerably under the stimulus of food and drink, and was looking remarkably pretty. I noticed that she made no effort to return the Prince's glances, in the manner she had employed at Mrs. Andriadis's party. Truscott was clearly doing wonders with Miss Walpole-Wilson, whose wide social contacts he must have regarded as of sufficient importance, possibly as an ancillary factor in publicising Donners-Brebner concerns, to justify, on his own part, slightly more than normal attention. It was even possible, though I thought on the whole improbable, that Miss Walpole-Wilson's rather unaccommodating exterior might, in itself, have been sufficient to put Truscott on his mettle to display, without ulterior motive, his almost unequalled virtuosity in handling intractable material of just the kind Miss Walpole-Wilson's personality provided. In rather another field, I had seen Archie Gilbert, on more than one occasion, do something of that sort; on the part of Truscott, however, such relatively frivolous expenditure of energy would have been unexpected.

Only Eleanor, still no doubt contemplating hound puppies and their diet, or perhaps disapproving in general of the assembled company's formal tone, appeared uncompromisingly bored. Sir Magnus himself did not talk much, save intermittently to express some general opinion. His

words, wafted during a comparative silence to the farther
end of the table, would have suggested on the lips of a
lesser man processes of thought of a banality so painful—
of such profound and arid depths, in which neither humour,
nor imagination, nor, indeed, any form of human understanding could be thought to play the smallest part—that
I almost supposed him to be speaking ironically, or teasing
his guests by acting the part of a bore in a drawing-room
comedy. I was far from understanding that the capacity of
men interested in power is not necessarily expressed in the
brilliance of their conversation. Even in daylight he looked
young for his age, and immensely, almost unnaturally,
healthy.

At the end of the meal, on leaving the dining-room, Sir
Gavin, who had one of his favourite schemes to discuss,
cornered Lord Huntercombe, and they went off together.
Lord Huntercombe, a small man, very exquisite in appearance and possessing a look of ineffable cunning, was trustee
of one, if not more, of the public galleries, and Sir Gavin
was anxious to interest him in a project, dear to his heart,
of which he had spoken at Hinton, regarding the organisation of a special exhibition of pictures to be thought of as
of interest in connection with the history of diplomatic
relations between England and the rest of the world. The
two of them retired among the yew hedges, Lord Huntercombe's expression presaging little more than sufferance at
the prospect of listening to Sir Gavin's plan. The rest of
the party broke up into groups. Jean, just as she used to
disappear from the scene in her own home, was nowhere
to be found on the terrace, to which most of the party now
moved. Peggy Stepney, too, seemed to have gone off on
her own. Finding myself sitting once more with Stringham
and Truscott, I asked when the wedding was to take place.

" Oh, any moment now," Stringham said. " I'm not sure it isn't this afternoon. To be precise, the second week in October. My mother can't make up her mind whether to laugh or cry. I think Buster is secretly rather impressed."

I found it impossible to guess whether he was getting married because he was in love, because he hoped by taking this step to find a more settled life, or because he was curious to experiment with a new set of circumstances. The absurdity of supposing that exact reasons for marriage can ever be assigned had not then struck me; perhaps excusably, since it is a subject regarding which everyone considers, at least where friends are concerned, the assumption of categorical knowledge to be an inalienable right. Peggy Stepney herself looked pleased enough, though the formality of her style was calculated to hide outward responses. There had been an incident—hardly that—while we had been talking before luncheon. She had let her hand rest on a table in such a way that it lay, at least putatively, in Stringham's direction. He had placed his own hand over hers, upon which she had jerked her fingers away, almost angrily, and begun to powder her face. Stringham had shown absolutely no sign of noticing this gesture. His first movement had been made, so it had appeared, almost automatically, not even very specifically as a mark of affection. It was possible that some minor quarrel had just taken place; that she was teasing him; that the action had no meaning at all. Thinking of the difficulties inherent in his situation, I began to turn over once more the meeting with Jean, and asked Stringham if he knew that Peter Templer's sister was one of the guests at Stourwater.

"Didn't even know he had a sister—of course, yes, I remember now—he had two at least. One of them, like my own, was always getting divorced."

"This is the younger one. She is called Mrs. Duport."

"What, Baby's friend?"

He did not show the least interest. It was inexplicable to me that he had apparently noticed her scarcely at all; for, although Widmerpool's love for Barbara had seemed an outrageous presumption, Stringham's indifference to Jean was, in the opposite direction, almost equally disconcerting. My own feelings for her might still be uncertain, but his attitude was not of indecision so much as complete unawareness. However, the thought of Mrs. Wentworth evidently raised other questions in his mind.

"What sort of progress is Theodoric making with Baby?" he asked.

Truscott smiled, making a deprecatory movement with his finger to indicate that the matter was better undiscussed: at least while we remained on the terrace.

"Not very well, I think," Stringham said. "It will be Bijou Ardglass, after all. I'll have a bet on it."

"Did the Chief strike you as being a bit off colour at luncheon, Charles?" Truscott asked, ignoring these suppositions.

He spoke casually, though I had the impression he might be more anxious about Sir Magnus's state of temper than he wished outwardly to admit.

"I heard him say once that it took all sorts to make a world," said Stringham. "He ought to write some of his aphorisms down so that they are not forgotten. Would it be an occasion for the dungeons?"

He made this last remark in that very level voice of his that I recognised, as of old, he was accustomed to employ when intending to convey covert meaning to some apparently simple statement or question. Truscott pouted, and lowered his head in rather arch reproof. I saw that he was amused about some joke shared in secret between them, and I knew that I had judged correctly in suspecting latent implication in what Stringham had said.

" Baby doesn't like it."

" Who cares what Baby likes?"

" The Chief is never unwilling," Truscott said, still smiling. " It certainly might cheer him up. *You* ask him, Charles."

Sir Magnus was talking to Lady Huntercombe only a short distance from us. Stringham moved across the terrace towards them. As he came up, Lady Huntercombe, whose features and dress had been designed to recall Gainsborough's Mrs. Siddons, turned, almost as if she had been expecting his arrival, and pointed, with an appropriately dramatic gesture, to the keep of the castle, as if demanding some historical or architectural information. I could see Stringham repress a smile. Her words had perhaps made his inquiry easier to present. Before answering, he inclined towards Sir Magnus, and, with perhaps more deference than had been common to his manner in former days, put some question. Sir Magnus, in reply, raised his eyebrows, and—like Truscott a few minutes earlier, who had perhaps unconsciously imitated one of his employer's mannerisms— made a deprecatory movement with his forefinger; his face at the same time taking on the very faintest suggestion of a deeper colour, as he in turn addressed himself to Lady Huntercombe, apparently requesting her opinion on the point brought to his notice by Stringham. She nodded at once in such a way as to indicate enthusiasm, the rather reckless gaiety of a great actress on holiday, one of the moods, comparatively limited in range, to which her hat and general appearance committed her. Stringham looked up, and caught Truscott's eye.

The result of the consultation was a public announcement by Truscott, as Sir Magnus's mouthpiece, that our host, who had by then spoken a word with Prince Theodoric, would himself undertake a personally conducted tour of the castle, "including the dungeons." This was the kind of exordium Truscott could undertake with much adroitness, striking an almost ideal mean between putting a sudden stop to conversation, and, at the same time, running no risk of being ignored by anyone in the immediate neighbourhood. No doubt most of those assembled round about had already made the inspection at least once. Some showed signs of unwillingness to repeat the performance. There was a slight stir as sightseers began to sort themselves out from the rest. The end of the matter was that about a dozen persons decided to make up the company who would undertake the tour. They were collected into one group and led indoors.

"I'll get the torches," said Truscott.

He went off, and Stringham returned to my side.

"What is the joke?"

"There isn't one, really," he said, but his voice showed that he was keeping something dark.

Truscott returned, carrying two electric torches, one of which he handed to Stringham. The party included Prince Theodoric, Lady Huntercombe, Miss Janet Walpole-Wilson, Eleanor, Rosie Manasch, and Pardoe : together with others, unknown to me. Stringham went ahead with Truscott, who acted as principal guide, supplying a conjunction of practical information and historical detail, in every way suitable to the circumstances of the tour. As we moved round, Sir Magnus watched Truscott with approval, but at first took no part himself in the exposition. I felt certain that Sir Magnus was secure in exact knowledge of the market price of every object at Stourwater: that kind of insight that men can develop without possessing any of the æsthete's, or specialist's cognisance of the particular category, or implication, of the valuable concerned. Barnby used to say that he knew a chartered accountant, scarcely aware even how pictures are produced, who could at the same time enter any gallery and pick out the most expensively priced work there "from Masaccio to Matisse," simply through the mystic power of his own respect for money.

We passed through room after room, apartments of which the cumulative magnificence seemed only to enhance the earlier fancy that, at some wave of the wand—somewhat in the manner of Peer Gynt—furniture and armour, pictures and hangings, gold and silver, crystal and china, could turn easily and instantaneously into a heap of withered leaves blown about by the wind. From time to time Prince Theodoric made an appreciative comment, or Miss Walpole-Wilson interjected a minor correction of statement; although, in the latter case, it was clear that Truscott's effective handling of the matter of sitting next to her at luncheon had greatly reduced the potential of her critical assault.

We made an end of that part of the interior of the castle to be regarded as "on show," returning to the ground floor, where we came at length to the head of a spiral staircase, leading down to subterranean depths. Here Sir Magnus was handed one of the torches by Truscott, and from this point he took over the rôle of showman. There was a slight pause. I saw Stringham and Truscott exchange a look.

"We are now descending to the dungeons," said Sir Magnus, his voice trembling slightly. "*I sometimes think that is where we should put the girls who don't behave."*

He made this little speech with an air almost of discomfort. A general titter rippled across the surface of the party, and there was a further pause, as of expectancy, perhaps on account of an involuntary curiosity to learn whether he would put this decidedly threatening surmise to practical effect. Truscott smiled gently, rather like a governess, or nanny, of wide experience who knows only too well that "boys will be boys." I could see from Stringham's face that he was suppressing a tremendous burst of laughter. It struck me, at this moment, that such occasions, the enjoyment of secret laughter, remained for him the peak of pleasure, for he looked suddenly happier; more buoyant, certainly, than when he had introduced me to Peggy Stepney. What perverse refinements, verbal or otherwise, were actually implied by Sir Magnus's words could only be guessed. It seemed that this remark, as an assertion of opinion, had always to be uttered at this point in the itinerary, and that its unfailing regularity was considered by his secretaries—if Stringham and Truscott could be so called—as an enormous hidden joke.

There was also the point to be remembered that Baby Wentworth, as Truscott had earlier reminded Stringham, "did not like" these visits to the dungeons. I recalled some of Barnby's speculations regarding the supposed relationship between her and Sir Magnus. While scarcely to be supposed that, in truth, he physically incarcerated Mrs. Wentworth, or his other favourites, in the manner contemplated, frequent repetition of the words no doubt drew attention to sides of his nature that a girl often seen in his company might reasonably prefer to remain unemphasised. Sir Magnus's eyes had, in fact, paused for a second on Rosie Manasch when he had spoken that sentence. Now they ranged quickly over the faces of Lady Huntercombe, Miss Janet Walpole-Wilson, and Eleanor : coming to rest on the ingenuous profile of a little fair girl whose name I did not know. Then, moistening his lips slightly, he beckoned us on. The party began to descend the stairs, Sir Magnus leading the way.

It so happened that at that moment my shoe-lace came unfastened. There was an oak bench by the side of the staircase, and, resting my foot on this, I stooped to retie the lace, which immediately, as is the way, re-knotted itself tightly, delaying progress for a minute or more. The heels of the women echoed on the stones as the people clattered down the stairs, and then the sound of voices grew fainter, until hum of chatter and shuffle of feet became dim, ceasing at last in the distance. As soon as the shoe-lace was tied once more, I started off quickly down the steps, beside which an iron rail had been fixed as a banister. The way was dark, and the steps cut deep, so that I had slowed up by the time I came, only a short way below, to a kind of landing. Beyond this space the stairs continued again. I had passed this stage, and had just begun on the second flight, when a voice—proceeding apparently from out of the walls of the castle—suddenly spoke my name, the sound of which echoed round me, as the footsteps of the party ahead had echoed a short time before.

" Jenkins?"

I have to admit that I was at that moment quite startled by the sound. The tone was thick and interrogative. It seemed to emerge from the surrounding ether, a voice from out of the twilight of the stair, isolated from human agency, for near approach of any speaker, up or down the steps, would have been audible to me before he could have come as close as the sound suggested. A second later I became aware of its place of origin, but instead of relief at the simple explanation of what had at first seemed a mysterious, even terrifying, phenomenon, a yet more nameless apprehension was occasioned by the sight revealed. Just level with my head—as I returned a step or more up the stair—was a narrow barred window, or squint, through the iron grill of which, his face barely distinguishable in the shadows, peered Widmerpool.

"Where is the Chief?" he asked, in a hoarse voice.

Once in a way, for a brief instant of time, the subconscious fantasies of the mind seem to overflow, so that we make, in our waking moments, assumptions as outrageous and incredible as those thoughts and acts which provide the commonplace of dreams. Perhaps Sir Magnus's allusion to the appropriate treatment of "girls who don't behave," presumably intended by him at least in a relatively jocular manner, as he had pronounced the sentence, although, it was true, his voice had sounded unnaturally serious, had, for some unaccountable reason, resulted in the conjuration of this spectre, as the image seemed to be, that took form at that moment before my eyes. It was a vision of Widmerpool, imprisoned, to all outward appearance, in an underground cell, from which only a small grating gave access to the outer world: even those wider horizons represented only by the gloom of the spiral staircase. I felt a chill at my heart in the fate that must be his, thus immured, while I racked my brain, for the same brief instant of almost unbearable anxiety, to conjecture what crime, or dereliction of duty, he must have committed to suffer such treatment at the hands of his tyrant.

I record this absurd aberration on my own part only because it had some relation to what followed, for, so soon as anything like rational thought could be brought to bear

on the matter, it was clear to me that Widmerpool was
merely speaking from an outer passage of the castle, constructed on a lower level than the floor from which, a short
time earlier, we had approached the head of the spiral stair.
He had, in fact, evidently arrived from the back entrance,
or, familiar with the ground plan of the building, had
come by some short cut straight to this window.

"Why are you staring like that?" he asked, irritably.

I explained as well as I could the circumstances that
caused me to be found in this manner wandering about
the castle alone.

"I gathered from one of the servants that a tour was in
progress," said Widmerpool. "I came over with the draft
speech for the Incorporated Metals dinner. I am spending
the week-end with my mother, and knew the Chief would
like to see the wording as soon as possible—so that I could
make a revision when one or two points had been settled.
Truscott agreed when I rang up."

"Truscott is showing the party round."

"Of course."

All this demonstrated clearly that arrangements initiated
by Truscott at Mrs. Andriadis's party had matured in such
a manner as to graft Widmerpool firmly on to the Donners-
Brebner organisation, upon the spreading branches of which
he seemed to be already positively blossoming. Before I
could make further inquiries, on the tip of my tongue,
regarding such matters as the precise nature of his job, or
the closeness of touch maintained by him with his chief in
tasks like the writing of speeches, Widmerpool continued
to speak in a lower and more agitated tone, pressing his
face between the iron bars, as if attempting to worm his
way through their narrow interstices. Now that my eyes
had become accustomed to the oddness of his physical

position, some of the earlier illusion of forcible confinement dissolved; and, at this later stage, he seemed merely one of those invariably power-conscious beings—a rôle for which his temperament certainly well suited him—who preside over *guichets* from which tickets are dispensed for trains or theatres.

"I am glad to have an opportunity for speaking to you alone for a moment," he said. "I have been worried to death lately."

This statement sent my thoughts back to his confession about Barbara on the night of the Huntercombes' dance, and I supposed that he had been suddenly visited with one of those spasms of frustrated passion that sometimes, like an uncured disease, break out with renewed virulence at a date when treatment seemed no longer necessary. After all, it was only in a fit of anger, however justifiable, that he had sworn he would not see her again. No one can choose, or determine, the duration of such changes of heart. Indeed, the circumstances of his decision to break with her after the sugar incident made such a renewal far from improbable.

"Barbara?"

He tried to shake his head, apparently in vehement negation, but was prevented by the bars from making this movement at all adequately to convey the force of his feelings.

"I was induced to do an almost insanely indiscreet thing about the girl you introduced me to."

The idea of introducing Widmerpool to any girl was so far from an undertaking I was conscious ever of having contemplated, certainly a girl in relation to whom serious indiscretion on his part was at all probable, that I began to wonder whether success in securing the Donners-Brebner

job had been too much for his brain, already obsessed
with self-advancement, and that he was, in fact, raving. It
then occurred to me that I might have brought him into
touch with someone or other at the Huntercombes', although no memory of any introduction remained in my
mind. In any case, I could not imagine how such a meeting
might have led to a climax so ominous as that suggested by
his tone.

" Gypsy," he said, hesitating a moment over the name,
and speaking so low as to be almost inaudible.

" What about her? "

The whole affair was hopelessly tangled in my head. I
could remember that Barnby had said something about
Widmerpool being involved with Gypsy Jones, but I have
already spoken of the way of looking at life to which, in
those days, I subscribed—the conception that sets individuals
and ideas in hermetically sealed receptacles—and the world
in which such things could happen at which Widmerpool
seemed to hint appeared infinitely removed, I cannot now
think why, from Stourwater and its surroundings. However, it was at last plain that Widmerpool had, in some
manner, seriously compromised himself with Gypsy Jones.
A flood of possible misadventures that could have played
an unhappy part in causing his distress now invaded my
imagination.

" A doctor was found," said Widmerpool.

He spoke in a voice hollow with desperation, and this
news did not allay the suspicion that whatever was amiss
must be fairly serious; though for some reason the exact
cause of his anxiety still remained uncertain in my mind.

" I believe everything is all right now," he said. " But
it cost a lot of money. More than I could afford. You know,
I've never even committed a technical offence before—like

using the untransferable half of somebody else's return ticket, or driving a borrowed car insured only in the owner's name."

Giving expression to his dismay seemed to have done him good : at least to have calmed him.

" I felt I could mention matters to you as you were already familiar with the situation," he said. " That fellow Barnby told me you knew. I don't much care for him."

Now, at last, I remembered the gist of what Mr. Deacon had told me, and, incredible as I should have supposed their course to be, the sequence of events began to become at least dimly visible: though much remained obscure. I have spoken before of the difficulties involved in judging other people's behaviour by a consistent standard—for, after all, one must judge them, even at the price of being judged oneself—and, had I been told of some similar indiscretion on the part, say, of Peter Templer I should have been particularly disturbed. There is, or, at least, should be, a fitness in the follies each individual pursues and uniformity of pattern is, on the whole, rightly preserved in human behaviour. Such unwritten regulations seemed now to have been disregarded wholesale.

In point of fact Templer was, so far as I knew, capable of conducting his affairs without recourse to such extremities; and a crisis of this kind appeared to me so foreign to Widmerpool's nature—indeed, to what might almost be called his station in life—that there was something distinctly shocking, almost personally worrying, in finding him entangled with a woman in such circumstances. I could not help wondering whether or not there had been, or would be, material compensation for these mental, and financial, sufferings. Having regarded him, before hearing of his feelings for Barbara, as existing almost in a vacuum so far as the emotion of love was concerned, an effort on my own part was required to accept the fact that he had been engaged upon so improbable, indeed, so sinister, a liaison. If I had been annoyed to find, a month or two earlier, that he considered himself to possess claims of at least, some tenuous sort on Barbara, I was also more than a trifle put out to discover that Widmerpool, so generally regarded by his contemporaries as a dull dog, had been, in fact, however much he might now regret it, in this way, at a moment's notice, prepared to live comparatively dangerously.

"I will tell you more some other time. Naturally my mother was distressed by the knowledge that I have had something on my mind. You will, of course, breathe a word to no one. Now I must find the Chief. I think I will go to the other end of this passage and cut the party off there. It is almost as quick as coming round to where you are."

His voice had now lost some of its funereal note, returning to a more normal tone of impatience. The outline of his face disappeared as suddenly as it had become visible a minute or two before. I found myself alone on the spiral staircase, and now hurried on once more down the steep steps, trying to digest some of the information just conveyed. The facts, such as they were, certainly appeared surprising enough. I reached the foot of the stair without contriving to set them in any very coherent order.

Other matters now intervened. The sound of voices and laughter provided an indication of the path to follow, leading along a passage, pitch-dark and smelling of damp, at the end of which light flashed from time to time. I found the rest of the party standing about in a fairly large vaulted chamber, lit by the torches held by Sir Magnus and Truscott. Attention seemed recently to have been directed to certain iron staples, set at irregular intervals in the walls a short way from the paved floor.

"Where on earth did you get to?" asked Stringham, in an undertone. "You missed an ineffably funny scene."

Still laughing quietly to himself, he went on to explain that some kind of horse-play had been taking place, in the course of which Pardoe had borrowed the dog-chain that was almost an integral part of Eleanor's normal equipment, and, with this tackle, had attempted by force to fasten Rosie Manasch to one of the staples. In exactly what manner this had been done I was unable to gather, but he seemed to have slipped the chain round her waist, producing in this manner an imitation of a captive maiden, passable enough to delight Sir Magnus. Rosie Manasch herself, her bosom heaving slightly, seemed half cross, half flattered by this attention on Pardoe's part. Sir Magnus stood by, smiling very genially, at the same time losing none of his accustomed air of asceticism. Truscott was smiling, too, although he looked as if the situation had been allowed to get farther out of control than was entirely comfortable for one of his own cautious temperament. Eleanor, who had recovered her chain, which she had doubled in her hand and was swinging about, was perhaps not dissatisfied to see Rosie, sometimes a little patronising in her tone, reduced to a state of fluster, for she appeared to be enjoying herself for the first time since our arrival at the castle. It was perhaps a pity that her father had missed the tour. Only Miss Janet Walpole-Wilson stood sourly in the shadows, explaining that the supposed dungeon was almost certainly a kind of cellar, granary, or storehouse; and that the iron rings, so far from being designed to shackle, or even torture, unfortunate prisoners, were intended to support and secure casks or trestles. However, no one took any notice of her, even to the extent of bothering to contradict.

"The Chief was in ecstasies," said Stringham. "Baby will be furious when she hears of this."

This description of Sir Magnus's bearing seemed a little exaggerated, because nothing could have been more matter-of-fact than the voice in which he inquired of Prince Theodoric: "What do you think of my private prison, sir?"

The Prince's features had resumed to some extent that somewhat embarrassed fixity of countenance worn when I had seen him at Mrs. Andriadis's; an expression perhaps evoked a second or two earlier by Pardoe's performance, the essentially schoolboy nature of which Prince Theodoric, as a foreigner, might have legitimately failed to grasp. He seemed at first to be at a loss to know exactly how to reply to this question, in spite of its evident jocularity, raising his eyebrows and stroking his dark chin.

"I can only answer, Sir Magnus," he said at last, "that you should see the interior of one of our new model prisons. They might surprise you. For a poor country we have some excellent prisons. In some ways, I can assure you, they compare very favourably, so far as modern convenience is concerned, with the accommodation in which my own family is housed—certainly during the season of the year when we are obliged to inhabit the Old Palace."

This reply was received with suitable amusement; and, as the tour was now at an end—at least the serious part of it—we moved back once more along the passage. Our host, in his good-humour, had by then indisputably lost interest in the few minor points of architectural considera-tion that remained to be displayed by Truscott on the ascent of the farther staircase. Half-way up these stairs, we encountered Widmerpool, making his way down. He retired before the oncoming crowd, waiting at the top of the stairway for Sir Magnus, who was the last to climb the steps. The two of them remained in conference together, while the rest of us returned to the terrace overlooking the garden, where Sir Gavin and Lord Huntercombe were standing, both, by that time, showing unmistakable signs of having enjoyed enough of each other's company. Peggy Stepney had also reappeared.

"Being engaged really takes up all one's time," said Stringham, after he had described to her the incidents of the tour. "Weren't you talking of Peter? Do you ever see him these days? I never meet anyone or hear any gossip."

"His sister tells me he ought to get married."

"It comes to us all sooner or later. I expect it's hanging over you, too. Don't you Peggy? He'll have to submit."

"Of course," she said, laughing.

They seemed now very much like any other engaged couple, and I decided that there could have been no significance in the withdrawal of her hand from his. In fact, everything about the situation seemed normal. There was not even a sense of the engagement being " on " again, after its period of abeyance, presumably covered by the interlude with Mrs. Andriadis. I wondered what the Bridgnorths thought about it all. I did not exactly expect Stringham to mention the Andriadis party, indeed, it would have been surprising had he done so; but, at the same time, he was so entirely free from any suggestion of having " turned over a new leaf," or anything that could possibly be equated with that state of mind, that I felt curious to know what the stages had been of his return to a more conventional form of life. We talked of Templer for a moment or two.

"I believe you have designs on that very strange girl you came over here with," he said. "Admit it yourself."

"Eleanor Walpole-Wilson?"

"The one who produced the chain in the dungeon. How delighted the Chief was. Why not marry her?"

"I think Baby will be rather angry," said Peggy Stepney, laughing again and blushing exquisitely.

"The Chief likes his few whims," said Stringham. "I don't think they really amount to much. Still, people tease Baby sometimes. The situation between Baby and myself is always rather delicate in view of the fact that she broke up my sister's married life, such as it was. Still, one mustn't let a little thing like that prejudice one. Here she is, anyway."

If Mrs. Wentworth, as she came up, heard these last remarks, which could have been perfectly audible to her, she made no sign of having done so. She was looking, it was true, not best pleased, so that it was to be assumed that someone had already taken the trouble to inform her of the dungeon tour. At the same time she carried herself, as ever, with complete composure, and her air of dissatisfaction may have been no more than outward expression of a fashionable indifference to life. I was anxious to escape from the group and look for Jean, because I thought it probable that we should not stay for tea, and all chance of seeing her again would be lost. I had already forgotten about Widmerpool's troubles, and did not give a thought to the trying time he might be experiencing, talking business while overwhelmed with private worry, though it could at least have been said in alleviation that Sir Magnus, gratified by Pardoe's antics, was probably in a receptive mood. This occurred to me later when I considered Widmerpool's predicament with a good deal of interest; but at the time the people round about, the beauty of the castle, the sunlight striking the grass and water of the moat, made such decidedly sordid difficulties appear infinitely far away.

Even to myself I could not explain precisely why I wanted to find Jean. Various interpretations were, of course, readily available, of which the two simplest were, on the one hand, that—as I had at least imagined myself to be when I had stayed with the Templers—I was once more " in love " with her; or, on the other, that she was an unquestionably attractive girl, whom any man, without necessarily ulterior motive, might quite reasonably hope to see more of. However, neither of these definitions completely fitted the case. I had brought myself to think of earlier feelings for her as juvenile, even insipid, in the approach, while, at the same time, I was certainly not disinterested enough to be able honestly to claim the second footing. The truth was that I had become once more aware of that odd sense of uneasiness which had assailed me when we had first met, while no longer able to claim the purely romantic conceptions of that earlier impact; yet so far was this feeling remote from a simple desire to see more of her that I almost equally hoped that I might fail to find her again before we left Stourwater, while a simultaneous anxiety to search for her also tormented me.

Certainly I know that there was, at that stage, no coherent plan in my mind to make love to her; if for no other reason, because, rather naïvely, I thought of her as married to someone else, and therefore removed automatically from any such sphere of interest. I was even young enough to think of married women as belonging, generically, to a somewhat older group than my own. All this must be admitted to be an altogether unapprehending state of mind; but its existence helps to interpret the strange, disconcerting fascination that I now felt: if anything, more divorced from physical desire than those nights lying in bed in the hot little attic room at La Grenadière, when I used to think of Jean, or Suzette, and other girls remembered from the past or seen in the course of the day.

Perhaps a consciousness of future connection was thrown forward like a deep shadow in the manner in which such perceptions are sometimes projected: a process that may well explain what is called " love at first sight ": that knowledge that someone who has just entered the room is going to play a part in our life. Analysis at that moment was in any case out of reach, because I realised that I had been left, at that moment, standing silently by Mrs. Wentworth, to whom I now explained, *à propos de bottes*, that I knew Barnby. This information appeared, on the whole, to please her, and her manner became less disdainful.

" Oh, yes, how is Ralph?" she said. "I didn't manage to see him before leaving London. Is he having lots of lovely love affairs?"

A sudden move on the part of the Walpole-Wilsons, made with a view to undertaking preparations for return to Hinton, exempted me then and there from need to answer this question; rather to my relief, because it seemed by its nature to obstruct any effort to present Barnby, as I supposed he would wish, in the condition of a man who thought exclusively of Mrs. Wentworth herself. The decision to leave was probably attributable in the main to Miss Janet Walpole-Wilson, evidently becoming restless in these surroundings, admittedly unsympathetic to her. She had been standing in isolation for some time at the far end of the terrace, looking rather like a governess waiting to bring her charges home after an unusually ill-behaved children's party. Sir Gavin, too, showed signs of depression,

H

after his talk with Lord Huntercombe. Even Prince Theodoric's friendliness, when we took leave of him did not succeed in lifting the cloud of his sense of failure in forwarding a favourite scheme.

"Getting on in life now, sir," he said, in answer to some
remark made by the Prince. "Got to make way for
younger men."

"Nonsense, Sir Gavin, nonsense."

Prince Theodoric insisted on coming to the door to say
a final good-bye. A number of other guests, with Sir
Magnus, followed to the place in the courtyard where the
cars were waiting. Among this crowd of people I suddenly
noticed Jean had reappeared.

"Bob is returning next month," she said, when I approached her. "Come to dinner, or something. Where do
you live?"

I told her my address, feeling at the same time that dinner
with the Duports was not exactly the answer to my problem.
I suddenly began to wonder whether or not I liked her at
all. It now seemed to me that there was something awkward and irritating about the manner in which she had
suggested this invitation. At the same time she reminded
me of some picture. Was it Rubens and *Le Chapeau de
Paille* : his second wife or her sister? There was that same
suggestion, though only for an instant, of shyness and sub-
mission. Perhaps it was the painter's first wife that Jean
resembled, though slighter in build. After all, they were
aunt and niece. Jean's grey-blue eyes were slanting and
perhaps not so large as theirs. Some trivial remarks passed
between us, and we said good-bye.

Turning from this interlude, I noticed a somewhat
peculiar scene taking place, in which Widmerpool was
playing a leading part. This was in process of enactment

in front of the steps. He must have completed his business with Sir Magnus and decided to slip quietly away, because he was sitting in an ancient Morris which now resolutely refused to start. Probably on account of age, and hard use suffered in the past, the engine of this vehicle would roar for a second or two, when the car would give a series of jerks; and then, after fearful, thunderous shaking, the noise would die down and cease altogether. Widmerpool, red in the face, could be seen through the thick grime of the almost opaque windscreen, now pressing the self-starter, now accelerating, now shifting the gears. The car seemed hopelessly immobilised. Sir Magnus, the ground crunching under his tread, stepped heavily across towards the spot.

" Is anything wrong?" he asked, mildly.

The question was no doubt intended as purely rhetorical, because it must have been clear to anyone, even of far less practical grasp of such matters than Sir Magnus, that something was very wrong indeed. However, obeying that law that requires most people to minimise to a superior a misfortune which, to an inferior, they would magnify, Widmerpool thrust his head through the open window of the car, and, smiling reverentially, gave an assurance that all was well.

" It's quite all right, sir, quite all right," he said. " She'll fire in a moment. I think I left her too long in the sun."

For a time, while we all watched, the starter screeched again without taking effect; the sound was decreasing and this time it stopped finally. It was clear that the battery had run out.

" We'll give you a push," said Pardoe. " Come on, boys."

Several of the men went over to help, and Widmerpool, in his two-seater, was trundled, like Juggernaut, round and

round the open space. At first these efforts were fruitless,
but suddenly the engine began to hum, this sound occurring
at a moment when, facing a wall, the car was so placed to
make immediate progress forward impossible. Widmerpool therefore applied the brake, "warming up" for several
seconds. I could see, when once more he advanced his head
through the window, that he was greatly agitated. He
shouted to Sir Magnus: "I must apologise for this, sir, I
really must. It is too bad."

Sir Magnus inclined his head indulgently. He evidently
retained his excellent humour. It was then, just as the
Walpole-Wilson party were settled in their two cars, that
the accident happened. My attention had been momentarily
distracted from the scene in which Widmerpool was playing
the main rôle by manœuvres on the part of Sir Gavin to
steer Rosie Manasch, this time successfully, into the seat
beside him; with the unforeseen result that Miss Janet Walpole-Wilson, as if by irresistible instinct, immediately seated
herself in the back of the same car. While these dispositions
were taking place, Widmerpool, making up his mind to
move, must have released the brake and pressed the
accelerator too hard. Perhaps he was unaware that his gear
was still in "reverse." Whatever the reason, the Morris
suddenly shot backward with terrific force for so small a
body, running precipitately into one of the stone urns where
it stood, crowned with geraniums, at the corner of the
sunken lawn. For a moment it looked as if Widmerpool
and his car would follow the flower-pot and its heavy base,
as they crashed down on to the grass, striking against each
other with so much force that portions of decorative mould-
ing broke from off the urn. Either the impact, or some
sudden, and quite unexpected, re-establishment of control
on Widmerpool's part, prevented his own wholesale descent

on to the lower levels of the lawn. The engine of the Morris stopped again, giving as it did so a kind of wail like the departure of an unhappy spirit, and, much dented at the rear, the car rolled forward a yard or two, coming to rest at an angle, not far from the edge of the parapet.

Before this incident was at an end, the Walpole-Wilson chauffeur had already begun to move off, and, looking back, the last I saw of the actors was a glimpse of the absolutely impassive face of Sir Magnus, as he strode with easy steps once more across the gravel to where Widmerpool was climbing out of his car. The sun was still hot. Its rays caught the sweat glistening on Widmerpool's features, and flashed on his spectacles, from which, as from a mirror, the light was reflected. There was just time to see him snatch these glasses from his nose as he groped for a handkerchief. We passed under the arch, reaching the portcullis, and crossing the causeway over the moat, before anyone spoke. Once more the car entered the lanes and byways of that romantic countryside.

"That was a near one," said Pardoe.

"Ought we to have stopped?" asked Lady Walpole-Wilson, anxiously.

"I wonder who it was," she continued a moment later.

"Why, didn't you see?" said Eleanor. "It was Mr. Widmerpool. He arrived at Stourwater some time after luncheon. Is he staying there, do you think?"

This information threw her mother into one of her not uncommon states of confusion, though whether the nervous attack with which Lady Walpole-Wilson was now visited could be attributed to some version, no doubt by that time hopelessly garbled, having come to her ears regarding Barbara and the sugar incident, it was not possible to say. More probably she merely looked upon Widmerpool and his mother as creators of a social problem with which she was consciously unwilling to contend. Possibly she had hoped that, in subsequent summers, the Widmerpools would find somewhere else in England to rent a cottage; or, at least, that after a single invitation to dinner the whole matter of Widmerpool's existence might be forgotten once and for all. Certainly she would not wish, over and above such strands as already existed, to be additionally linked to his mother. That was certain. Nor could there be any doubt that she would not greatly care for the idea of Widmerpool himself being in love with her niece. At the same time, nothing could be more positive than the supposition that Lady Walpole-Wilson would, if necessary, have shown the Widmerpools, mother and son, all the kindness and consideration that their presence in the locality—regarded, of course, in relation to his father's former agricultural connection with her brother-in-law— might, in the circumstances, justly demand.

" Oh, I hardly think Mr. Widmerpool would be staying at Stourwater," she said; adding almost immediately: " Though I don't in the least know why I should declare that. Anyway . . . he seemed to be driving away from the castle when we last saw him."

This last sentence was the product of instinctive kindness of heart, or fear that she might have sounded snobbish : the latter state of mind being particularly abhorrent to her at that moment because the attitude, if existent, might seem applied to an establishment which she could not perhaps wholly respect. She looked so despairing at the idea of Widmerpool possessing, as it were, an operational base in extension to the cottage from which he, and his mother, could already potentially molest Hinton, that I felt it my duty to explain with as little delay as possible that

Widmerpool had recently taken a job at Donners-Brebner, and had merely come over that afternoon to see Sir Magnus on a matter of business. This statement seemed, for some reason, to put her mind at ease, at least for the moment.

"I was really wondering whether we should ask Mr. Widmerpool and his mother over to tea," she said, as if the question of how to deal with the Widmerpools had now crystallised in her mind. "You know Aunt Janet likes an occasional talk with Mrs. Widmerpool—even though they don't always see eye to eye."

What followed gave me the impression that Lady Walpole-Wilson's sudden relief may have been to some extent attributable to the fact that she had all at once arrived at a method by which the Widmerpools might be evaded, or a meeting with them at least postponed. If this was her plan —and, although in many ways one of the least disingenuous of women, I think she must quickly have devised a scheme on that occasion—the design worked effectively, because, at this suggestion of her mother's, Eleanor at once clenched her teeth in a manner that always indicated disapproval.

"Oh, don't let's have them over when Aunt Janet is here," she said. "You know I don't really care for Mr. Widmerpool very much— and Aunt Janet has plenty of opportunity to have her gossips with his mother when they are both in London."

Lady Walpole-Wilson made a little gesture indicating "So be it," and there the matter seemed to rest, where, I suppose, she had intended it to rest. Disturbed by mixed feelings set in motion by benevolence and conscience, she had been no doubt momentarily thrown off her guard. Comparative equilibrium was now restored. We drove on; and, by that evening, Widmerpool was forgotten by the rest of the party at Hinton Hoo. However, although nothing further was said about Widmerpool, other aspects of the visit to Stourwater were widely discussed. The day had left Sir Gavin a prey to deep depression. The meeting with Prince Theodoric had provided, naturally enough, a re-minder of former grandeurs, and the congenial nature of their reunion, by agreeable memories aroused, had no doubt at the same time equally called to mind the existence of old, unhealed wounds.

"Theodoric is a man of the middle of the road," he said. "That, in itself, is sympathetic to me. In my own case, such an attitude has, of course, been to a large extent a pro-fessional necessity. All the same it is in men like Károlyi and Sforza that I sense a kind of fundamental reciprocity of thought."

"He seems a simple young man," said Miss Walpole-Wilson. "I find no particular fault in him. No doubt he will have a difficult time with that brother of his."

"Really, the Prince could not have been more friendly," said Lady Walpole-Wilson, "and Sir Magnus, too. He was so kind. I can't think why he has never married. So nice to see the Huntercombes. Pretty little person, Mrs. Wentworth."

"So your friend Charles Stringham is engaged again," said Rosie Manasch, rather maliciously. "I wonder why it hasn't been in the papers. Do you think his mother is holding up the announcement for some reason? Or the Bridgnorths? They sound rather a stuffy pair, so it may be them."

"How long ought one to wait until one puts an engage-ment in print?" asked Pardoe.

"Are you secretly engaged, Johnny?" said Rosie. "I'm sure he is, aren't you?"

"Of course I am," said Pardoe. "To half a dozen girls,

at least. It's just a question of deciding which is to be the
lucky one. Don't want to make a mistake."

" I've arranged to see the hound puppies on Tuesday,"
said Eleanor. " What a pity you will all be gone by then."

However, she spoke as if she could survive the disband-
ment of our party. I pondered some of the events of the
day, especially the situations to which, by some inexorable
fate, Widmerpool's character seemed to commit him. This
last misfortune had been, if anything, worse than the matter
of Barbara and the sugar. And yet, like the phœnix, he
rose habitually, so I concluded, recalling his other worries,
from the ashes of his own humiliation. I could not help
admiring the calm manner in which Sir Magnus had
accepted damage of the most irritating kind to his property : violation which, to rich or poor, must always represent, to a greater or lesser degree, assault upon themselves and their feelings. From this incident, I began to
understand at least one small aspect of Sir Magnus's pre-
scriptive right to have become in life what Uncle Giles
would have called " a person of influence." The point
about Jean that had impressed me most, I thought, was
that she was obviously more intelligent than I had previously supposed. In fact she was almost to be regarded as
an entirely new person. If the chance arose again, it was in
that capacity that she must be approached.

Sir Gavin straightened the photograph of Prince Theodoric's father, wearing hussar uniform, that stood on the
piano in a plain silver frame, surmounted by a royal crown.

" His helmet now shall make a hive for bees . . ." he remarked, as he sank heavily into an arm-chair.

FOUR

A sense of maturity, or at least of endured experience, is conveyed, for some reason, in the smell of autumn; so it seemed to me, passing one day, by chance, through Kensington Gardens. The eighteen months or less since that Sunday afternoon on the steps of the Albert Memorial, with the echoing of Eleanor's whistle, and Barbara's fleeting grasp of my arm, had become already measureless as an eternity. Now, like scraps of gilt peeled untidily from the mosaic surface of the neo-Gothic canopy, the leaves, stained dull gold, were blowing about in the wind, while, squatting motionless beside the elephant, the Arab still kept watch on summer's mirage, as, once more, the green foliage faded gradually away before his displeased gaze. Those grave features implied that for him, too, that year, for all its monotony, had also called attention, in different aspects, to the processes of life and death that are always on the move. For my own part, I felt myself peculiarly conscious of these unalterable activities. For example, Stringham, as he had himself foreshadowed, was married to Peggy Stepney in the second week of October; the same day, as it happened, that saw the last of Mr. Deacon.

"Don't miss Buster's present," Stringham just had time to remark, as the conveyor-belt of wedding guests evolved sluggishly across the carpet of the Bridgnorths' drawing-room in Cavendish Square.

There was opportunity to do no more than take the hand, for a moment, of bride and bridegroom; but Buster's present could hardly have remained invisible: a grand-

father clock, gutted, and fitted up with shelves to form a
" cocktail cabinet," fully equipped with glasses, two shakers,
and space for bottles. A good deal of money had evidently
been spent on this ingenious contrivance. There was even
a secret drawer. I could not make up my mind whether the
joke was not, in reality, against Stringham. The donor
himself, perhaps physically incapacitated by anguish of
jealousy, had been unable to attend the church; and, since
at least one gossip column had referred to " popular Commander Foxe's temporary retirement to a nursing home,"
there seemed no reason to disbelieve in the actuality of
Buster's seizure.

Stringham's mother, no less beautiful, so it seemed to me,
than when, as a schoolboy, I had first set eyes on her—
having at last made up her mind, as her son had put it,
" whether to laugh or cry "—had wept throughout the
whole of the service into the corner of a small, flame-
coloured handkerchief. By the time of the reception, however, she had made a complete recovery. His sister, Flavia,
I saw for the first time. She had married as her second
husband an American called Wisebite, and her daughter,
Pamela Flitton, a child of six or seven, by the earlier marriage, was one of the bridesmaids. Well dressed, and good-
looking, Mrs. Wisebite's ties with Stringham were not
known to me. She was a few years older than her brother,
who rarely mentioned her. Miss Weedon, rather pale in
the face, and more beaky than I remembered, sat in one
of the back pews. I recalled the hungry looks she used to
dart at Stringham on occasions when I had seen them together years before.

Neither of Peggy Stepney's parents looked specially cheer-
ful, and rumours were current to the effect that objections
had been raised to the marriage by both families. It

appeared to have been Stringham himself who had insisted upon its taking place. Such opposition as may have existed had been, no doubt, finally overcome by conviction on the Bridgnorths' part that it was high time for their elder daughter to get married, since she could not subsist for ever on the strength of photographs, however charming, in the illustrated papers; and they could well have decided, in the circumstances, that she might easily pick on a husband less presentable than Stringham. Lord Bridgnorth, a stout, red-faced man, wearing a light grey stock and rather tight morning clothes, was notable for having owned a horse that won the Derby at a hundred to seven. His wife—daughter of a Scotch duke, to one of the remote branches of whose house Sir Gavin Walpole-Wilson's mother had belonged—was a powerful figure in the hospital world, where she operated, so I had been informed, in bitter competition with organisations supported by Mrs. Foxe: a rivalry which their new relationship was hardly likely to decrease. The Walpole-Wilsons themselves were not present, but Lady Huntercombe, arrayed more than ever like Mrs. Siddons, was sitting with her daughters on the bride's side of the church, and later disparaged the music.

Weddings are notoriously depressing affairs. It looked as if this one, especially, had been preceded by more than common display of grievance on the part of persons regarding themselves as, in one way or another, fairly closely concerned, and therefore possessing the right to raise difficulties and proffer advice. Only Lady Anne Stepney appeared to be, for once, enjoying herself unreservedly. She was her sister's chief bridesmaid, and, as a kind of public assertion of rebellion against convention of all kind, rather in Mr. Deacon's manner, she was wearing her wreath back to front; a disorder of head-dress that gravely prejudiced the general appearance of the cortège as it passed up the aisle. Little Pamela Flitton, who was holding the bride's train, felt sick at this same moment, and rejoined her nurse at the back of the church.

I returned to my rooms that evening in rather low spirits; and, just as I was retiring to bed, Barnby rang up with the news—quite unexpected, though I had heard of his indisposition—that Mr. Deacon had died as the result of an accident. Barnby's account of how this had come about attested the curious fitness that sometimes attends the manner in which people finally leave this world; for, although Mr. Deacon's end was not exactly dramatic within the ordinary meaning of the term, its circumstances, as he himself would have wished, could not possibly be regarded as commonplace. In many ways the embodiment of bourgeois thought, he could have claimed with some justice that his long struggle against the shackles of convention, sometimes inwardly dear to him, had, in the last resort, come to his aid in releasing him from what he would have considered the shame of a bourgeois death.

Although the demise was not a violent one in the most usual sense of the word, it unquestionably partook at the same time of that spirit of carelessness and informality always so vigorously advocated by Mr. Deacon as a precept for pursuing what Sillery liked to call " The Good Life." Sillery's ideas upon that subject were, of course, rather different, on the whole, from Mr. Deacon's, in spite of the fact that both of them, even according to their own lights, were adventurers. But, although each looked upon himself as a figure almost Promethean in spirit of independence— godlike, and following ideals of his own, far from the well-worn tracks of fellow men—their chosen roads were also acknowledged by each to be set far apart.

Mr. Deacon and Sillery must, in fact, have been just about the same age. Possibly they had known each other in their troubled youth (for even Sillery had had to carve out a career for himself in his early years), and some intersection of those unrestricted paths to which each adhered no doubt explained at least a proportion of Sillery's disapproval of Mr. Deacon's habits. Any such strictures on Sillery's part were at least equally attributable to prudence: that sense of self-preservation, and desire to " keep on the safe side," of which Sillery, among the many other qualities to which he could lay claim, possessed more than a fair share.

When, in an effort to complete the picture, I had once asked Mr. Deacon whether, in the course of his life, he had ever run across Sillery, he had replied in his deep voice, accompanied by that sardonic smile : " My father, a man of modest means, did not send me to the university, I sometimes think—with due respect, my dear Nicholas, to your own *Alma Mater*—that he was right."

In that sentence he avoided a direct answer, while framing a form of words not specifically denying possibility of the existence of an ancient antagonism; his careful choice of phrase at the same time excusing him from commenting in any manner whatsoever on the person concerned. It was as if he insisted only upon Sillery's status as an essentially academical celebrity : a figure not properly to be discussed by one who had never been—as Mr. Deacon was accustomed to put it in the colloquialism of his own generation—" a 'varsity man." There was also more than a hint of regret implicit in the deliberately autobiographical nature of this admission, revealing an element to be taken into account in any assessment of Mr. Deacon's own outlook.

At the time of his death, few, if any, of Mr. Deacon's

friends knew the jealously guarded secret of his age more exactly than within a year or two; in spite of the fatal accident having taken place on his birthday—or, to be pedantic about chronology, in the small hours of the day following his birthday party. I was myself not present at the latter stages of this celebration, begun at about nine o'clock on the evening before, having preferred, as night was already well advanced, to make for home at a moment when Mr. Deacon, with about half a dozen remaining guests, had decided to move on to a night-club. Mr. Deacon had taken this desertion—my own and that of several other friends, equally weak in spirit—in bad part, quoting: "Blow, blow, thou winter wind . . ." rather as if enjoyment of his hospitality had put everyone on his honour to accept subjection to the host's will for at least a period of twelve hours on end. However, the dissolution of the party was clearly inevitable. The club that was their goal, newly opened, was expected by those conversant with such matters to survive no more than a week or two, before an impending police raid : a punctual visit being, therefore, regarded as a matter of comparative urgency for any amateur of " night life." In that shady place, soon after his arrival there, Mr. Deacon fell down the stairs.

Even in this undignified mishap there had been, as ever, that touch of martyrdom inseparable from the conduct of his life, since he had been on his way, so it was learnt afterwards, to lodge a complaint with the management regarding the club's existing sanitary arrangements : universally agreed to be deplorable enough. It was true that he might have taken a little more to drink than was usual for some-one who, after the first glass or two, was relatively abstemious in his habit. His behaviour at Mrs. Andriadis's, occasioned, of course, far more by outraged principles than un-

accustomed champagne, had been, so I discovered from
Barnby, quite exceptional in its unbridled nature, and had
proved, indeed, a source of great worry to Mr. Deacon
in the weeks that followed.

As a matter of fact, I had never learnt how the question
of his exit from the house in Hill Street had been finally
settled. Whether Mr. Deacon had attempted to justify himself with Mrs. Andriadis, or whether she, on her part, compelled him—with, or without, the assistance of men-servants, Max Pilgrim, or the Negro—to clear up the litter of
papers in the hall, the future never revealed. Mr. Deacon
himself, on subsequent occasions, chose to indicate only in
the most general terms that he had found Mrs. Andriadis's
party unenjoyable. When her name had once cropped up in
conversation, he echoed a sentiment often expressed by
Uncle Giles, in remarking: "People's manners have
changed a lot since the war—not always for the better." He
did not disclose, even to Barnby, who acted in some respects
almost as his conscience, the exact reason for his quarrel
with the singer, apart from the fact that he had taken
exception to specific phrases in the song, so that the nature
of his difference with Pilgrim on some earlier occasion remained a matter for speculation.

However, if undeniable that at Hill Street Mr. Deacon
had taken perhaps a glass or two more of champagne than
was wise, the luxurious style of the surroundings had no
doubt also played their part in stimulating that quixotic
desire, never far below the surface in all his conduct, to
champion his ideals, wherever he found himself, however
unsuitable the occasion. At the night-club he was, of course,
in more familiar environment, and it was agreed by everyone present that the fall had been in no way attributable to

anything more than a rickety staircase and his own habitual impetuosity. The truth was that, as a man no longer young, he would have been wiser in this, and no doubt in other matters too, to have shown less frenzied haste in attempting to bring about the righting of so many of life's glaring wrongs.

At such an hour, in such a place, nothing much was thought of the fall at the time, neither by Mr. Deacon nor the rest of his party. He had complained, so it was said, only of a bruise on his thigh and a " shaking up " inside. Indeed, he had insisted on prolonging the festivities, if they could be so called, until four o'clock in the morning: an hour when Barnby, woken at last after repeated knocking, had been roused to admit him, with Gypsy, once more to the house, because the latch-key had by that time been lost or mislaid. Mr. Deacon had gone into hospital a day or two later. He must have sustained some internal injury, for he died within the week.

We had met fairly often in the course of renewed acquaintance, for I had taken to dropping in on Barnby once or twice a week, and we would sometimes descend to the shop, or Mr. Deacon's sitting-room, for a talk, or go across with him to the pub for a drink. Now he was no more. Transition between the states of life and death had been effected with such formidable rapidity that his anniversary seemed scarcely completed before he had been thus silently called away; and, as Barnby remarked some time later, it was " hard to think of Edgar without being overwhelmed with moralisings of a somewhat banal kind." I certainly felt sad that I should not see Mr. Deacon again. The milestones provided by him had now come suddenly to an end. The road stretched forward still.

"Edgar's sister is picking up the pieces," Barnby said. "She is a clergyman's wife, living in Norfolk, and has already had a shattering row with Jones."

He had made this remark when informing me by telephone of arrangements made for the funeral, which was to take place on a Saturday: the day, as it happened, upon which I had agreed to have supper with Widmerpool and his mother at their flat. This invitation, arriving in the form of a note from Mrs. Widmerpool, had added that she was looking forward to meeting "so old a friend" of her son's. I was not sure that this was exactly the light in which I wished, or, indeed, had any right, to appear; although I had to admit to myself that I was curious to learn from Widmerpool's lips, as I had not seen him since Stourwater, an account, told from his own point of view, of the course events had taken in connection with himself and Gypsy Jones. I had already received one summary from Barnby on my first visit to Mr. Deacon's shop after return from the Walpole-Wilsons'. He had spoken of the subject at once, so that no question of betraying Widmerpool's confidence arose.

"Your friend paid," Barnby had said. "And that was all."

"How do you know?"

"Jones told me."

"Is she to be believed?"

"No statement on that subject can ever be unreservedly accepted," said Barnby. "But he has never turned up here since. Her story is that he left in a rage."

"I don't wonder."

Barnby shook his head and laughed. He did not like Gypsy, nor she him, and so far as he was concerned, that was an end of the matter. I saw his point, though personally I did not share the obduracy of his views. In fact there were moments when Gypsy turned up at the shop and we seemed to get on rather well together. Her egotism was of that entirely unrestrained kind, always hard to resist when accompanied by tolerable looks, a passionate self-absorption of the crudest kind, extending almost far enough to threaten the limits of sanity: with the added attraction of unfamiliar ways and thought. Besides, there was something disarming, almost touching, about her imperfectly concealed respect for " books," which played a considerable part in her conversation when not talking of " chalking " and other political activities. However—as Barbara might have said—there was no need to become sentimental. Gypsy usually showed herself, on the whole, more agreeable than on the first night we had met, but she could still be tiresome enough if the mood so took her.

" Jones is an excellent specimen of middle-class female education brought to its logical conclusions," Barnby used to say. " She couldn't be more perfect even if she had gone to the university. Her head is stuffed full of all the most pretentious nonsense you can think of, and she is incapable —but literally incapable—of thought. The upper and lower classes can sometimes keep their daughters in order—the middle classes rarely, if ever. I belong to the latter, and I know."

I felt this judgment unnecessarily severe. Claiming, as she did, some elementary knowledge of typing and short-hand, Gypsy was temporarily employed in some unspeci-fied capacity, next-door to Mr. Deacon's, at the offices of the Vox Populi Press: duties alleged by Barnby to be con-tingent on " sleeping with Craggs," managing director of that concern. There seemed no reason either to accept or refute this statement, for, as Mr. Deacon used to remark,

not without a touch of pride in his voice: "Indiscretion is
Gypsy's creed." There could be no doubt that she lived up
to this specification, although, as a matter of fact, shared
political sympathies might equally well have explained close
association with Craggs, since the Press (which was, in
truth, merely a small publishing business, and did not, as
its name implied, print its own publications) was primarily
concerned with producing books and pamphlets of an in-
surgent tone.

Mr. Deacon had talked a lot about his birthday party
before it had taken place, discussing at great length who
should, and who should not, be invited. He had determined, for some reason, that it was to be a " respectable "
gathering, though no one, not even Barnby and Gypsy Jones
knew where—or rather at whom—Mr. Deacon was likely
to draw the line. Naturally, these two were themselves to
be present, and they were to ask, at Mr. Deacon's suggestion, some of their own friends. However, when the
names of prospective candidates for invitation were actually
put forward, there had been a good deal of argument on
Mr. Deacon's part as to whether or not he could agree to
allow some of the postulants " in the house "—using the
phrase I remembered Stringham attaching to Peter Templer
years before—because a great many people, often unknown
to themselves, had, at one time or another, caused offence
to him in a greater or lesser degree. In the end he relented,
vetoing only a few of Barnby's female acquaintances: pro-
cedure which certainly caused no hard feelings on Barnby's
part.

Speaking for myself, I had been prepared for anything
at Mr. Deacon's party. I was conscious, as it happened, of
a certain sense of disappointment, even of annoyance, in my
own life, and weariness of its routine. This was because,

not many days before, I had rung up the Duports' house in
Hill Street, and a caretaker, or whoever had answered the
telephone, had informed me that the Duports had gone
abroad again, and were coming back in the spring. This
statement was accompanied by various hypotheses and sug-
gestions on the part of the speaker, embedded in a suitable
density of hesitation and subterfuge, that made the fact
that Jean was, as my informant put it, " expecting," no
longer a secret even before this definitive word itself
dropped into our conversation. This eventuality, I realised
at once, was something to be inevitably associated with the
married state; certainly not to be looked upon as unreasonable, or—as Mr. Deacon would say—" indiscreet."

All the same, I felt, as I have said, disappointed, although
aware that I could hardly claim that anything had taken
place to justify even the faintest suspicion of a broken
" romance." In fact, I could not even explain to myself
why it was, for some reason, necessary to make this denial
—that a relatively serious hope had been blighted—sufficiently clear in my own mind. In short, the situation encouraged the kind of mood that made the prospect of an entertainment such as Mr. Deacon's party promised to be,
acceptable rather than the reverse. The same pervading
spirit of being left, emotionally speaking, high and dry on a
not specially Elysian coast, had also caused a faint pang,
while having my hair cut, at seeing a picture of Prince
Theodoric, sitting on the sands of the Lido between Lady
Ardglass and a beautiful Brazilian, a reminder of the visit
to Stourwater that now seemed so long past, and also of the
perennial charm of female companionship in attractive surroundings. On thinking over this photograph, however, I
recalled that, even apart from circumstances inherent in our
different walks of life, the Prince's own preferred associate

had been Mrs. Wentworth, so that he, too, had probably
suffered a lack of fulfilment. Barnby had been delighted
when his attention had been drawn to this snapshot.

"I knew Baby would ditch Theodoric," he said. "I
wonder who the Brazilian girl was."

He had even expressed a hope that he might succeed in
bringing Mrs. Wentworth to Mr. Deacon's party.

"Somewhere where she would at least be sure of not
meeting Donners," he had added.

Certainly, Sir Magnus had not turned up at Mr.
Deacon's, nor, for that matter, anyone at all like him. The
sitting-room had been largely cleared of the many objects
over-flowed from the shop that were usually contained
there. Chairs and sofa had been pushed back to the walls,
which were hung on all sides, frame to frame, with his
own paintings, making a kind of memorial hall of Mr.
Deacon's art. Even this drastic treatment of the furniture
did not entirely exempt the place from its habitually old-
maidish air, which seemed, as a rule, to be vested in the
extraordinary number of knick-knacks, tear-bottles and tiny
ornamental cases for needles or toothpicks, that normally
littered every available space.

At either end of the mantelpiece stood a small oval frame
—the pair of them uniformly ornamented with sea shells—
one of which contained a tinted daguerreotype of Mr.
Deacon's mother, the other enclosing a bearded figure, the
likeness, so it appeared, of Walt Whitman, for whom Mr.
Deacon possessed a profound admiration. The late Mrs.
Deacon's features so much resembled her son's as for the
picture, at first sight, almost to cause the illusion that he
had himself posed, as a *jeu d'esprit*, in crinoline and pork-
pie hat. Juxtaposition of the two portraits was intended, I
suppose, to suggest that the American poet, morally and

intellectually speaking, represented the true source of Mr. Deacon's otherwise ignored paternal origins.

The atmosphere of the room had already become rather thick when I arrived upstairs that night, and a good many bottles and glasses were set about on occasional tables. After the meticulous process of selection to which they had been subjected, the first sight of the people assembled there came as something of an anti-climax; and Mr. Deacon's method of choosing was certainly not made at once apparent by a casual glance round the room. A few customers had been invited, picked from the ranks of those specially distinguished in buying expensive " antiques." These were mostly married couples, middle-aged to elderly, their position in life hard to define with any certainty. They laughed rather uneasily throughout the evening, in due course leaving early. The rest of the gathering was predominantly made up of young men, some of whom might reasonably have been considered to fall within Mr. Deacon's preferential category of " respectable," together with others whose claim to good repute was, at least outwardly, less pronounced : in some cases, even widely open to question.

There were, however, two persons present who, as it now seems to me, first revealed themselves at Mr. Deacon's party as linked together in that mysterious manner that circumscribes certain couples, and larger groups of human beings : a subject of which I have already spoken in connection with Widmerpool and myself. These two were Mark Members and Quiggin; although at that period I was, of course, unable to appreciate that this pair had already begun the course of their long pilgrimage together, regarding them as no more connected with each other than with myself. I had not set eyes upon Quiggin since coming down from the university, although, as it happened, I had already learnt that he was to be invited as the result of a chance remark let fall by Gypsy during discussion of arrangements to be made for the party.

" Don't let Quiggin get left over in the house at the end of the evening," she had said. " I don't want him snuffling round downstairs after I have just dropped off to sleep."

" Really, the ineffable vanity of woman," Mr. Deacon had answered sharply. " Quiggin will not molest you. He thinks too much about himself, for one thing, to bother about anyone else. You can set your mind at rest on that point."

" I'd rather be safe than sorry," said Gypsy. " He showed signs of making himself quite a nuisance the other night, you may like to know. I'm just warning you, Edgar."

Thinking the person named might well be the same Quiggin I had known as an undergraduate, I inquired about his personal appearance.

" Very plain, I'm afraid, poor boy," said Mr. Deacon. " With a shocking North-Country accent—though I suppose one should not say such a thing. He is a nephew of a client of mine in the Midlands. Rather hard up at the moment, he tells me, so he lends a hand in the shop from time to time. I'm surprised you have never run across him here. It gives him a pittance—and leisure to write. That's where his heart is."

" He is J. G. Quiggin, you know," said Gypsy. " You must have read things by him."

She may have thought that the importance she had ascribed to Quiggin as a potential source of nocturnal persecution of herself had been under-estimated by me, through ignorance of his relative eminence as a literary figure; and it was certainly true that I was unfamiliar with the name of the magazine mentioned by her as the organ to which he was said most regularly to contribute.

"No doubt about Quiggin's talent," said Mr. Deacon. "Though I don't like all his ideas. He's got a rough manner, too. All the same, he made himself very useful disposing of some books of a rather awkward sort—you need not snigger like that, Barnby—that I wanted to get rid of."

Trying to recall terms of our mutual relationship when we had last seen anything of each other, I could remember only that I had met Quiggin from time to time up to the early part of my second year at the university, when, for some reason, he had passed completely out of my life. In this process of individual drifting apart, there was, where university circles were concerned, of course, nothing out of the way: undergraduate acquaintance flourishing and decaying often within a matter of weeks. I could remember commenting at one of Sillery's tea-parties that Quiggin seemed not to have been about for some time, at which, so far as I could recall, Sillery, through the medium of considerable verbal convolution, had indicated, or at least implied, that Quiggin's scholarship had been withdrawn by his college on grounds of idleness, or some other cause of dissatisfaction to the authorities; and that, not long after this had happened, he had been "sent down." That story had been, I thought, more or less substantiated by Brightman, a don at Quiggin's college. Certainly Brightman, at some luncheon party, had referred to "that path trodden by scholarship boys whose mental equipment has been somewhat over-taxed at an earlier stage of their often injudiciously promoted education," and it was possible that he had used the case of Quiggin as an illustration.

I was rather impressed to hear that in the unfamiliar form of " J. G. Quiggin " this former acquaintance was already known as a " writer "; and admired, if only by Gypsy Jones. I also felt a little ashamed, perhaps merely on account of this apparent notoriety of his, to think, after finding in him something that had interested, if not exactly attracted, me, I had so easily forgotten about his existence.

My first sight of him at the party suggested that he had remained remarkably unchanged. He was still wearing his shabby black suit, the frayed trousers of which were maintained insecurely by a heavy leather belt with a brass buckle. His hair had grown a shade sparser round the sides of his dome-like forehead, and he retained that look of an undomesticated animal of doubtful temper. At the same time there was also his doggy, rather pathetic look about the eyes that had reminded me of Widmerpool, and which is a not uncommon feature of those who have decided to live by the force of the will. When we talked, I found that he had abandoned much of the conscious acerbity of manner that had been so much a part of social equipment at the university. It was not that he was milder—on the contrary, he seemed more anxious than ever to approach on his own terms every matter that arose—but he appeared to have come much nearer to perfection of method in his particular method of attacking life, so that for others there was not, as in former days, the same field of conversational pitfalls to be negotiated. No doubt this greater smoothness of intercourse was also to be explained by the fact that we had both " grown up " in the year or two that had passed. He asked some searching questions, comparable to Widmerpool's, regarding my firm's publications, almost immediately suggesting that he should write a preface for a book to be included in one or other of some series mentioned to him.

It was at that stage we had been joined by Members, rather to my surprise, because, as undergraduates, Members and Quiggin had habitually spoken of each other in a far from friendly manner. Now a change of relationship seemed to have taken place, or, it would perhaps be more exact to say, appeared desired by each of them; for there was no doubt that they were prepared, at least momentarily, to be on the best of terms. The three of us talked together, at first perhaps with a certain lack of ease, and then with greater warmth than I remembered in the past.

I had, in fact, met Members with Short, who was a believer in what he called "keeping up with interesting people," soon after I had come to live in London. This taste of Short's, with whom I occasionally had dinner or saw a film—as we had planned to do on the night when I had cut him for the Walpole-Wilson dinner-party—resulted in running across various former acquaintances not seen regularly as a matter of course, and Members, by now of some repute as a *littérateur*, was one of these. To find him at Mr. Deacon's was unexpected, however, for I had supposed Members, for some reason, to frequent literary circles of a more sedate kind, though quite why I should have thus regarded him I hardly know.

In contrast with Quiggin, Mark Members had altered considerably since his undergraduate period, when he had been known for the relative flamboyance of his dress. Him too I remembered chiefly from my first year at the university, though this was not because he had left prematurely, but rather on account of his passing into a world of local hostesses of more or less academical complexion, which I did not myself frequent. If I had considered the matter, it was to some similar layer of society in London that I should have pictured him attached : perhaps a reason for supposing him out of place at Mr. Deacon's. Possibly these ladies, most of them hard-headed enough in their own way, had been to some extent responsible for the almost revolutionary changes that had taken place in his appearance; for, even since our meeting with Short, Members had worked hard on his own exterior, in much the same manner that Quiggin had effected the interior modifications to which I have already referred.

There had once, for example, been at least a suggestion of side-whiskers, now wholly disappeared. The Byronic collar and loosely tied tie discarded, Members looked almost as neat round the neck as Archie Gilbert. His hair no longer hung in an uneven fringe, but was brushed severely away from his forehead at an acute angle; while he had also, by some means, ridded himself of most of his freckles, acquiring a sterner expression that might almost have been modelled on Quiggin's. In fact, he looked a rather distinguished young man, evidently belonging to the world of letters, though essentially to the end of that world least well disposed to Bohemianism in its grosser forms. He had been brought—Mr. Deacon had finally declared himself resigned to a certain number of uninvited guests, " modern manners being what they are "—by a strapping, black-haired model called Mona, a friend of Gypsy's belonging, so Barnby reported, to a stage of Gypsy's life before she was known to Mr. Deacon.

Short had told me that Members did occasional work for one of the " weeklies "—the periodical, in fact, that had commented rather disparagingly on Prince Theodoric's visit to England—and I had, indeed, read, with decided respect, some of the pieces there written by him. He had, I believed, failed to secure the "first" expected of him, by Sillery and others, at the end of his university career, but, like Bill Truscott in another sphere, he had never relinquished the reputation of being "a coming young man." Speaking of reviews written by Members, Short used to say: "Mark handles his material with remarkable facility," and, not without envy, I had to agree with that judgment; for this matter of writing was beginning to occupy an increasing amount of attention in my own mind. I had even toyed with the idea of attempting myself to begin work on a novel: an act that would thereby have brought to pass the assertion made at La Grenadière, merely as a conversational pretext to supply an answer to Widmerpool, to the effect that I possessed literary ambitions.

As I have already said of Mrs. Andriadis's party, such latitudes are entered by a door through which there is rarely if ever a return. In rather the same manner, that night at Mr. Deacon's seemed to crystallise certain matters. Perhaps this crystallisation had something to do with the presence there of Members and Quiggin, though they themselves were in agreement as to the displeasure they both felt in the company assembled.

"You must admit," said Members, looking round the room, "it all looks rather like that picture in the Tate of the Sea giving up the Dead that were in It. I can't think why Mona insisted on coming."

Quiggin concurred in finding Mr. Deacon's guests altogether unacceptable, at the same time paying suitable commendation to the aptness of the pictorial allusion. He looked across the room to where Mona was talking to Barnby, and said: "It is a very unusual figure, isn't it? Epstein would treat it too sentimentally, don't you think?,

Something more angular is required, in the manner of Lipchitz or Zadkine."

" She really *hates* men," said Members, laughing dryly.

His amusement was no doubt directed at the impracticability of the unspoken desires of Quiggin, who, perhaps with the object of moving to ground more favourable to himself, changed the subject.

" Did I hear that you had become secretary to St. John Clarke?" he asked, in a casual voice.

Members gave his rather high laugh again. This was evidently a matter he wished to be approached delicately. He seemed to have grown taller since coming to London. His slim waist and forceful, interrogative manner rather suggested one of those strong-willed, elegant young salesmen, who lead the customer from the shop only after the intention to buy a few handkerchiefs has been transmuted into a reckless squandering on shirts, socks, and ties, of patterns to be found later fundamentally unsympathetic.

" At first I could not make up my mind whether to take it," he admitted. " Now I am glad I decided in favour. St. J. is rather a great man in his way."

" Of course, one could not exactly call him a very great novelist," said Quiggin, slowly, as if deliberating the question carefully within himself. " But he is a *personality,* certainly, and some of his critical writing might be labelled as—well—shall we say ' not bad '?"

" They have a certain distinction of thought, of course, in their rather old-fashioned manner."

Members seemed relieved to concede this. He clearly felt that Quiggin, catching him in a weak position, had let him off lightly. St. John Clarke was the novelist of whom Lady Anne Stepney had spoken with approval. I had read some of his books towards the end of my time at school with great enjoyment; now I felt myself rather superior to his windy, descriptive passages, two-dimensional characterisation, and, so I had come to think, the emptiness of the writing's inner content. I was surprised to find someone I regarded as so impregnable in the intellectual field as I supposed Members to be, saddled with a figure who could only be looked upon by those with literary pretensions of any but the crudest kind as an Old Man of the Sea; although, in one sense, the metaphor should perhaps have been reversed, as it was Members who had, as it were, climbed upon the shoulders of St. John Clarke.

I can now see his defence of St. John Clarke as an interesting example of the power of the will, for his disinclination for St. John Clarke's works must have been at least equal to my own: possibly far in excess. As Members had made up his mind to accept what was probably a reasonable salary—though St. John Clarke was rather well known for being " difficult " about money—his attitude was undoubtedly a sagacious one; indeed, a great deal more discerning than my own, based upon decidedly romantic premises. The force of this justification certainly removed any question of Quiggin, as I had at first supposed he might, opening up some sort of critical attack on Members, based on the charge that St. John Clarke was a " bad writer." On the contrary, Quiggin now seemed almost envious that he had not secured the post for himself.

" Of course, if I had a job like that, I should probably say something one day that wouldn't go down," he commented, rather bitterly. " I've never had the opportunity to learn the way successful people like to be treated."

" St. J. knows your work," said Members, with quiet emphasis. " I brought it to his attention."

He watched Quiggin closely after saying this. Once more

I wondered whether there was any truth in Sillery's story, never verified in detail, to the effect that the two of them lived almost next-door in the same Midland town. In spite of Quiggin's uncouth, drab appearance, and the new spruceness of Members, there could be no doubt that they had something in common. As Quiggin's face relaxed at these complimentary words, I could almost have believed that they were cousins. Quiggin did not comment on the subject of this awareness of his own status as a writer now attributed to St. John Clarke, but, in friendly exchange, he began to question Members about his books, in process of being written or already in the press: projected works that appeared to be several in number—at least three, possibly four—consisting of poems, a novel, a critical study, together with something else, more obscure in form, the precise nature of which I have forgotten, as it never appeared.

" And you, J.G.?" asked Members, evidently not wishing to appear grudging.

" I am trying to remain one of the distinguished few who have not written a novel," said Quiggin, lightly. " The Vox Populi may be doing a fragment of autobiography of mine in the spring. Otherwise I just keep a few notes—odds and ends I judge of interest. I suppose they will find their way into print in due course. Everything does these days."

" No streams of consciousness, I hope," said Members, with a touch of malignity. " But the Vox Populi isn't much of a publishing house, is it? Will they pay a decent advance?"

" I get so sick of all the ' fine ' typography you see about," said Quiggin, dismissing the matter of money. " I've told Craggs to send it out to a jobbing printer, just as he would one of his pamphlets—print it on lavatory paper, if he likes. At least Craggs has the right political ideas."

"I question if there is much of the commodity you mention to be found on the premises of the Vox Populi," said Members, giving his thin, grating laugh. "But no doubt that *format* would ensure a certain sale. Don't forget to send me a copy, so that I can try and say something about it somewhere."

In leaving behind the kind of shell common to all undergraduates, indeed to most young men, they had, in one sense, taken more definite shape by each establishing conspicuously his own individual identity, thereby automatically drawing farther apart from each other. Regarded from another angle, however, Quiggin and Members had come, so it appeared, closer together by their concentration, in spite of differences of approach, upon the same, or at least very similar, aims. They could be thought of, perhaps, as representatives, if not of different cultures, at least of opposed traditions; Quiggin, a kind of abiding prototype of discontent against life, possessing at the same time certain characteristics peculiar to the period : Members, no less dissatisfied than Quiggin, but of more academic derivation, perhaps even sharing some of Mr. Deacon's intellectual origins.

Although he had already benefited from the tenets of what was possibly a dying doctrine, Members was sharp enough to be speedily jettisoning appurtenances, already deteriorated, of an outmoded æstheticism. Quiggin, with his old clothes and astringent manner, showed a similar sense of what the immediate future intimated. This was to be a race neck-and-neck, though whether the competitors themselves were already aware of the invisible ligament binding them together in apparently eternal contrast and

I

comparison, I do not know. Certainly the attitude that was to exist mutually between them—perhaps best described as " love-hate "—must have taken root long before anything of the sort was noticed by me. At the university their eclectic personalities had possessed, I had thought, a curious magnetism, unconnected with their potential talents. Now I was almost startled by the ease with which both of them appeared able to write books in almost any quantity; for Quiggin's relative abnegation in that field was clearly the result of personal choice, rather than lack of subject matter, or weakness in powers of expression.

Quiggin was showing no public indication of the attempts to ingratiate himself with Gypsy suggested by her earlier remarks. On the contrary, he seemed to be spending most of his time talking business or literary gossip of the kind in which he had indulged with Members. On the whole, he restricted himself to the men present, though once or twice he hovered, apparently rather ill at ease, in the vicinity of the model, Mona, in whom Barnby was also showing a certain interest. Gypsy had taken manifest steps to clean herself up for the party. She was wearing a bright, fussy little frock that emphasised her waif-like appearance. When I noticed her at a later stage of the evening's evolution, sitting on the knee of Howard Craggs, a tall, baldish man, in early middle age, with a voice like a radio announcer's, rich, oily, and precise in its accents, this sight made me think again of her brush with Widmerpool, and wish for a moment that I knew more of its details. Perhaps some processes of thought-transference afforded at that moment an unexpected dispensation from Gypsy herself of further enlightenment to my curiosity.

Craggs had been making fairly free for a considerable time in a manner that certainly suggested some truth in the aspersions put forward by Barnby. However, this perseverance on his part had apparently promoted no very ardent feeling of sympathy between them, there and then, for she was looking sullen enough. Now she suddenly scrambled out of his lap, straightening her skirt, and pushed her way across the room to where I was sitting on the sofa, talking—as I had been for some time—to a bearded man interested in musical-boxes. This person's connection with Mr. Deacon was maintained purely and simply through their common interest in the musical-box market, a fact the bearded man kept on explaining: possibly fearing that his reputation might otherwise seem cheap in my eyes. At the arrival of Gypsy, probably supposing that the party was getting too rough for a person of quiet tastes, he rose from his seat, remarking that he must be " finding Gillian and making for Hampstead." Gypsy took the deserted place. She sat there for a second or two without speaking.

" We don't much like each other, do we?" she said at length.

I replied, rather lamely, that, even supposing some such mutual hostility to exist between us, there was no good reason why anything of the sort should continue; and it was true that I was conscious, that evening, of finding her notably more engaging than upon earlier meetings, comparatively amicable though some of these had been.

" Have you been seeing much of your friend Widmerpool lately?" she asked.

" I've just had a letter from his mother inviting me to dine with them next week."

She laughed a lot at this news.

" I expect you heard he forked out," she said.

" I gathered something of the sort."

" Did he tell you himself?"

"In a manner of speaking."

"Was he fed up about it?"

"He was, rather."

She laughed again, though less noisily. I wondered what unthinkable passages had passed between them. It was evident that any interest, emotional or venal, invested by her in Widmerpool was now expended. There was something odious about her that made her, at the same time—I had to face this—an object of desire.

"After all, somebody had to cough up," she said, rather defensively.

"So I suppose."

"In the end he went off in a huff."

This statement seemed explicit enough. There could be little doubt now that she had made a fool of Widmerpool. I felt, at that moment, she was correct in assuming that I did not like her. She was at once aware of this disapproval.

"Why are you so stuck up?" she asked, truculently.

"I'm just made that way."

"You ought to fight it."

"I can't see why."

As far as I can remember, she went on to speak of the "social revolution," a subject that occupied a great deal of her conversation and Cragg's, too, while even Mr. Deacon could not hold his own in such discussions, though representing a wilder and less regimented point of view than the other two. I was relieved of the necessity of expressing my own opinions on this rather large question—rivalling in intensity Lady Anne Stepney's challenge to the effect that she was herself "on the side of the People" in the French Revolution—by the sudden appearance of Howard Craggs himself in the neighbourhood of the sofa upon which we were sitting; or rather, by then, lying, since for some reason she had put up her feet in such a manner as to require, so it seemed at the time, a change of position on my own part.

"I'm going soon, Gypsy," said Craggs in his horrible voice, as if speaking lines of recitation for some public performance, an illusion additionally suggested by the name itself. "Should you be requiring a lift?"

"I'm dossing down here," she said. "But I've got one or two things to tell you before you leave."

"All right, Gypsy, I'll have one more drink."

He shambled off. We chatted for a time in a desultory manner—and some sort of an embrace may even have taken place. Soon after that she had said that she must find Craggs and tell him whatever information she wished to pass on. The party was by then drawing to close, or at least changing its venue, with such disastrous consequences for its host. I did not see Mr. Deacon again, after saying good night to him on the pavement: nor Barnby until we met at the cremation.

Most funerals incline, through general atmosphere, to suggest the presence, or at least the more salient characteristics of the deceased; and, in the case of Mr. Deacon, the ceremony's emphasis was on the disorganised, undisciplined aspect of his character, rather than an echo of the shrewdness and precision that certainly made up the opposite side of his nature. Matters had been arranged by his sister, a small, grey-haired woman, whose appearance hardly at all recalled her brother. There had been some question as to what rites would be appropriate, as Mr. Deacon, latterly agnostic, was believed to have been a Catholic convert for some years as a young man. His sister had ruled out the suggestion of an undenominational service in favour of that

of the Church of England. Upon this subject, according to
Barnby, she had words with Gypsy Jones; with the result
that Gypsy, on anti-religious grounds, had finally refused to
attend the funeral. This withdrawal had not worried Mr.
Deacon's sister in the least. Indeed, it may have relieved
her, since there was reason to suppose that she suspected,
perhaps not unreasonably, the propriety of Gypsy's connection with the shop. However, Barnby was extremely annoyed.

" Just like the little bitch," he said.

The weather had turned warmer, almost muggy. About
a dozen or fifteen people showed up, most of them belonging to that race of shabby, anonymous mourners who form
the bulk of the congregation at all obsequies, whether high
or low, rich or poor; almost as if the identical band trooped
round unceasingly—like Archie Gilbert to his dances—
from interment to interment. Among the leaden-coloured
garments of these perpetual attendants upon Death, the
lightish suit of a tall young man in spectacles stood out.
The face was, for some reason, familiar to me. During
the responses his high, quavering voice, repeating the words
from the row behind, resounded throughout the little
chapel. The sound was churchly, yet not of the Church.
Then I remembered that this young man was Max Pilgrim,
the " public entertainer "—as Mr. Deacon had called him—
with whom the scene had taken place at the end of Mrs.
Andriadis's party. At the close of the service, his willowy
figure shuddering slightly as he walked, Pilgrim hurried
away. The reasons that had brought him there, however
commendable, were only to be conjectured, and could be
interpreted according to taste.

" That was a desperate affair," Barnby had said, as we returned to the shop together.

We climbed the stairs to his studio, where, in preparation for tea, he put a kettle on a gas-ring, and, although it was still warm, lighted the fire; then, changing into overalls, began to prepare a canvas. I lay on the divan. We talked of Mr. Deacon for a time, until conversation fell into more general channels, and Barnby began to discourse on the subject of love.

"Most of us would like to be thought of as the kind of man who has a lot of women," he said. "But take such fellows as a whole, there are few enough of them one would wish to be at all like."

"Do you wish to change your identity?"

"Not in the least. Merely to improve my situation in certain specific directions."

"Which particular Don Juan were you thinking of?"

"Oh, myself, of course," said Barnby. "Funerals make one's mind drift in the direction of moral relaxation—though it's unaccountable to me the way intimate relations between the sexes are always spoken of, and written about, as if of necessity enjoyable or humorous. In practice they might much more truly be described as encompassing the whole range of human feeling from the height of bliss to the depths of misery."

"Is something on your mind?"

Barnby agreed that this diagnosis was correct. He was about to enter into some further explanation, when as if making a kind of rejoinder to the opinion just expressed, the bell of the telephone began to ring from below. Barnby wiped his hands on a cloth, and went off down the stairs to where the instrument stood on a ledge by the back entrance to the shop. For a time I heard him talking. Then he returned to the room, greatly exhilarated.

"That was Mrs. Wentworth," he said. "I was about to

tell you when the telephone went that she was, in fact, the matter on my mind."

" Is she coming round here?"

" Better than that. She wants me to go round and see her right away. Do you mind? Finish your tea, of course, and stay here as long as you like."

He tore off his overalls, and, without attempting to tidy up the material of his painting, was gone almost immediately. I had never before seen him so agitated. The front door slammed. A sense of emptiness fell on the house.

In the circumstances, I could not possibly blame Barnby for absenting himself so precipitately, experiencing at the same time a distinct feeling of being left in a void, not less so on account of the substance of our conversation that had been in this way terminated so abruptly. I poured out another cup of tea, and thought over some of the things he had been saying. I could not help envying the opportune nature, so far as Barnby himself was concerned, of the telephone call, which seemed an outward indication of the manner in which he had—so it seemed to me in those days—imposed his will on the problem at hand.

His life's unusual variety of form provided a link between what I came, in due course, to recognise as the world of Power, as represented, for example, by the ambitions of Widmerpool and Truscott, and that imaginative life in which a painter's time is of necessity largely spent: the imagination, in such a case, being primarily of a visual kind. In the conquest of Mrs. Wentworth, however, other spheres—as the figures of Sir Magnus Donners and Prince Theodoric alone sufficiently illustrated—had inevitably to be invaded by him. These hinterlands are frequently, even compulsively, crossed at one time or another by almost all who practise the arts, usually in the need to earn a living;

but the arts themselves, so it appeared to me as I considered the matter, by their ultimately sensual essence, are, in the long run, inimical to those who pursue power for its own sake. Conversely, the artist who traffics in power does so, if not necessarily disastrously, at least at considerable risk. I was making preparations to occupy my mind with such thoughts until it was time to proceed to the Widmerpools', but the room was warm, and, for a time, I dozed.

Nothing in life can ever be entirely divorced from myriad other incidents; and it is remarkable, though no doubt logical, that action, built up from innumerable causes, each in itself allusive and unnoticed more often than not, is almost always provided with an apparently ideal moment for its final expression. So true is this that what has gone before is often, to all intents and purposes, swallowed up by the aptness of the climax, opportunity appearing, at least on the surface, to be the sole cause of fulfilment. The circumstances that had brought me to Barnby's studio supplied a fair example of this complexity of experience. There was, however, more to come.

When I awoke from these sleepy, barely coherent reflections, I decided that I had had enough of the studio, which merely reminded me of Barnby's apparent successes in a field in which I was then, generally speaking, feeling decidedly unsuccessful. Without any very clear idea of how I would spend my time until dinner, I set off down the stairs, and had just reached the door that led from the back of the shop to the foot of the staircase, when a female voice from the other side shouted: "Who is that?"

My first thought was that Mr. Deacon's sister had returned to the house. After the cremation, she had announced herself as retiring for the rest of the day to her hotel in Bloomsbury, as she was suffering from a headache.

I supposed now that she had changed her mind, and decided to continue the task of sorting her brother's belongings, regarding some of which she had already consulted Barnby, since there were books and papers among Mr. Deacon's property that raised a number of questions of disposal, sometimes of a somewhat delicate kind. She had probably come back to the shop and again sought guidance on some matter. It was to be hoped that the point would not prove an embarrassing one. However, when I said my name, the person beyond the door turned out to be Gypsy.

"Come in for a moment," she called.

I turned the handle and entered. She was standing behind the screen, in the shadows, at the back of the shop. My first impression was that she had stripped herself stark naked. There was, indeed, good reason for this misapprehension, for a second look showed that she was wearing a kind of bathing-dress, flesh-coloured, and of unusually sparing cut. I must have showed my surprise, because she burst into a paroxysm of laughter.

"I thought you would like to see my dress for the Merry Thought fancy-dress party," she said. "I am going as Eve."

She came closer.

"Where is Barnby?" she asked.

"He went out. Didn't you hear him go? After he spoke on the telephone."

"I've only just come in," she said. "I wanted to try out my costume on both of you."

She sounded disappointed at having missed such an opportunity to impress Barnby, though I thought the display would have annoyed rather than amused him; which was no doubt her intention.

" Won't you be cold?"

" The place is going to be specially heated. Anyway, the weather is mild enough. Still, shut the door. There's a bit of a draught."

She sat down on the divan. That part of the shop was shut off from the rest by the screen in such a way as almost to form a cubicle. As Mr. Deacon had described, shawls or draperies of some sort were spread over the surface of this piece of furniture.

" What do you think of the fig leaf?" she asked. " I made it myself."

I have already spoken of the common ground shared by conflicting emotions. As Barnby had remarked, the funeral had been " hard on the nerves," and a consciousness of sudden relief from pressure was stimulating. Gypsy, somewhat altering the manner she had adopted on my first arrival in the shop, now managed to look almost prim. She had the air of waiting for something, of asking a question to which she already knew the answer. There was also something more than a little compelling about the atmosphere of the alcove : the operation perhaps of memories left over as a residue from former states of concupiscence, although so fanciful a condition could hardly be offered in extenuation. I asked myself whether this situation, or something not far from it, was not one often premeditated, and, although I still felt one half awake, not to be lightly passed by.

The lack of demur on her part seemed quite in accordance with the almost somnambulistic force that had brought me into that place, and also with the torpid, dream-like atmosphere of the afternoon. At least such protests as she put forward were of so formal and artificial an order that they increased, rather than diminished, the impression

that a long-established rite was to be enacted, among
Staffordshire figures and *papier-mâché* trays, with the compelling, detached formality of nightmare. Perhaps some
demand, not to be denied in its overpowering force, had
occasioned simultaneously both this summons and Mrs.
Wentworth's telephone call; each product of that slow
process of building up of events, as already mentioned,
coming at last to a head. I was conscious of Gypsy changing her individuality, though at the same time retaining
her familiar form : this illusion almost conveying the extraordinary impression that there were really three of us—
perhaps even four, because I was aware that alteration had
taken place within myself too—of whom the pair of active
participants had been, as it were, projected from out of our
normally unrelated selves.

In spite of the apparently irresistible nature of the circumstances, when regarded through the larger perspective that
seemed, on reflection, to prevail—that is to say of a general
subordination to an intricate design of cause and effect—I
could not help admitting, in due course, the awareness of a
sense of inadequacy. There was no specific suggestion that
anything had, as it might be said, "gone wrong", it was
merely that any wish to remain any longer present in those
surroundings had suddenly and violently decreased, if not
disappeared entirely. This feeling was, in its way, a shock.
Gypsy, for her part, appeared far less impressed than myself by consciousness of anything, even relatively moment-
ous, having occurred. In fact, after the brief interval of
extreme animation, her subsequent indifference, which
might almost have been called torpid, was, so it seemed to
me, remarkable. This imperturbability was inclined to
produce an impression that, so far from knowing each other
a great deal better, we had progressed scarcely at all in that

direction; perhaps, become more than ever, even irretrievably, alienated. Barbara's recurrent injunction to avoid any question of " getting sentimental " seemed, here in the embodiment of Gypsy, now carried to lengths which might legitimately be looked upon as such a principle's logical conclusion.

This likeness to Barbara was more clearly indicated, however, than by a merely mental comparison of theory, because, while Gypsy lay upon the divan, her hands before her, looking, perhaps rather self-consciously, a little like Goya's *Maja nude*—or possibly it would be nearer the mark to cite that picture's derivative, Manet's *Olympia*, which I had, as it happened, heard her mention on some former occasion—she glanced down, with satisfaction, at her own extremities.

" How brown my leg is," she said. " Fancy sunburn lasting that long."

Were Barbara and Gypsy really the same girl, I asked myself. There was something to be said for the theory; for I had been abruptly reminded of Barbara's remark, uttered under the trees of Belgrave Square earlier in the year: "How blue my hand is in the moonlight." Self-admiration apart, there could be no doubt now that they had a great deal in common. It was a concept that made me feel that, in so far as I was personally involved in matters of sentiment, the season was, romantically speaking, autumn indeed, and that the leaves had undeniably fallen from the trees so far as former views on love were concerned: even though such views had been held by me only so short a time before. Here, at least, at the back of Mr. Deacon's shop, some conclusion had been reached, though even that inference, too, might be found open to question. At the same time, I could not help being struck, not only by a kind of wonder that I now found myself, as it were, with Barbara in conditions once pictured as beyond words vain of achievement, but also at that same moment by a sense almost of solemnity at this latest illustration of the pattern that life forms. A new phase in conversation was now initiated by a question from Gypsy.

"What was the funeral like?" she asked, as if making a deliberate return to every-day conditions.

"Short."

"I think I was right not to go."

"You didn't miss much."

"It was a matter of conscience."

She developed for a time this line of thought, and I agreed that, regarded in the light of her convictions, her absence might be looked upon as excusable, if any such severity of doctrine was indeed insurmountable. I agreed further that Mr. Deacon himself might have appreciated such scruples.

"Max Pilgrim was there."

"The man who sings the songs?"

"He didn't at the cremation."

"There comes a moment when you've got to make a stand."

I presumed that she had returned to the problems of her own conscience rather than to refer to Pilgrim's restraint in having kept himself from breaking into song at the crematorium.

"Where will you stay now that the shop is coming to an end?"

"Howard says he can put me up once in a way at the Vox Populi. They've got a camp-bed there. He's taking me to the party to-night."

"What's he going as?"

"Adam."

"Is he arriving here in that guise?"

"We're dining early, and going back to his place to dress up. Only I thought I must try out my costume first. As a matter of fact he is picking me up here fairly soon."

She looked rather doubtful, and I saw that I must not overstay my welcome. There was nothing to be said for allowing time to slip by long enough for Craggs to arrive. It appeared that Gypsy was going to the country—it was to be presumed with Craggs—in the near future. We said good-bye. Later, as I made my way towards the Widmerpools', association of ideas led inevitably to a reminder, not a specially pleasant one, of Widmerpool himself and his desires; parallel, it appeared, in their duality, with my own, and fated to be defrauded a second time. The fact that I was dining at his flat that evening in no way reduced the accentuation given by events to that sense of design already mentioned. Whatever the imperfections of the situation from which I had just emerged, matters could be considered with justice only in relation to a much larger configuration, the vast composition of which was at present —that at least was clear—by no means even nearly completed.

There is a strong disposition in youth, from which some individuals never escape, to suppose that everyone else is having a more enjoyable time than we are ourselves; and, for some reason, as I moved southwards across London, I was that evening particularly convinced that I had not yet succeeded in striking a satisfactory balance in my manner of conducting life. I could not make up my mind whether the deficiencies that seemed so stridently to exist were attributable to what had already happened that day, or to a growing certainty in my own mind that I should much prefer to be dining elsewhere. The Widmerpools—for I felt that I had already heard so much of Widmerpool's mother that my picture of her could not be far from the truth—were the last persons on earth with whom I wished to share the later part of the evening. I suppose I could have had a meal by myself, thinking of some excuse later to explain my absence, but the will to take so decisive a step seemed to have been taken physically from me.

They lived, as Widmerpool had described, on the top floor of one of the smaller erections of flats in the neighbourhood of Westminster Cathedral. The lift, like an ominously creaking funicular, swung me up to these mountainous regions, and to a landing where light shone through frosted panes of glass. The door was opened by a depressed elderly maid, wearing cap and pince-nez, who showed me into a drawing-room, where Widmerpool was sitting alone, reading *The Times*. I was dimly aware of a picture called *The Omnipresent* hanging on one of the walls, in which three figures in bluish robes stand or kneel on the edge of a precipice. Widmerpool rose, crumpling the paper, as if he were surprised to see me, so that for a painful moment I wondered whether, by some unhappy mistake, I had arrived on the wrong night. However, a second later, he made some remark to show I was expected, and asked me to sit down, explaining that " in a minute or two " his mother would be ready.

" I am very much looking forward to your meeting my mother," he said.

He spoke as if introduction to his mother was an experience, rather a vital one, that every serious person had, sooner or later, to undergo. I became all at once aware that this was the first occasion upon which he and I had met anywhere but on neutral ground. I think that Widmerpool, too, realised that a new relationship had immediately risen between us from the moment when I had entered the drawing-room; for he smiled in a rather embarrassed way, after making this remark about his mother, and seemed to make an effort, more conscious than any he had ever shown before, to appear agreeable. In view of the embarrassments he had spoken of when we had last met—and their apparent conclusion so far as he were concerned—I had expected to find him depresed. On the contrary, he was in unusually high spirits.

"Miss Walpole-Wilson is supping with us," he said.

"Eleanor?"

"Oh, no," he said, as if such a thing were unthinkable. "Her aunt. Such a knowledgeable woman."

Before any comment were possible, Mrs. Widmerpool herself came through the door, upon the threshold of which she paused for a moment, her head a little on one side.

"Why, Mother," said Widmerpool, speaking with approval, "you are wearing your bridge-coat."

We shook hands, and she began to speak at once, before I could take in her appearance.

"And so you were both at Mr. Le Bas's house at school," she said. "I never really cared for him as a man. I expect he had his good qualities, but he never quite appreciated Kenneth."

"He was an odd man in many ways."

"Kenneth so rarely brings the friends of his school days here."

I said that we had also stayed together with the same French family in Touraine; for, if I had to be regarded as a close friend of her son's, it was at La Grenadière that I had come to know him best, rather than at school, where he had always seemed a figure almost too grotesque to take seriously.

"At the Leroys'?" she asked, as if amazed at the brilliance of my parents in having hit on the only possible household in the whole of France.

"For six weeks or so."

She turned to Widmerpool.

"But you never told me that," she said. "That was naughty of you!"

"Why should I?" said Widmerpool. "You didn't know him."

Mrs. Widmerpool clicked her tongue against the roof of her mouth. Her large features distinctly recalled the lineaments of her son, though she had perhaps been good looking when younger. Even now she seemed no more than in her late forties, though I believe she was, in fact, older than that. However, her well-preserved appearance was in striking contrast with Widmerpool's own somewhat decaying youth, so that the pair of them appeared almost more like contemporaries, even husband and wife, rather than mother and son. Her eyes were brighter than his, and she rolled them, expanding the pupils, in comment to any remark that might be thought at all out of the ordinary. Her double row of firm teeth were set between cheeks of brownish red, which made her a little resemble Miss Walpole-Wilson, with whom she clearly possessed something discernibly in common that explained their friendly connection. She seemed a person of determination, from whom no doubt her son derived much of his tenacity of purpose. The garment to which he referred was of flowered velvet, with a fringe, and combined many colours in its pattern.

"I hear you know the Gorings," she said. "It seems such

a pity they have allowed Barbara to run so wild. She used
to be such a dear little girl. There really appears to be
something a trifle queer about Lord Aberavon's grand-
children."

"Oh, shut up, Mother," said Widmerpool, changing his
almost amatory manner unexpectedly. "You don't know
anything about it."

He must have felt, not entirely without reason, that his
mother was on delicate ground in bringing up so early,
and in such a critical spirit, the subject of Gorings and
Walpole-Wilsons. Mrs. Widmerpool seemed not at all put
out by the brusque form of address used by her son, continuing to express herself freely on the characteristics, in
her eyes, good, bad and indifferent, of Barbara and Eleanor,
adding that she understood that neither of the Goring
sons were "very much of a hand at their books." She felt
perhaps that now was the time to unburden herself upon
matters hardly to be pursued with the same freedom after
the arrival of Miss Janet Walpole-Wilson. From her comments, I supposed that Widmerpool must have given his
mother, perhaps involuntarily, some indication that the
Gorings were out of favour with him; although it was
impossible to guess how accurately she might be informed
about her son's former feelings for Barbara: even if she
knew of them at all. It was possible that she had attributed
the anxiety he had gone through with Gypsy Jones to a later
aggravation of his entanglement with Barbara: in fact,
the same conclusion to which I had myself first arrived,
when, at Stourwater, he had spoken of the troubles that
were oppressing him.

"There doesn't seem any sign of Eleanor getting married
yet," said Mrs. Widmerpool, almost dreamily, as if she were
descrying in the depths of the gas-fire a vision invisible to

the rest of us, revealing the unending cavalcade of Eleanor's potential suitors.

"Perhaps she doesn't want to," said Widmerpool, in a tone evidently intended to close the subject. "I expect you two will like a talk on books before the end of the evening."

"Yes, indeed, for I hear you are in the publishing trade," said his mother. "You know, I have always liked books and bookish people. It is one of my regrets that Kenneth is really too serious minded to enjoy reading for its own sake. I expect you are looking forward to those articles in *The Times* by Thomas Hardy's widow. I know I am."

While I was making some temporising answer to these reassurances on Mrs. Widmerpool's part regarding her inclination towards literature, Miss Walpole-Wilson was announced, who excused her lateness on the grounds of the chronic irregularity of the bus service from Chelsea, where her flat was situated. She was wearing a mackintosh, of which, for some reason, she had refused to divest herself in the hall; exemplifying in this manner a curious trait common to some persons of wilful nature, whose egotism seems often to make them unwilling, even incapable, of shedding anything of themselves until they can feel that they have safely reached their goal. She now removed this waterproof, folding and establishing it upon a chair—an act watched by her hostess with a fixed smile that might have signified disapproval—revealing that she, too, was wearing a richly-coloured coat. It was made of orange, black, and gold silk : a mandarin's coat, so she explained, that Sir Gavin had given her years before.

The relationship between Mrs. Widmerpool and Miss Walpole-Wilson, in general an amicable one, gave the impression of resting not exactly upon planned alliance so much as community of interest, unavoidable from the nature of the warfare both waged against the rest of the world. Miss Walpole-Wilson was, of course, as she sometimes described herself, "a woman of wide interests," while Mrs. Widmerpool concerned herself with little that had not some direct reference to the career of her son. At the same time there was an area of common ground where disparagement of other people brought them close together, if only on account of the ammunition with which each was able to provide the other : mutual aid that went far to explain a friendship long established.

Miss Walpole-Wilson's manner that evening seemed intended to notify the possession of some important piece of news to be divulged at a suitable moment. She had, indeed, the same air as Widmerpool : one, that is to say, suggesting that she was unusually pleased with herself. We talked for a time, until the meal was despondently announced by the decrepit house-parlourmaid, who, a minute or two later, after we had sat down to cold food in a neighbouring room, hurried plates and dishes round the table with reckless speed, as if she feared that death—with which the day seemed still associated in my mind—would intervene to terminate her labours. There was a bottle of white wine. I asked Miss Walpole-Wilson whether she had been seeing much of Eleanor.

"Eleanor and I are going for a sea trip together," she said. "A banana boat to Guatemala."

"Rather wise to get her away from her family for a bit," said Mrs. Widmerpool, making a grimace.

"Her father is full of old-fashioned ideas," said Miss Walpole-Wilson, "and he won't be laughed out of them."

"Eleanor will enjoy the free life of the sea," Mrs. Widmerpool agreed.

"Of course she will," said Miss Walpole-Wilson; and,

pausing for a brief second to give impetus to her question, added: "You have heard, I expect, about Barbara?"

It was clear from the way she spoke that she felt safe in assuming that none of us could possibly have heard already whatever her news might be. I thought, though the supposition may have been entirely mistaken, that for an instant she fixed her eyes rather malignantly on Widmerpool; and certainly there was no reason to suggest that she knew anything of his former interest in Barbara. However, if she intended to tease him, she scored a point, for at mention of the name his face at once took on a somewhat guilty expression. Mrs. Widmerpool inquired curtly what had happened. She also seemed to feel that Miss Walpole-Wilson might be trying to provoke her son.

"Barbara is engaged," said Miss Walpole-Wilson, smiling, though without good-humour.

"Who to?" asked Widmerpool, abruptly.

"I can't remember whether you know him," she said. "He is a young man in the Guards. Rich, I think."

I felt certain, immediately, that she must refer to someone I had never met. Many people can never hear of any engagement without showing envy, and no one can be quite disinterested who has been at one time an implicated party. The thought that the man would turn out to be unknown to me was, therefore, rather a relief.

"But what is the name?" said Widmerpool, insistently.

He was already nettled. There could be no doubt that Miss Walpole-Wilson was deliberately tormenting him, although I could not decide whether this was simply her usual technique in delaying the speed at which she passed on gossip with the object of making it more appetising, or because she knew, either instinctively or from specific information in her possession, that he had been concerned with Barbara. For a moment or two she smiled round the table frostily.

"He is called Pardoe," she said, at last. "I think his other name is John."

"Her parents *must* be pleased," said Mrs. Widmerpool. "I always thought that Barbara was becoming—well—almost a problem in a small way. She got so noisy. Such a pity when that happens to a girl."

I could see from Widmerpool's pursed lips and glassy eyes that he was as astonished as myself. The news went some way to dispel his air of self-satisfaction, that had seemed only momentarily displaced by irritation with Miss Walpole-Wilson before this announcement. I was myself conscious of a faint sense of bitterness, rather indefinite in its application. Among the various men who had, at one time or another, caused me apprehension, just or unjust, in connection with Barbara, Pardoe had never at any moment, figured in the smallest degree. Why this immunity from my jealousy should have attached to him, I was now quite unable to understand, when, in the light of the information just imparted, I considered past incidents. Even after deciding that I was no longer in love with Barbara, I could still slightly resent her attitude towards Tompsitt; but objection—like Widmerpool's—to her crossing the supper-room to sit with Pardoe would never have entered my mind.

In fact, Widmerpool's instinct on the matter, if not his action, had, in one sense, been sound, so it now appeared; though it was true that his own emotions were still at that time deeply involved, a condition having a natural tendency to sharpen all perceptions in that particular direction. The manner in which jealousy operates is, indeed, curious enough, having perhaps relatively little bearing on the

practical menace offered by a rival. Barnby used to describe a husband and lover known to him, who had both
combined against a third—or rather fourth—party, found
to be intervening. However, that situation was, of course,
poles apart from the one under examination. Widmerpool
now made an effort to control his voice.

"When did this happen?" he asked, speaking casually.

"I think they actually became engaged in Scotland," said
Miss Walpole-Wilson, pleased with the impression she had
made. "But it has not been made public yet."

There was a pause. Widmerpool had failed to rise above
the situation. For the moment he had lost all his good-
humour. I think he was cross not only at Barbara's engagement, but also at the inability he was experiencing to conceal his own annoyance. I felt a good deal of sympathy for
him in what he was going through.

"Rather a ridiculous little man," he said, after a time.
"Still, the fortune is a large one, and I have been told it is
a nice house. I hope she will be very happy."

"Barbara has great possibilities," said Miss Walpole-
Wilson. "I don't know how she will like being an officer's
wife. Personally, I always find soldiers so dull."

"Oh, not in the *Guards*, surely?" said Mrs. Widmerpool,
baring her teeth, as if in expectation, or memory, of behaviour on the part of Guardsmen infinitely removed from
anything that could be regarded as dull, even by the most
satiated.

"Of course, one of Barbara's brothers went into the
Army," said Miss Walpole-Wilson, as if that might be
calculated to soften the blow.

Discussion of the engagement continued in a desultory
manner. Such matters are habitually scrutinised from
angles that disregard almost everything that might be truly

looked upon as essential in connection with a couple's married life together; so that, as usual, it was hard to think with even moderate clearness how the marriage would turn out. The issues were already hopelessly confused, not only by Miss Walpole-Wilson and Mrs. Widmerpool, but also by anarchical litter enveloping the whole subject, more especially in the case of the particular pair concerned: a kind of phantasmagoria taking possession of the mind at the thought of them as husband and wife. The surroundings provided by the Widmerpool flat were such as to encourage, for some reason, the wildest flights of imagination, possibly on account of some inexplicable moral inadequacy in which its inhabitants seemed themselves to exist. Barbara's engagement lasted as a topic throughout the meal.

" Shall we leave the gentlemen to their port?" said Mrs. Widmerpool, when finally the subject had been picked bone-dry.

She mouthed the words " gentlemen " and " port " as if they might be facetiously disputable as strictly literal descriptions in either case. Widmerpool shut the door, evidently glad to be rid of both women for the time being. I wondered whether he would begin to speak of Barbara or Gypsy. To my surprise, neither girl turned out to be his reason for his so impatiently desiring a *tête-à-tête* conversation.

"I say, I've had an important move up at Donners-Brebner," he said. " That speech at the Incorporated Metals dinner had repercussions. The Chief was pleased about it."

" Did he forgive you for knocking his garden about?"

Widmerpool laughed aloud at the idea that such a matter should have been brought up against him.

"You know," he said, " you sometimes make me feel

that you must live completely out of the world. A man like
Sir Magnus Donners does not bother about an accident of
that sort. He has something more important to worry
about. For example, he said to me the other day that he
did not give tuppence what degrees a man had. What he
wanted was someone who knew the ropes and could think
and act quickly."

"I remember him saying something of the sort when
Charles Stringham went into Donners-Brebner."

"Stringham is leaving us now that he is married. Just
as well, in my opinion. I believe Truscott really thinks
so too. People talk a great deal about 'charm,' but something else is required in business, I can assure you. Perhaps
Stringham will settle down now. I believe he had some
rather undesirable connections."

I inquired what Stringham was going to do now that
he was departing from Donners-Brebner, but Widmerpool
was ignorant on that point. I was unable to gather from
him precisely what form his own promotion, with which
he was so pleased, would take, though he implied that he
would probably go abroad in the near future.

"I think I may be seeing something of Prince Theodoric," he said. "I believe you just met him."

"Sir Gavin Walpole-Wilson could tell you all about
Theodoric."

"I think I may say I have better sources of information
at hand than to be derived from diplomats who have
been 'unstuck'," said Widmerpool, with complacency. "I
have been brought in touch recently with a man you probably know from your university days, Sillery—'Sillers'—
I find him quite a character in his way."

Feeling in no mood to discuss Sillery with Widmerpool,
I asked him what he thought about Barbara and Pardoe.

" I suppose it was only to be expected," he said, reddening a bit.

" But had you any idea?"

" I really do not devote my mind to such matters."

In saying this, I had no doubt that he was speaking the truth. He was one of those persons capable of envisaging others only in relation to himself, so that, when in love with Barbara, it had been apparently of no interest to him to consider what other men might stand in the way. Barbara was either in his company, or far from him; the latter state representing a kind of void in which he was uninterested except at such a moment as that at the Huntercombes', when her removal was brought painfully to his notice. Turning things over in my mind, I wondered whether I could be regarded as having proved any more sentient myself. However, I felt now that the time had come to try and satisfy my curiosity about the other business.

" What about the matter you spoke of at Stourwater?"

Widmerpool pushed back his chair. He took off his spectacles and rubbed the lenses. I had the impression that he was about to make some important pronouncement, rather in the manner of the Prime Minister allowing some aspect of governmental policy to be made known at the Lord Mayor's Banquet or Royal Academy Dinner.

" I am glad you asked that," he said, slowly. " I wondered if you would. Will you do me a great favour?"

" Of course—if I can."

" Never mention the subject again."

" All right."

" I behaved unwisely, perhaps, but I gained something."

" You did?"

I had accented the question in the wrong manner. Widmerpool blushed again.

" Possibly we do not mean the same thing," he said. " I referred to being brought in touch with a new side of life—even new political opinions."

" I see."

" I am going to tell you something else about myself."

" Go ahead."

" No woman who takes my mind off my work is ever to play a part in my life in the future."

" That sounds a wise decision so far as it goes."

" And another thing . . ."

" Yes?"

" If I were you, Nicholas—I hope, by the way, you will call me Kenneth in future, we know each other well enough by now to use Christian names—I should avoid all that set. Deacon and the whole lot of them. You won't get any good out of it."

" Deacon is dead."

" What?"

" I went to the funeral this afternoon. He was cremated."

" Really," said Widmerpool.

He demanded no details, so I supplied none. I felt now that we were, in a curious way, fellow-conspirators, even though Widmerpool might be unaware of this, and I was myself not unwilling to connive at his desire to draw a veil over the matter of which we had spoken. For a time we talked of other things, such as the arrangements to be made when he went abroad. After a while we moved into the next room, where Miss Walpole-Wilson was describing experiences in the Far East. When I left, at a comparatively early hour, she was still chronicling the occasion when she had trudged across the face of Asia.

" You must come again soon," said Mrs. Widmerpool. " We never managed to have our chat about books."

During the descent in the lift, still groaning precariously, thinking over Widmerpool and his mother, and their life together, it came to me in a flash who it was Mrs. Andriadis had resembled when I had seen her at the party in Hill Street. She recalled, so I could now see, two persons I had met, and although these two were different enough from each other, their elements, or at least some of them, were combined in her These two were Stringham's mother and her former secretary, Miss Weedon. I remembered the dialogue that had taken place when Stringham had quarrelled with Mrs Andriadis at the end of that night. "As you wish, Milly," he had said; just as I could imagine him, in his younger days, saying to Miss Weedon: "As you wish, Tuffy," at the termination of some trivial dispute at his home.

It was a moonlight night. That region has an atmosphere peculiar to itself, separated in spirit as far from the historic gloom of Westminster's more antique streets as from the *louche* seediness and Victorian decay of the wide squares of Pimlico beyond Vauxhall Bridge Road. For some reason, perhaps the height of the tower, or more probably the prodigal inappropriateness to London of the whole structure's architectural style, the area immediately adjacent to the cathedral imparts a sense of vertigo, a dizziness almost alarming in its intensity: lines and curves of red brick appearing to meet in a kind of vortex, rather than to be ranged in normal forms of perspective. I had noticed this before when entering the terrain from the north, and now the buildings seemed that evening almost as if they might swing slowly forward from their bases, and downward into complete prostration

Certain stages of experience might be compared with the game of Russian billiards, played (as I used to play with Jean, when the time came) on those small green tables, within the secret recesses of which, at the termination of a given passage of time—a quarter of an hour, I think—the hidden gate goes down; after the descent of which, the white balls and the red return no longer to the slot to be replayed; and all scoring is doubled. This is perhaps an image of how we live. For reasons not always at the time explicable, there are specific occasions when events begin suddenly to take on a significance previously unsuspected, so that, before we really know where we are, life seems to have begun in earnest at last, and we ourselves, scarcely aware that any change has taken place, are careering uncontrollably down the slippery avenues of eternity.

Anthony Powell

'Powell is very like a drug, the more compelling the more you read him.' *Sunday Times*

A Dance to the Music of Time

'The most remarkable feat of sustained fictional creation in our day.' *Guardian*

A Question of Upbringing
A Buyer's Market
The Acceptance World
At Lady Molly's
Casanova's Chinese Restaurant
The Kindly Ones
The Valley of Bones
The Soldier's Art
The Military Philosophers
Books Do Furnish a Room
Temporary Kings
Hearing Secret Harmonies

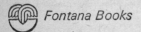 *Fontana Books*

Fontana Books

Fontana is a leading paperback publisher of fiction and non-fiction, with authors ranging from Alistair MacLean, Agatha Christie and Desmond Bagley to Solzhenitsyn and Pasternak, from Gerald Durrell and Joy Adamson to the famous Modern Masters series.

In addition to a wide-ranging collection of internationally popular writers of fiction, Fontana also has an outstanding reputation for history, natural history, military history, psychology, psychiatry, politics, economics, religion and the social sciences.

All Fontana books are available at your bookshop or newsagent; or can be ordered direct. Just fill in the form and list the titles you want.

FONTANA BOOKS, Cash Sales Department, G.P.O. Box 29, Douglas, Isle of Man, British Isles. Please send purchase price, plus 8p per book. Customers outside the U.K. send purchase price, plus 10p per book. Cheque, postal or money order. No currency.

NAME (Block letters)

ADDRESS